PRAISE FOR *A MAN*

"Hirano has continued to grapple with new themes ever since his debut. In this work, he has arrived at the primal question of what validates human existence."

—Yoko Ogawa, author of *The Memory Police*

"A riveting examination of desire and identity, *A Man* patiently unpicks the nature of unfulfilled aspirations. Keiichiro Hirano has written a multilayered tale of human reinvention, at once eminently readable and deeply moving."

—Tash Aw, author of *The Harmony Silk Factory* and
Five Star Billionaire

"There is no doubt that Keiichiro Hirano is an author with an extremely pioneering and modern spirit. His works have opened up a very imaginative space in analyzing and exploring the spiritual world of humanity."

—Sheng Keyi, author of *Northern Girls* and *Death Fugue*

"But to you," Kido-san continued, "I will tell the truth from now on."

Aside from this initial exchange revolving around his lie, Kido-san was an unaffected, affable, collected person. He had a sensitive and receptive mind, and in his every word one could sense a character of great depth and complexity.

I felt comfortable talking with him. Whatever I wanted to get across he understood well, and his meaning in turn was as clear as day to me. We also found commonality in our love for music. I appreciated how rare it was to come across someone like this, and I sensed that there had to be extenuating circumstances that explained his need to lie.

The next time I visited that bar on the same night of the week, Kido-san was drinking alone again as I'd expected, and I sat down beside him at his invitation, in a seat somewhat removed from the bartender's post. A number of times afterward, we shared each other's company in those same seats and grew intimate enough that we would talk late into the night.

His drink of choice was vodka. Despite his lean build, he could definitely hold his liquor and would claim to be pleasantly tipsy even though he never seemed to change, his tone of voice remaining always composed.

The two of us became something like friends. Making a new drinking buddy with whom you form a deep connection is surprisingly rare in middle age. But our relationship was limited to the counter of that establishment, and neither of us sought the other's contact information. He probably felt uncomfortable asking. For my part, the truth is that I was still wary of him. In fact, I have not seen him in quite some time and doubt that I ever will again. His no longer visiting that bar—no longer feeling the need to do so—I interpret as a positive sign.

Novelists, whether consciously or unconsciously, are always on the lookout for people that can serve as models for their novels. That is, we eagerly await the serendipity of someone like Meursault or Holly Golightly appearing out of the blue one day.

For a person to be appropriate to serve as such a model, he or she needs to be highly out of the ordinary while possessing something that might be seen as a kind of template for humanity or for the age and must be purified via fiction until they reach the dimension of the symbol.

When I hear the stories of people who have lived dramatic and tumultuous lives, I think to myself that they might work as novels. Some of these individuals even encourage me by way of subtle circumlocution, as if to say, "You can use me if you want, you know." Yet whenever I give serious consideration to writing such ostentatious yarns, I find myself balking, though I suppose my novels might sell better if only I could go through with it.

Where I usually find my models is among the people I already know. Since I try to associate as little as possible with those who don't interest me, everyone that I maintain a long relationship with has a certain something. And sometimes I am astonished to discover all of a sudden that one of them is the protagonist of my next novel for whom I was searching all along. Individuals such as these, about whom my understanding slowly deepens over time, are ideal for full-length novels, since the protagonist is together with the reader for the long haul.

✕

Starting the second time I met him, Kido-san gradually began to explain the reason he had used a fake name, and it turned out to be a very intricate story indeed. I found myself utterly captivated, often keeping my arms crossed as I considered what he told me carefully, and soon grasped why he had wanted to divulge it to me. While he may never

PROLOGUE

The protagonist of this story is someone that I have been fondly calling "Kido-san." You may be wondering where the fondness comes in, as using a family name with the addition of "san" isn't always the warmest way to address someone, but I think you will soon understand why I hesitate to call him anything else.

I first met Kido-san on my way back from a talk at a bookstore. My head was buzzing after having spoken continuously for two and a half hours and, wanting to settle down somewhat before returning home, I had stopped in at a certain drinking establishment that I happened to stumble upon. Kido-san was drinking alone at the bar.

At first I listened vaguely as he chatted with the bartender. But at some juncture, I couldn't help but laugh and found myself joining the conversation.

The initial introduction he gave me—his name, his background—I would soon learn was all lies. But as I had no reason to doubt him then, I believed every word.

Wearing square black-rimmed glasses, the man wasn't what you would call strikingly handsome, but his face had a certain air of sophistication that went well with a dim bar. I thought to myself that if I had looks like his, I might remain attractive well into middle age, even if I were to develop a few more wrinkles and gray hairs. But when I told him so, he merely cocked his head to the side with an expression of disbelief and said, "No, not at all . . ."

I told him I was a novelist. He hadn't heard of me and seemed embarrassed by that fact, which made me ashamed in turn, an all-too-common occurrence. But he had a profound interest in my profession, and after interrogating me about various details, something like admiration suddenly filled his face, and he said, "I'm sorry." I frowned, unsure why he was apologizing, when he told me that his real name was Akira Kido, thereby admitting that the name he had just told me was a false one. He then asked that I keep this secret from the bartender and went on to explain that he was a lawyer, born in the same year that I was, 1975.

Having once been a, shall we say, less-than-studious law school student, I often feel self-conscious when faced with a bona fide legal expert. But after his confession, I felt no such drop in stature, as the personal history he had until then claimed as his own had been unfortunate enough to arouse my sympathy.

His behavior struck me as tasteless, and I asked him what he was doing telling such lies. This left him searching for words with a pensive frown.

"I keep myself together by living other people's pain," he said eventually with an indescribably lonesome smile. "It's like the expression 'the man who goes mummy hunting ends up a mummy himself . . .' Do you understand what it's like to be honest through lies? I mean, of course, just for brief stints at places like this. Somehow I can't seem to let go of myself entirely.

"What I truly want is to think directly about myself, but that just makes me sick. It's the one thing I can't help. I've done everything I can. And I believe that soon enough my need to act like this will pass—I never would have guessed things would turn out like this . . ."

I was put off by his intentionally mysterious way of speaking but found the content of what he had told me fascinating. Moreover, I could not deny my budding affection for the man.

A MAN

A MAN

KEIICHIRO HIRANO

TRANSLATED BY ELI K.P. WILLIAM

AMAZON **CROSSING**

Previously published as *Aru Otoko* in the magazine *Bungakukai* and then in book form by Bungeishunju in Japan in 2018. Translated from the Japanese by Eli K. P. William. First published in English by Amazon Crossing in 2020.

Published by Amazon Crossing, Seattle

www.apub.com

Amazon, the Amazon logo, and Amazon Crossing are trademarks of Amazon.com, Inc., or its affiliates.

ISBN-13: 9781542006880 (hardcover)
ISBN-10: 1542006880 (hardcover)

ISBN-13: 9781542006873 (paperback)
ISBN-10: 1542006872 (paperback)

Cover design by David Drummond

Printed in the United States of America

First edition

A | MAN

have actually said, "You can use me if you want," the proposition was surely on his mind. But my decision to actually do so didn't come about until after I happened to meet a lawyer elsewhere that knew him well.

"He's a great man," this lawyer said without hesitation, "and incredibly kind to people of all stripes. Like taxi drivers. If they don't know the route, he tells them with such warmth and care it's amazing."

I laughed, but had to agree that it was an admirable quality in this day and age—and in a rich man to boot!

The other stories this lawyer related were surprising, involving as they did a number of moving incidents about which Kido-san himself had never spoken, and I finally came to understand in full living color this unmistakably isolated and lonely middle-aged man. It might sound trite, but he was, after all, a real character.

In writing this novel, I spoke again with the lawyer and other concerned parties, investigated for myself various details that Kido-san had left vague in the interest of confidentiality, embellished it all with my imagination, and made it into fiction. I doubt Kido-san would have ever disclosed so much of what he had learned on the job to anyone, but I followed through with what the novel required.

With all the unique characters that make an appearance, some of you might wonder why on earth I didn't pick one of the bit players to be the protagonist. While Kido-san will in fact become obsessed with the life of a man, it is in Kido-san, viewed from behind as he chases this man, that I sensed something that needed to be seen.

There's a painting by René Magritte entitled *Not to Be Reproduced* in which a man with his back turned is looking into a mirror at the back of another version of himself inside the mirror, who is likewise looking into the depths of the reflection. This story is similar in some ways. And perhaps the reader will spot the central theme of this work in the back of me, the artist, obsessing over Kido-san absorbed in his own obsession.

What's more, you may take issue with this prologue and doubt that the man I met at the bar was really "Kido-san" to begin with. That is perfectly understandable, but personally I believe he is who he says he is.

It would seem natural to begin the story with him, but before that I would like to write about a woman named Rié. For you see, the bewilderingly strange and tragic ordeals that she underwent are where everything in this tale finds its origin.

CHAPTER ONE

It was in mid-September 2011 that news spread among the people of a certain Town S that the husband of Rié from the stationery shop had passed away.

While everyone in Japan associates 2011 with the Great East Japan Earthquake, there are some in Town S, tucked away in the center of Miyazaki Prefecture, for whom this death of no national significance holds a more prominent place in their recollections. It was not uncommon for those residing in the small, rustic community of around thirty thousand, Rié's mother among them, to never have met anyone from the devastated Tohoku region.

Looking at a map, one finds a thoroughfare of some antiquity called Mera Road cutting through the middle of town along its course over the Kyushu Mountains to its eventual terminus in Kumamoto. Visiting in person, one discovers a settlement of simple appearance, about a forty-minute drive from Miyazaki City to the southeast.

Town S is undoubtedly a place of many unique qualities. For ancient history buffs, its name reportedly conjures the enormous burial mounds within its precincts, while fans of professional baseball recognize it as the site of one team's spring camp and dam aficionados for its boasting the largest in Kyushu. Like a good local, Rié never had much interest in any of this. Though she would, nonetheless, develop a sentimental attachment to a certain cherry tree in the park with the burial mounds.

Upon the release of a documentary in 2007 about a secluded mountain village that was abandoned en masse in the 1980s after severe depopulation left it difficult to sustain, a certain kind of tourist began to descend on Town S. Previously unknown in these parts, they would waltz about with a condescending air, possessive of a perverse fascination with ghost towns.

While the center of Town S flourished after it was redeveloped during the economic bubble of the Showa era, the combination of a low birth rate and aging population left many businesses on the main shopping stretch along Mera Road permanently shuttered, earning it the rueful nickname "Showa Burial Mound." One of the few shops that remained was Rié's family business, Seibundo Stationery.

※

Rié's late husband, Daisuké Taniguchi, moved to town just before the documentary began to generate buzz. Wanting to start a career in forestry at the age of thirty-five without any experience in the industry, he found employment at Ito Lumber, and after working there for four years with enough diligence to earn the admiration of the company president, he was crushed by a cryptomeria tree that he himself had felled and there met his end. His age at time of death was thirty-nine.

Daisuké was a reticent man. As he hardly spoke to any of his coworkers and had no friends of note, the only townspeople that learned the details of his past were Rié and her family. One might even call him an enigma, though it wasn't unusual for migrants to depopulating areas to have issues about which they could not speak. What set Daisuké apart was that, within a single year of his arrival, he had married one of the locals: Rié from the stationery shop.

Rié was the only daughter of the proprietors of a stationery shop that had been in the family since her grandfather's generation and was known by everyone in town. While somewhat eccentric, she was thought to be sensible and trustworthy. So, although her decision aroused universal surprise, everyone assumed that a woman like Rié would only have decided to tie the knot after thoroughly sussing Daisuké out and concluding that he presented no harm. This was enough to bring all prying into his past to an indeterminate hiatus.

Ito, president of Ito Lumber, was pleased by the development, as it raised the likelihood that Daisuké, who had far exceeded his expectations, might stay permanently. At the same time, officials in charge of migration between urban and rural areas at the town office treated the union as an ideal case study.

※

In part due to his being Rié's husband, no one ever had bad things to say about Daisuké Taniguchi. On the contrary, even hinting at ill-intentioned gossip would provoke disapproval, and most of the townspeople were quick to defend him. One might even go so far as to call him cherished.

Better described as introverted than standoffish, Daisuké wasn't the type to go out of his way to socialize, but if someone struck up a conversation with him, he would engage them with surprising cheerfulness. He had a distinctive, laid-back air about him, and Ito would often cross his arms and say, "Now that man is going places."

While Daisuké was never angry, sulky, or otherwise in bad temper, he wasn't afraid to speak up, albeit gently, about inefficiency and danger in his work. Occupational accidents are an all-too-frequent occurrence on logging sites, and talk has an unfortunate tendency to be gruff and dire. Somehow, the mere presence of this newbie reduced conflict.

They say it takes approximately three years for a forester to come into their own, beginning with chainsaw felling and moving on to the operation of processors and grapples. Daisuké was a reliable hand within a year and a half. A prudent judge of circumstances, steadfast, and both physically and psychologically healthy, he poured himself quietly into his work, whether under the scorching sun of midsummer or the sleet of a chilly winter day, and completed his tasks so utterly without complaint that experienced site supervisors would often advise him to pipe up if he was uncomfortable.

It can be hard to predict the capabilities of a new hire until they are actually put to the test, but Ito bragged on a number of occasions to others in the industry about what a find Daisuké turned out to be and tended to attribute his exemplary performance to his university degree. In the whole history of Ito Lumber, going back three generations, there had never been another employee like him.

After Daisuké's death, neighbors who had known Rié for many years expressed their sympathy by saying of her, "That girl is badly marked . . ." To be "badly marked" means to be unfortunate. Apparently, this is something of an anachronism, but the phrase remains in use in the Kyushuian vernacular. It is often intoned by elders with intense commiseration derived from reflection on their long life experience. None of which is to imply that the people of Kyushu have exceptionally bad luck or that they are especially fatalistic.

Misfortune can visit itself upon anyone. But when it comes to serious misfortune, we have a tendency to presume that, if it happens at all, it can only happen once in a lifetime. The fortunate imagine this to be so out of a certain kind of naivety. Those who have actually experienced misfortune pray for it to be so as a desperate wish. And yet, the sort of major misfortune for which once is plenty, sadly, has something in common with the stray dog that persistently chases the same person around, twice and then thrice. It is in the midst of such recurrent misfortune that people visit shrines for purification ceremonies or have their names changed.

Including Daisuké, Rié lost three of the people she most loved one after the next.

Rié was raised in Town S and lived in her family home until leaving after high school graduation to attend university in Kanagawa Prefecture. There she found a steady job and, at the age of twenty-five, married her first husband, an assistant at an architecture firm. Their first son was named Yuto, and their second, Ryo.

At the age of two, Ryo was diagnosed with a brain tumor and died six months later. This was the first deep sorrow Rié had ever experienced.

Rié and her husband fought over Ryo's treatment, and she was never able to put the hurt she suffered in the process behind her. At her husband's insistence that they forge onward as a family, she could only shake her head. Their divorce mediation lurched from argument to argument, and it took eleven months for them to reach an agreement. Thanks to the efforts of a capable lawyer, Rié managed to secure custody of their remaining child, which had been a sticking point for her husband in the negotiations. Then a vitriolic postcard arrived from her in-laws, with whom she had always been on good terms, denouncing her as "inhuman."

Just as the dust was settling, her own father suddenly died, prompting Rié to return with Yuto to her family home in Town S.

Her predicament aroused great pity as the townspeople had all been fond of Rié since she was a child, remembering her as a well-behaved little darling. A lovely, subdued, petite girl with the sort of eyes that seem to harbor idiosyncratic thoughts, her friends would often tease her about the faraway look that appeared on her face whenever her mind wandered.

While she wasn't exactly an overachiever, Rié had good grades, and when her friends learned that she would begin commuting to a university prep school in Miyazaki City an hour away by bus instead of to their local high school, they took it as a matter of course. Despite the fact that she wasn't the most talkative student, there were two or three boys every school year, in both junior high and high school, who watched her in the hallways or classroom, nursing a secret crush.

Her parents were immensely proud of their only daughter, who had graduated from university in the big city of Yokohama, married a man on track to be an architect, and even been blessed with children. One would have been hard pressed to find anyone who looked upon that joyful face of hers with anything like bitterness or contempt.

In other words, Rié's life fell far short of how everyone imagined it would turn out. No one—not the grown-ups, not her old classmates— had doubted for a second that she was happy, so when the townspeople heard that she had lost a young child, gotten a divorce, and returned home, their reaction did not stop at mere sympathy; they were profoundly disturbed by the injustice of it all. That the world in which they lived was the sort of place where such things could happen was an unsettling idea. When on top of all this she lost her second partner after only three years and nine months of marriage, it's hardly surprising that they would say nothing to demean the memory of Daisuké, if for no other reason than that he was Rié's husband.

When Rié met Daisuké, she had taken over management of the stationery shop from her mother. Delivering office supplies to her old middle school, the town office, local corporations, and other customers; seeing to the checkout counter; and fulfilling the various tasks required, Rié watched each day pass in a blur. While she found some consolation in familiar faces, it was less stressful to deal with new clients. Of these they had no shortage, thanks to their serving as a distributor for a mail-order company since the days her father was in charge.

As soon as Rié was alone, she thought of the son she had lost and often cried. She could never forget the time, perhaps one month before he died, when she'd left his ward to talk with the doctor and returned to find him staring quietly at the ceiling. *What could he be thinking and feeling?* she wondered as she studied him in profile. The capacity for thought he had been endowed with was supposed to have served him in leading his life for many decades more. Instead it was functioning merely to recognize his impending doom. But there was just no way he could possibly understand the terrible process occurring in his body, not even at the bitter end . . . Whenever Rié recalled Ryo at that moment, she lost even the power to stand, sitting down wherever she happened to be and covering her face.

Inevitably, her thoughts would turn to Yuto, the growing son that had been left to her, and she would remind herself to continue on as cheerfully as she could. Lacking the maturity to be troubled by his brother's death, Yuto had grown into an unexpectedly energetic boy since Rié's return, and this was her one solace.

She also remembered her father. Not once in his life had he ever raised his voice to her or stopped loving her with everything he had.

Rié had no faith in any particular religion. Her family were so-called "funeral Buddhists," belonging to the Jodo sect only insofar as they employed its funerary services. Nevertheless, she often imagined her father as a kindly old man watching over Ryo in heaven, and this never failed to bring her a touch of relief.

"Father only went to heaven a little bit early to keep Ryo company," drawled her mother, who truly believed such things. "He followed after that boy so as he won't worry till you're ready to go yourself. That's Father, alright."

※

Living in her hometown for the first time since high school fourteen years earlier was the source of some comfort for Rié. But sometimes, when idling at her desk in the shop, she was beset by a feeling of emptiness so powerful, she worried for her own well-being. Her moorings to the world came loose, time slipping by insensibly around her. Then suddenly, like long-sunken garbage bobbing up inexplicably from the bottom of a pond, the thought would come to her that maybe death wasn't that scary after all. I mean, if such a small child as Ryo could go through it, then why not her? And wasn't her father waiting patiently with him on the other side . . . ? Whenever she caught herself thinking this way, the core of her body would fill with the luminous chill of dread.

For the first while after her return, Rié looked with envy at the social media pages of her friends from her university days. But after taking a break for a week, she was surprised to find that her interest in the interplay of text and photos was gone.

Visitors to the shop were scant. It was their mail-order clients that supported Rié's life with her son and mother. The future of the family business was not looking bright.

She had seen the main street lined with shuttered stores on her annual visits for New Year's and the Obon Festival. But it wasn't until she resettled permanently that the town began to make her feel lonesome, as though she had been abandoned alone in a big, empty, dilapidated house.

On the second floor of a building across the street from the shop was the piano studio where she had studied for eight years. It was now deserted, the building utterly neglected. The town lacked even the young people to spray-paint it with graffiti.

Once a week, Rié had crossed the street for her lesson and then returned to the shop, where she did homework while waiting for her father to finish work. The ride back to their nearby home, with her sitting shotgun while her father drove, just the two of them, she now looked back on with fierce longing . . .

Could I start fresh in Yokohama or another area around Tokyo? Or how about somewhere closer like Hakata? Maybe I could go look for a new job there? Such thoughts crossed her mind from time to time. She could never be bothered to even reach out and touch them, leaving them instead to simply fade away.

It was in the February of the year after Rié's return that Daisuké first visited Seibundo Stationery.

That winter, Rié and Yuto had both come down with colds twice. Although Town S was supposed to be much warmer than Yokohama, Rié had gotten used to living in a modern condo, and her drafty family home was simply too much for her, especially the frigid bathing room. It had been up to her mother, the only one in the family who remained well, to take care of them on both occasions.

Rié had just recovered from one of these colds when Daisuké stepped into the shop alone. It was evening, around the time that children come to buy pens and notebooks on their way home from school. Darkness had fallen already, and Rié was just then considering letting her mother take over so she could go home to make dinner.

Especially given the dearth of customers, it was hard not to notice an unfamiliar man around Rié's age. Also conspicuous were the sketchbook and watercolor set he brought to the counter along with a planner. Skinny, he was just tall enough that Rié with her small stature had to look up at him slightly and, dressed plainly in a navy-blue windbreaker and jeans, he gave the vague impression of not being from around there.

As she was peeling off the planner's price tag for him, Rié imagined this man starting a new life in the town and wondered what would compel him to do so. Any of the townspeople surely would have been just as curious. When he left the store, she said thank you for the second time and, with her eyes on his back as he walked away, inexplicably sensed a life teeming with stories that needed to be told.

Before a month had elapsed, Daisuké visited the store again. It had been raining torrentially since morning, and an old acquaintance of Rié's mother's, Okumura-san, had just stopped by, carrying some bamboo shoots to while away the time.

"Go ahead," said Rié, as Daisuké was making his way timidly toward the counter to buy a sketchbook and a small amount of paint as before.

"Oh, I'm very sorry, young man," said Okumura-san. "Looks like I'm in your way."

When she stepped aside, Daisuké gave a slight bow and put his items on the counter.

"That is some storm," said Okumura-san, trying to make conversation.

"Yes." Daisuké gave a faint smile. His white car was parked in front of the store.

"Do you need a receipt?" Rié asked.

"Um . . . I'm fine," Daisuké replied, lowering his head. Then, with palpable self-consciousness, he straightened up abruptly and looked Rié straight in the eye for a moment.

Rié opened her eyes wide, as though she had just been addressed. But Daisuké merely averted his gaze without a word, gave another slight bow, and left the shop, driving off into the downpour.

⋊

From then on, this nameless customer visited the shop about once a month, usually in the evening. Invariably he purchased painting supplies and sketchbooks, only the large A3 size at first, then the little A5 ones as well. They were the sorts of items that hardly anyone but high school art club students wanted, so whenever Rié stocked up on inventory, he began to pop into her head.

One of his visits was on another day of pouring rain about six months later, when Yuto's summer break was coming to an end. Thick turbulent clouds blanketed the town, and Rié was repeatedly startled by ground-rumbling booms that followed close behind lightning.

He opened the door of the shop around three o'clock. The sound of cicadas—buzzing from the lush sidewalk trees in spite of the weather— filled the room, along with sultry air, before both were cut off as the door closed.

Okumura-san was sitting in a chair eating a steamed bun, absorbed in conversation with Rié's mother. She had stopped in not long before to blather away while taking shelter from the rain.

"I take it art is your hobby?" Okumura-san asked Daisuké in the local dialect as he approached the checkout counter with his usual sketchbook and paint.

Startled, Daisuké paused before replying yes with a faint smile.

"A customer of mine says he saw you painting outdoors. On the lawn by the Hitotsuse River? Bet you've built up some collection by now, huh?"

Daisuké gave only a slight nod, still smiling.

"Next time you could show them to us. What do you say? You want to see his paintings too, don't you, Rié?"

Rié could tell that Okumura-san wasn't making this request purely for curiosity's sake. She was trying to ferret out information about this unknown repeat customer. It reminded Rié why she'd spent her adolescence desperate to escape this country town, as tranquil and close to her heart as it was supposed to be.

"Okumura-san, you're putting him on the spot," said Rié. "Sorry about that. Forget what she said and please come again."

"Oh . . . It's fine. I mean, they're not really worth showing to anyone . . ." Saying this, the man nodded and made his usual abrupt exit.

Okumura-san looked to Rié and her mother, giving them each a sly smile in turn.

CHAPTER TWO

Rié doubted that the customer would ever come again. And the thought made her feel vaguely lonely. Not because she yearned to see him. Not at this stage. Rather, she felt bad to think that this apparently solitary man might leave town because of Okumura-san's prying. It was like the sadness of watching someone accidently knock over a fragile treasure you had always handled with great care.

But contrary to her expectations, he returned the following week, alone on a weekday evening as always. Her guess was that he wanted to allay the suspicions of the townspeople.

"Here . . ." Daisuké proffered two of his sketchbooks to Rié. As he carried them with him everywhere, the green covers were dog-eared, the corners whitened. With no other customers in the shop and Rié's mother out, it was just the two of them.

"You brought these for me?" A smile spread across Rié's face.

On the first page of the sketchbook, she opened to what appeared to be the landscape of an island in Miyazaki City called Aoshima. Depicted were a rocky beach nicknamed "Devil's Washboard" with rolling terrain like ripples on water, the gate of Aoshima Shrine, a great expanse of ocean that seemed to perfectly reflect the blue sky stretching overhead, and the coast in the distance.

Rié raised her head and looked at the Regular, whose name she didn't even know. He stood there, wearing a stiff expression. The slight quivering of his jaw seemed to be impeding his efforts to smile.

Turning the pages, Rié found cherry trees in full bloom on a burial mound, the dam at the edge of town, the Hitotsuse River that Okumura-san had mentioned, a nearby park . . . The scenery captured was the sort someone not from around there might pick out, from tourist spots to ordinary places in which locals would have found nothing unique. Some were black-and-white sketches while others were in color.

His drawings and paintings didn't suggest any kind of special talent. But they weren't terrible either. They made Rié think of the pictures drawn by the boy who had been the best artist in her class at middle school. For most people, drawing pictures was something you did during arts and crafts time until you graduated from middle school and then immediately gave it up. His work was what you would expect from a random adult if you handed them a paintbrush and drawing paper out of the blue, employing technique that had not evolved since adolescence.

Yet while everyone else had stopped, for some reason this man had kept on going. And so what if his artistic proficiency remained frozen. But what about his level of maturity? Whether you wanted to call it growing up or growing old, wasn't hanging on to such innocence supposed to be against the rules? I mean, here was a full-grown adult, probably in his mid-thirties, around the same age as Rié herself. And he had not stopped at drawing just one of these pure, carefree pictures for a laugh. He had gone on silently filling whole sketchbooks with them. Rié found this deeply touching.

Was this how the world revealed itself to his eyes, so open and unfettered? What would life be like to calmly face such a reality?

For nearly fifteen minutes, Rié took her time turning the pages, hoping that no one would interrupt her. Right then, she didn't want any customers to walk in.

Eventually her gaze fell on a painting at the end of the second sketchbook. It depicted the bus terminal she had used every day to commute to high school in Miyazaki City. Although she had been passing by on a regular basis again, as she was studying the picture, tears began to well up inexplicably in her eyes, and she brushed them away in annoyance.

For a long time afterward, Rié would sometimes wonder why she had cried at that moment. All she could think in the end was that she had been profoundly psychologically unstable. It was as though her feelings about the circumstances of her life, including her sadness over the deaths of Ryo and her father, had been building up imperceptibly since her return until, with the addition of these last trifling drops of emotion, the surface tension had finally broken and it had all spilled out.

In the days when she had sat each morning in the waiting room of that bus terminal, she had never dreamed for a moment that in the future she might find a job in Yokohama, live a married life there, lose one of the two children she bore all too soon, split up with her husband, and return home. And somehow, even though fifteen long years had passed, this dripping watercolor of the bus terminal depicted the building just as it appeared wistfully in her memory. The sole difference being that teenage Rié in her school uniform was no longer there.

This may have all been nothing more than a fleeting thought that arose much later, in the process of reflecting back on this event again and again. What she experienced in the moment was something swelling within her, filling her breast and crushing all other emotions.

"You're very talented," said Rié. "I'm sorry. It's a place I know well. It seems to have reminded me of something from long ago . . ."

She smiled and wiped her cheeks with her upturned fingers. Then, carefully closing the sketchbook so as not to wet it, she covered her mouth with her hand and took a few moments to regain her composure before beaming another smile. But to her surprise, the Regular, who until then had merely stood there in silence, was looking straight at her when tears suddenly spilled from his reddened eyes in the same way. Frantically, he cowered to hide his face, not so much out of shame but as though some secret had been exposed, and fled behind a nearby shelf.

When he came back after a while with a red pen that he seemed to have picked out at random, the tears were gone.

While Daisuké waited for her to ring him up, he kept his lips pursed firmly. Rié too said nothing. For though she could make no sense of what was happening, the lucid serenity revealed by the lights of the town in the gathering dusk suffused her with tenderness, and she could not bear to rupture that moment.

X

Daisuké returned a week later. Instead of calling out "welcome" as she did with normal customers, Rié greeted him with the friendlier "good afternoon." Daisuké responded with a "good afternoon" of his own and, after paying for some printing paper and other office supplies, raised his head.

"Um . . ."

"Yes?" Rié widened her big eyes expectantly.

"If it's not too much trouble, will you be my friend?"

"Huh? Um, OK . . ." Rié nodded, bewildered. Her chest began to throb with a feeling that was not quite surprise and not quite joy. How long had it been since she heard the word "friend"? It seemed like ages, but that couldn't be. She ought to have come across it countless times, both in Yokohama and since her return. She had as many Facebook friends as your average person, even if she wasn't logging in these days, and the town practically crawled with her childhood friends everywhere she went.

Yet, from this man's lips, the word seemed to mean something new. She didn't think anyone had ever asked her so directly, not even in childhood. Viewed objectively, it should have creeped her out coming from someone his age. The only reason her guard didn't immediately go up was that she had seen those sketchbooks. But hold on, what could he have meant by "be my friend"? It wasn't clear to her what exactly she had consented to.

"May I ask your name?"

"I'm Daisuké Taniguchi." Daisuké took out his business card, trying to hide the trembling of his hands. Listed was the name of a company, Ito Lumber, a mobile phone number, and an email address.

"Sorry, I don't have any business cards with me at the moment, but my name is Rié Takemoto. Here, let me write it for you." Rié reached for a yellow sticky note beside the cash register.

"If it's alright with you, this Sunday, how about dinner or . . ."

"On Sunday I have to look after my son." Rié's tone left no room for misunderstanding.

"Are you married?"

"I was—I got divorced, and now I've come back to my parents' place with my child."

"I see. Sorry, I had no idea."

"It would be pretty freaky if you did! I know we said friends, but I can't do anything except talk with you here—is that OK?"

"Yes, of course . . . That's plenty."

"I go out on errands sometimes, but I'm in the store almost every day. As you can see, I've got a lot of free time on my hands, so come by and show me your pictures whenever you like. Don't worry about buying anything."

From then on, Daisuké visited about once every ten days, and the length of their conversations steadily grew, until before Rié knew it she was having her mother watch the shop while she went with him for tea and other outings. Daisuké explained that he worked in forestry. Logging sites usually shut down before four and he was currently working on a nearby mountain, so he always zipped over as soon as he was done.

For a time, Rié respectfully stayed off the topic of Daisuké's past, sensing his discomfort. But she began to pick up on what she thought were hints that there was something he wanted her to ask him about and finally decided to give it a try.

On the day she asked him about his past, Daisuké was off work due to heavy rain. The two of them were having lunch at the neighborhood eel restaurant. It was after the meal while they were drinking hot tea that Daisuké, following a moment of hesitation, began to tell his story.

Daisuké was the second son of the owners of an inn in a hot springs town in Gunma Prefecture called Ikaho Onsen; he had a brother who was one year his senior. This brother was what is sometimes called a "dawdling master." While he wasn't bad at heart, the knowledge that, being the first-born son, he'd inherit the inn no matter what made him complacent. As a result, he'd slacked off at his studies, becoming something of a hoodlum in middle school and driving his parents out of their minds. He nonetheless managed to get into a private university in Tokyo before studying abroad in America for two years, but upon returning to Japan, went straight back to the capital, where he began to run a restaurant with his friends.

As Daisuké's mother and father both loved his brother dearly, they persevered for a time in trying to persuade him to come home. Eventually, though, they gave up and reluctantly decided to leave the inn to their second son. For better or for worse, Daisuké was less adventurous than his brother and had graduated from the economics department of a public university in the countryside.

Once he started at his father's company, Daisuké applied himself diligently. He wanted nothing more than to cheer up his disappointed parents and gradually reconciled them to the idea that they would entrust their legacy to him. But soon Daisuké's brother came crying to their father, burdened with a large debt from the failure of his restaurant, and their father agreed to pay it off only on the condition that he take over the inn. Their mother was in full agreement, and they promised their sons that Daisuké's brother would one day become "managing director" while Daisuké would be "vice president."

Whatever their titles, Daisuké knew that he was the one who would have to carry the business in practice. What scared him was that this arrangement might sour his relationship with his brother. For many years, he had struggled to understand why his parents had to love his brother so much simply because he was the eldest male. That confusion had never gone away. He loved his brother too. But the feeling was not entirely mutual.

Several years later, their father was diagnosed with liver cancer at the age of seventy-one. As the cancer was at an advanced stage, he would need a transplant if he was going to survive, but even then, his prognosis was poor. With no time to wait for a liver from a brain-dead donor, his one chance was a live-donor transplant from a relative. The test results disqualified Daisuké's brother as he had a fatty liver. But Daisuké's liver was healthy. It hardly seemed fair that he would be the one called upon, precisely because he had not lived immoderately like his brother . . .

Live liver transplantation posed a risk of lingering complications not just for the recipient but for the donor as well. In some cases, this could mean death. Daisuké's father bowed to him for the first time ever and asked him to fulfill his duty as a son while he gripped his hand and cried. Although Daisuké's brother and mother never said explicitly that he ought to grant this request, they never reassured him that he was under no obligation either, and both told him that they wanted his father to live a long life. They made no attempt to urge his father to reconsider, and the three of them were always having discussions when Daisuké wasn't around. It was awkward when Daisuké went to the hospital for a visit and walked in on such meetings. But he understood their urgency; time was of the essence, and he wanted his father to live out his years as much as they did.

In the end, Daisuké consented to serving as the donor. Rather than simply capitulate to the pressure of his family, he would provide his liver of his own free choice, without any hard feelings.

His father was overjoyed. It was the only time that he would ever say thank you to Daisuké. His brother promised him the entire inheritance when the time came. Their mother looked happy as well.

But sadly, his father's cancer had progressed faster than predicted, and while Daisuké wavered over consenting to the transplant, it had already become too late. His father died wearing a horrendously irritated expression, almost brimming with hatred. The three surviving family members mourned together, but neither Daisuké's brother nor his mother had any kind words regarding his ultimately pointless resolution.

"As you can probably imagine, I was relieved. I wanted to save my father's life, but the more I looked into the procedure, the more scared I got . . . And after his death, I realized that something inside me was broken beyond repair. So I cut off all contact with my family and left town. I wanted to get as far away as possible . . . I have no intention of ever seeing them again. This is the last time I talk about my family."

Rié listened to Daisuké's story from start to finish without interrupting him once. She tried to imagine what might have been going through his mind when he came to this remote town; took up employment in, of all things, the strenuous and hazardous forestry industry; drew pictures by himself on his days off; and, after more than six months, finally asked Rié to be his friend.

She sympathized with his predicament and began to feel that, as a friend, she ought to divulge a secret of comparable weight. So she told him that she had lost a son to disease, that a disagreement surrounding his medical treatment had been the cause of her divorce, and that her decision to return immediately after was due to her father's death.

Daisuké stared at Rié without moving until she had finished, then he lowered his head slightly and gave her three nods. The patrons in the restaurant had thinned out, and a server came to take away the tray with the lacquered boxes that had held their eel. They were both silent. Eventually Daisuké summoned the courage to reach across and squeeze the back of Rié's hand resting on the tabletop. Or perhaps it's more accurate to say that he gently sheltered it. Rié had not seen this coming. Nevertheless, the warmth of that palm—blistered as it was from chainsaw work—was comforting, and she found that she was happy. If he hadn't taken the initiative, she might have done the same thing herself.

Rié remained still like that for a time. And looking down at a once-clear plastic cup now clouded from long use, she thought about whether she ought to give in to this change that had arrived in her life.

⋊

After they were married, Daisuké went to live in Rié's family home, and they had a girl they named Hana. By the time Daisuké met with his accident in the mountains, Yuto was twelve and Hana was three. When Rié heard the news, she rushed to the hospital, but Daisuké was already dead.

Given his risky line of work, they had discussed the eventuality of something happening to him on several occasions. Daisuké had told her that under no condition did he ever want her to contact his family in Gunma or associate with them in any way even if he passed away. Rié respected his wishes until the first anniversary of his death. Then, after consulting with her mother and her friends, she decided to notify his family by letter. Her main purpose was to ask them what to do about his grave. She still had nowhere to entomb his ashes.

Rié wondered if she should have insisted her husband make amends with his family and regretted not pushing him more. His death had been far too abrupt, leaving many things unfinished.

⋊

Daisuké's elder brother, Kyoichi Taniguchi, flew to Miyazaki as soon as he received the letter.

When Kyoichi stepped out of his rented car in front of their house, Rié went out to greet him at the front door. She had only ever seen his photo, and in person, he seemed different than she had imagined him. Wearing white pants with a navy-blue jacket and a belt embossed with a big brand-name logo, Kyoichi bore no resemblance to Daisuké. This accorded with what she had been told. But he didn't come off as the sort of well-meaning slob Daisuké had made him out to be. To the contrary, he struck her as standoffish and arrogant.

"Thank you for coming all this way," said Rié. Her manner was genial, meant to let him know that he was family. But Kyoichi gave her a look like he had touched something monstrous.

"The weather's warm down here," he said, staring unwaveringly at this woman who now went by his family name. Rié's gaze stopped on the sunglasses dangling from his chest, where she saw the reflection of herself and her mother wearing disconcerted smiles.

As her mother led Kyoichi into the sitting room, the scent of cologne incongruous with the daytime trailed him down the hall, making Rié conscious of all the rustic smells of their daily life at home. Kyoichi seemed restless as he sat on the couch, rotating his head to take in the low ceiling, the cupboard decorated with photos, and the rest of their abode. In her letter, Rié had already told Kyoichi when Daisuké had arrived in town and how he had lived since. But he seemed on the verge of marveling aloud that his brother had died in such a place. When Rié served him coffee, Kyoichi made no move to touch it.

"Sorry for all the trouble he's caused you," he said.

"No . . . ," said Rié, surprised that he would apologize. "I'm sorry for not inviting you to the funeral."

"Let me cover the ceremony, the grave, and any other expenses you had to shoulder."

"No, don't worry about it."

"I bet he talked shit about me, right?" Kyoichi started to draw a pack of cigarettes from his pocket and then stopped himself.

Rié studied his face for a few seconds.

"He said almost nothing about his past. Just that . . ."

"He never wanted to see us again? That's fine. I know. That bastard was like a big ball of inferiority complex on legs, just full of envy all the time, and it warped him to the core. We didn't get along, OK? Our personalities were off from day one. This kind of thing happens even with family, right? Why couldn't he have led a decent life? Getting crushed to death by a tree in a place like this . . . I'll respect my parents to the end. I haven't even told Mother about this yet."

Rié made sure not to let it show on her face, but she rebelled at both what Kyoichi had said and how he had said it. There was no way this rudeness was just a cover for sadness. She'd loved Daisuké's soft-spoken kindness from the bottom of her heart and decided that if Kyoichi saw Daisuké the way he seemed to, then there had to be something wrong with him. At last she understood why her husband had been so insistent about staying away from his elder brother and suddenly wished that she could apologize for urging him on several occasions to contact his family.

"You had a kid, right? With Daisuké?"

"Yes. Our child is at day care now."

"It's got to be tough, being a parent on your own. I have three little ones myself—yours is a girl, right?"

"Yes."

"That would make her my niece . . . I would have liked to see her face, but I better not overstay my welcome. Before I take off, maybe I'll just burn some incense for him."

"By all means. It's this way to the altar."

"Oh yeah. Here are some pastries we make at the inn." Kyoichi held out a paper bag with a wrapped box inside. "Please give them a try.

They're fantastic. I know they're the traditional kind, but they go well with black tea or coffee or really anything."

✗

Rié led Kyoichi to their Buddhist altar room and ushered him inside while her mother watched the two of them from a short distance. Kyoichi knelt on the tatami floor in front of the altar. After staring at the memorial photo of the deceased for a while, he looked over his shoulder and said, "What's this?"

"That's a photo from about a year before he passed away."

"Uh-huh. Who is it?"

"Which one do you mean? Oh, that's my father and my son."

"Your son . . . ? No, not that one—this one. You don't have a memorial photo of Daisuké?"

"That's it. That's the one."

Kyoichi scowled in astonishment. Then he glanced once more at the photo and looked up suspiciously at Rié.

"That isn't Daisuké."

"Huh?"

Kyoichi looked back and forth between Rié and her mother with angry, disgusted eyes. Then he smiled awkwardly, his cheeks twitching.

"Oh boy. I really don't get it . . . What? This guy went around using my brother's name? Um, it was Daisuké Taniguchi, right?"

"That's right . . . You mean he looks different from when he was younger?"

"No. I'm not saying he's changed or anything like that. This guy is someone else entirely."

"This isn't Daisuké? Wait, you are his elder brother, Kyoichi Taniguchi, aren't you?"

"That's me."

They were silent for a time.

"Have you submitted the marriage registration, death notification, and all the other paperwork to the local office?" Kyoichi asked.

"Of course. He kept a photo of you and your family, you know."

"I don't mean to be rude, but can you show it to me, like, now?"

When Rié brought him the photo album, Kyoichi took it and sat cross-legged on a floor cushion.

"Who the hell is this? What the . . . ?" From the first page onward, Kyoichi kept making such remarks under his breath, craning his neck over the album.

Despite her confusion, Rié felt insulted when Kyoichi let out a laugh, as though mocking her and Daisuké's marriage. She was getting creeped out, less due to doubts about Daisuké than worries about who this man in their house was supposed to be. Her mother seemed to have likewise grown scared and came over to take Rié's arm.

The album was assembled by Daisuké from printouts of his digital shots. Kyoichi studied page after page of photos in which the man who had claimed to be Daisuké appeared alongside Rié, Yuto, and Hana, until he turned to the final page. There, his eyes went wide at an old photo of Kyoichi himself together with his parents at their family home. He could still remember why Daisuké didn't appear in the photo: he'd been the one who took it.

When Kyoichi eventually raised his head, he looked up at Rié, the muscles around his mouth twitching, before immediately averting his gaze. Then, wearing a dumbfounded expression, he said, "So, unless you're up to some weird scheme . . . I hate to say it, but this creep had you fooled. Because that is not my brother. Somebody was impersonating Daisuké."

"What are you saying?" Rié asked gravely. "Then who was he?"

"You tell me. Like, I just saw his photo for the first time right now . . . Anyways, I guess the only thing we can do is go to the police. Don't you think it's got to be a scam or something?"

CHAPTER THREE

Riding the Tokyu Toyoko Line back to his home in Yokohama, Akira Kido was standing beside one of the doors, lost in thought.

He had been lucky enough to get a seat when he boarded at Shibuya Station but had given it up to a pregnant woman he noticed nearby. She appeared to be about eight months into her term, as far as he could tell under the coat she was wearing. Although the train was not especially crowded, none of the passengers had seemed at all concerned about her. To them, the unborn child might as well not have existed.

The woman got off at Tamagawa Station and gave Kido a polite bow for the second time as she passed.

"Thank you." She mouthed the words almost soundlessly with a look of sympathy.

"Take care," Kido responded without thinking, his manner of speech more casual than he would have liked.

The soft smile they traded left him with a pleasant, lingering charge. Now his thoughts turned to the baby inside her who would never know of their fleeting interaction. He or she would need countless such anonymous acts of goodwill to safely enter the world and grow up. And he found it comforting to know that he had been able to offer one of them.

This reminded him of a conversation he'd had at the firm the other day. He and the other lawyers had been talking about middle-aged depression, which was becoming increasingly common around them, as it was in society more generally. Since there was no predicting when one might fall into such bottomless self-loathing, Kido had made the

KEIICHIRO HIRANO

tongue-in-cheek suggestion that they begin to "gather evidence" to prove to themselves that they were not terrible people as insurance against such an eventuality.

Each time the train moved past a stretch of buildings, Kido watched as the windows took on the fading colors of twilight. The last glimmer of light on the horizon melted away too fast for his eyes to catch. Then his reflection in the glass grew distinct, and looking away, he began to brood over the predicament of his client, Rié Taniguchi.

⬭

It was nearly eight years ago now, back in 2004, that Kido had agreed to serve as Rié's divorce attorney. In the beginning, she went by her husband's family name, Yoneda, and once she had returned to her maiden name, Takemoto, after a yearlong mediation process, his job for her was complete. They had not been in contact since, and when he'd received an email the previous month, he did not at first put it together that it was from her, because her family name had changed once again, this time to Taniguchi. As soon as he realized it was the same Rié, he rejoiced for her in his heart. She had remarried.

But upon speaking with her on the phone, he learned that her new husband, "Daisuké Taniguchi," had already passed away and had since turned out to be a different person. That is, someone had masqueraded as "Daisuké Taniguchi," lived in matrimony with Rié, and even fathered a child with her. What's more, "Daisuké Taniguchi" was apparently not a made-up name but a person, according to census information listed on his family register, who actually existed.

Kido was skeptical of the story. Cases of identity concealment through use of a false name were common enough, and he could understand why people might want to hide their real name in some circumstances. In fact, this was all too easy for Kido to relate to because he was third-generation Zainichi. Many such ethnically Korean residents whose families had settled in Japan before the end of World War II had taken up Japanese names, and some chose to hide their heritage. Kido himself had only become a naturalized Japanese citizen in high school. So what perplexed him wasn't that someone would pretend to be a fictional person but that they would pretend to be a real one.

To make matters even more baffling, this man had not merely gone around introducing himself by another person's name. His identity had been legally verified by government officials when they updated his family register upon receipt of his notification of marriage and then again with his notification of death. He had driven a car with his license and gone to the doctor with his health insurance card while making all his pension contributions punctually. Every public record attested to the deceased man being Daisuké Taniguchi, and there appeared to be no discrepancies in his own account of his upbringing in Gunma. Yet he did not look like Daisuké Taniguchi, whose brother had visited Rié a year after her husband's death and sworn, upon seeing his photograph, that they were different people.

What on earth could this all be about? Kido was still trying to work out how he might contribute to the situation as a lawyer. But he had decided, first of all, to help sort out any inheritance-related issues, and was now on his way home from a meeting with said actual brother, Kyoichi Taniguchi.

※

After completing the trial hearing for a different case at the Tokyo District Court earlier that day, Kido had gone to speak with Kyoichi in the lounge of the Cerulean Hotel in Shibuya. Kyoichi, the fourth-generation inheritor of an inn in Ikaho Onsen, had his permed hair styled in a spiky, wet look. Either on account of the hairspray or his cologne, a choking smell assaulted Kido before they had even exchanged greetings. Dressed in an outfit straight out of a men's magazine fashion column with a caption like "Middle-Aged Playboy Essentials," Kyoichi explained that he frequently visited Tokyo for business meetings. In fact, later on he would be going to the Roppongi nightclub district to, as he put it, "catch up with an old friend," and Kido was shocked by the lewd overtones in the way he said this with a suggestive smile. Although the inn's home page included a photograph of Kyoichi's wife, describing her as the "Beautiful Proprietress," Kido now wondered if Kyoichi kept a mistress from his Tokyo days—not that it mattered. Kido was simply amazed that the man felt compelled to imply such possibilities to a lawyer that he was meeting for the first time.

Kyoichi's story itself, however, setting aside his chatty self-introduction—or perhaps even when factoring it in after all—was to the point, businesslike, and unfaltering, giving Kido the impression that he wasn't lying. That is to say, it appeared that the man Rié married truly hadn't been Daisuké Taniguchi.

At one point, Kyoichi leaned close with theatrical furtiveness and lowered his voice as though concerned about being overheard.

"You think Daisuké's alive? You don't think the guy that switched places with him might've bumped him off? You never know. That wife of his, she even had a photo of my family in Gunma. One that Daisuké took back in the day. It's creepy . . . Yeah, me and her went to the police. But to be honest, I wouldn't want this to get out. We've got our customers to think about, you know. That wife of his, if everything she says is true, I guess she's a victim, but, like, she did get his life insurance. Shouldn't they investigate her too?"

Since Kido had a younger brother of his own and had grown accustomed to family disagreements as part of his job, he understood how complicated the relationship between middle-aged brothers could be. Even so, Kyoichi's attitude toward his brother came across as oddly callous.

Kido tried asking about the conflict among the Taniguchis surrounding the liver transplant, but Kyoichi interrupted, obviously upset.

"No. Not true. The guy that impersonated him got it all wrong! I bet he looked it up online or something, right? Or maybe Daisuké told him about it in his messed-up way.

"Of course we wanted Dad to live a long life, the whole family did. Even Daisuké. Obviously, right? But there's no way my old man would ever have twisted his arm to become the donor! Not in a million years. That little shit decided to step forward of his own free choice. Then he goes and warps it all so he can whine about it after the fact. He was always like that! Like when he said he wanted to inherit the business, I handed it over to him! It's not like I had any interest in some hot spring inn out in the boonies, to tell the truth. But my parents came crying to me, saying it was hopeless with him, so I had no choice but to go back. Yup. And instead of thanks, what do I get from Daisuké? Bitterness and him being all jealous of me like a brat because the eldest male is more important or some shit. What an idiot, right?

"Honestly, I don't know if I should be saying this kind of thing to a lawyer, but let me tell you, I've had it up to here with that asshole. Do you have any idea how much trouble he's caused the family? How worried Mother has been since he disappeared all of a sudden? Forget what would happen if he's been murdered, if Daisuké's gone hoodlum and got himself mixed up in some wacked-out crime or something, our inn is finished!"

Despite being worked up, Kyoichi just managed to keep himself from shouting and only let loose some flailing gestures at the very end.

"Don't get me wrong, I am worried about the guy. No question about that. He is family after all . . . But, you know . . ." Kyoichi sighed as though he lacked the energy to finish what he was saying.

After this, although Kido wasn't sure how they got on to the topic, Kyoichi went on a long spiel about how tasty the soft-shelled turtle served at their inn was. Kido nodded along and made polite noises to show he was listening, until deciding he should at least contribute *something* to the conversation and began to say, "There's a historic restaurant in Kyoto . . ." But Kyoichi, as though he had been waiting for just such an opportunity, immediately stated the name of this well-known restaurant, which had been frequented by famous literary figures for many years.

"The turtle in those old joints stinks so bad you can't eat it. They're just not keeping up with the times," said Kyoichi. "I had to go on an epic tour sampling food all over the place to find our chef. He's basically a culinary genius. And I'm not just bragging. I mean it."

Kido had done his legal apprenticeship in Kyoto and a senior lawyer who took him under his wing had treated him once at that restaurant. The subtle flavors had so impressed him that Kido still occasionally reminisced with this mentor about their visit, and it was all he could do not to cringe at Kyoichi's speech. Kido didn't know much about Daisuké Taniguchi, but with a blowhard brother like this, who wouldn't want to leave home?

Kido lived on the ninth floor of a condo just around the corner from the Chinatown in Yokohama. He had purchased it four years earlier with his wife, Kaori, each of them taking out a thirty-five-year mortgage. Three years younger than Kido, Kaori was an office worker at a car company, and they had a four-year-old son named Sota. The two of them had wanted to have a second child immediately, and the layout of their home was meant for two children, but this hadn't gone as planned and recently they had both stopped talking about it.

When Kido returned home that night, they sat down for a meal of deep-fried chicken and savory steamed buns that he had picked up in Chinatown, during which he had to keep reminding Sota to stay in his chair. It was a dinner much like always, but for some reason this quotidian scene stirred up Kido's emotions like never before.

After they were finished, it was Kido's turn to give Sota a bath. At day care, they had been reading a picture book of Greek myths for young children, and Sota asked Kido, as he haltingly described the plot, why Narcissus transformed into a flower.

"That's a tough one, son. With a story like this, I guess they must have started off with a narcissus flower and then used it to imagine stuff. Like, hey, I wonder why it's so beautiful? Hey, I wonder why its neck is all droopy? Then someone would go, 'I know, it must have happened like this.'"

Kido made an honest effort to reply, but Sota seemed to feel that he was skirting the question. The upshot was that it became Kido's homework to look up the answer.

After the bath, the two of them went to Sota's room and sat together, browsing an illustrated guide to the Ultraman series. That was when Kido realized why his son had been fixating on the transformation of Narcissus; Ultraman went through his own kind of transformation, from a human into a giant alien.

Presently Kido turned out the light and, while putting his son to bed, fell asleep beside him. When he woke up in the middle of the night, the light was out in the master bedroom, and the door was shut. He had temporarily converted the room intended for their second child into his study, and ever since putting in a bed for the purpose of taking naps, he and his wife had been sleeping separately. In the end, both of them rested better that way. So aside from telling her about the day care Christmas party over dinner, the day ended without them talking.

Alone in the living room, Kido sat in a chair by the window holding an ice-cold bottle of Finlandia vodka, in the mood to get a bit tipsy. The space the bottle occupied in their chronically food-crammed freezer was the frequent source of his wife's complaints. As he gripped it, the frost turned to water in the exact shape of his hand and dripped gradually down the sides.

Kido poured himself a glass. The vodka was so deliciously cold the consistency was thick, and it had a kick to it like a sweet blaze in his mouth. The scent went up into his nose, recalling faint flashes of the doctor swabbing his arm before a shot in childhood, when he had for the first time discovered the existence of something called "alcohol."

Kido put on a live V.S.O.P. album at low volume and finished his first glass listening to an encore medley of "Stella by Starlight" and "On Green Dolphin Street." The notes of Wayne Shorter's tenor sax, reaching what struck him as perhaps the pinnacle of sensuality, stretched out so long it was painful and pierced Kido through. He listened to the medley three times before stopping the CD. That was enough music for him, for he felt both his inner and outer worlds grow placid while maintaining their separateness.

He loved dearly the angle he took when he was getting drunk on vodka. As though diving with no oxygen tank, he sunk in a straight line, heading toward the abyss of inebriation. His path along the way was transparent, words could never catch up with him, and even the flavor was like light sparkling on the distant surface of the water when he looked back.

After drinking two glasses in succession, Kido had become completely removed from the mundane at last, attaining the solitude in its depths. He flopped back in his easy chair like a rag doll. And for a while, he remained with his neck tilted in the same posture, pleasantly drunk.

I'm happy . . . , thought Kido, remembering the intense feeling of joy that had come upon him suddenly when he was holding his son's hand in the dark bedroom earlier.

I am the father of that child, he said to himself, and each of these words—not just "father" and "child" but every syllable that wove them into relation—transported him into ecstasy. It was an epiphany so huge that Kido thought he might lose himself in it, while sensing simultaneously that the incredible specialness that banal moment with his son had assumed was ultimately the flip side of his anxiety. Overwhelmed, he had a premonition that he might even look back on this night as the happiest of his life . . .

Although the official story of Kido and Kaori's first meeting was that they had been "introduced by an acquaintance," they would never have dreamed of going into detail about the frivolous party where it actually occurred. Amidst conversation that indulged in obscenity at every turn, full of forced laughter and raps of pretend enthusiasm on the tables, they had just barely discovered each other's existence.

Every time Kido recalled the event, he wished ruefully that they'd met under circumstances more fitting to the serious spouses they had become. The fact that their relationship had been utterly sexless since the Great East Japan Earthquake the previous year only contributed a sardonic bitterness to his recollections. Truth be told, they had never reminisced once about their initial encounter, and in the process of repeating their story about the acquaintance's introduction, had begun to half believe it themselves.

Kaori was the daughter of a well-to-do dentist whose family had lived for generations in Yokohama. Her brother, who was four years older, had become a doctor of internal medicine instead of following in their father's footsteps and had recently renovated their father's office to open his own practice. They were a conservative but generous family and had helped considerably with the down payment on Kido and Kaori's condo.

When Kido went to ask Kaori's father for permission to marry her, he had smiled and said, "Zainichi or not, after three generations you're a full-blown Japanese." At these words of welcome lacking any hint of animosity, Kido could only bow and say that he was looking forward to being part of the family. As for Kaori's mother, she used to ask him questions about Korea whenever she could fit them into the conversation, probably in an effort to show polite interest. This was during the Korean Wave of pop culture that caught on in the 2000s. But once she realized that he could barely give passable answers and couldn't even read the Korean alphabet, she gave up on all such queries.

Kido only began to give more than a passing thought to the connection between his ancestry and his in-laws after the Great East Japan Earthquake, when the media made mention several times of the massacre of Koreans in the aftermath of the 1923 Great Kanto Earthquake nearly ninety years earlier. As Kido had paid little attention to such issues, this was the first time he learned that Yokohama had been one of the main places where the incendiary false rumors about a "Korean riot" had originated. He was reminded then of his father-in-law's surprising words and wondered whether they had implied more than he realized.

Kaori's grandfather, who was now in a home, would have experienced the Great Kanto Earthquake as a young child, while her long-dead great-grandfather would have been an adult in his prime. The earthquake had reportedly devastated Yokohama, with 80 percent of urban areas lost to fire, and Kido wondered what the two of them might have been doing in the maelstrom of brutal violence in its aftermath . . .

Obviously he had not asked his wife's parents about these matters. He hadn't even asked Kaori. Since the Great East Japan Earthquake, they had discussed the major earthquake expected to strike the Tokyo region directly, but never even touched upon the Great Kanto Earthquake in comparison.

※

What is the past to love? Kido wondered as he thought about Rié's late husband. *I suppose it's a fact that the present is a result of the past. In other words, one is able to love someone in the present thanks to the past that made them the way they are. While genetics are surely a factor too, if that person had lived under different circumstances, they would have probably become a different person—but people are incapable of telling others their entire past, and regardless of their intentions, the past explained in words is not the past itself. If the past someone told diverged from the true past, would the love for that person be mistaken somehow? If it was an intentional lie, would that make it all meaningless? Or could it give rise to new love?*

Unlike Kido, who was from Kanazawa, all the way up on the Sea of Japan, Kaori had remained in the area where she was born and raised, graduating from nearby Keio University, and had thus been able to stay in touch with her friends from both middle school and high school. She had told him about a number of her memories from as far back as childhood, and Kido knew the incidents well. He had never suspected, of course, that they might be lies.

But supposing his wife had related the life story of a complete stranger as though it were her own, Kido would have undoubtedly believed her just the same. And his understanding of her would have been shaped in accordance with the type of person the story portrayed her to be. It was Kaori who might have been more justified in doubting Kido's past since he had grown up far away, though his early "confession" of the fact that he was third-generation Zainichi would have given her a rationale for thinking that he was sincere.

The only chance Kido might have had to clue in to any contradictions would have been when meeting those who knew Kaori's past. If she had been living in an unfamiliar place, having cut off all contact with her family and friends, there would have been no way to verify her past short of hiring a detective. Daisuké Taniguchi had apparently avoided all social media because he had been in just such a situation.

No, not Daisuké Taniguchi, Kido told himself, trying to sort out the confusion taking hold in his mind. Rié's husband had been a different man who had merely impersonated Daisuké Taniguchi. In keeping with the practices of his profession, he decided for the time being to call him X.

Ever since Kido had heard the story of X from Rié, the man's existence had haunted him. Whether walking, riding the train, or having a meal with his family, Kido found himself thinking about X, like when a melody won't stop playing in your head.

What was such a phenomenon called? In the case of music, it was an earworm, but here . . . ?

To start your life over as a completely different person—Kido had never found the notion compelling before. Of course, in his teenage years, he had frequently idolized and wanted to be like all sorts of people. Once he had even burned with envy to become a boy that the girl he had a crush on liked. But none of these wishes had been anything more than passing fantasies.

All day today, he had felt blessed by the life he was leading, as he had told himself repeatedly. Through his job, he came into contact with the misfortunes of the world more often than most. This was especially true of criminal cases, where the ins and outs were often so tragic that they almost seemed cordoned off in a universe apart from the everyday, making him reflect on the significance of his life being different.

I am happy right now, he reiterated in his mind, but this was merely an irritated call for the strange emotions stirring in his chest to relent.

To throw away everything and become someone else—imagining doing this undeniably aroused in Kido a certain beguiling excitation. It was not necessarily only in the midst of despair that someone might be placed at the mercy of such a yearning but also when happiness was interrupted by ennui. And though he remained wary of this danger, Kido delved into his heart no further.

If the impersonation was a fact, then X had committed several crimes, including making a false entry on a notarized public document—whether the police would actually go to the trouble of pressing charges was another question. If, on the other hand, it turned out that he had committed homicide or a comparably serious act as Kyoichi had tried to claim, then Kido would have to seek advice from a colleague at the firm who was better versed in criminal cases.

※

This will be my last glass, Kido thought as he poured a third. The water that dripped off the bottle had left a circular stain on the table. It looked to him like a misshapen simulacrum of the crescent moon in the distant night sky.

Kido considered the predicament of Rié, who had lost three family members—her small child, her not-so-elderly father, and her young husband—one after the next. In his mind's eye, he saw her girlish face and her big eyes, as she nodded only to the parts of Kido's explanation that she truly understood and accepted. Although her figure was petite overall, she had somewhat thickset shoulders that seemed to support her unflinching spirit. He deeply pitied the poor woman. What despair she must have felt to lose a two-and-a-half-year-old child to illness. It was beyond imagining for Kido, but Rié was strong-minded and somehow managed to smile whenever her surviving child was present. If Kido wasn't mistaken, the boy would be entering middle school soon.

Rié's wishes regarding her divorce had been firm, and she had unswervingly rejected the possibility of mending her relationship with her husband. The cause of their falling-out had been a clash over their child's sickness and its treatment. The boy, Ryo, grew ill just as he was approaching his second birthday, and was initially diagnosed with a kind of brain tumor called a germinoma. This terrible news had been a shock to both Rié and her husband, but they had been encouraged by the prognosis: a survival rate of 98 percent over five years with radiation treatment and chemotherapy.

The surgical biopsy usually performed at this stage was cancelled due to Rié's husband's fierce opposition. The doctor had explained that the procedure presented some risk to such a young patient and that if it turned out Ryo didn't have a germinoma, the most likely diagnosis would be a malignant tumor in an inoperable location. Rié thought that they should go through with the biopsy, but her husband insisted that it was irrational to expose their son to danger for the sole purpose of knowing whether or not it was a disease that could not in any case be cured. And unable to hold her ground in a debate surrounding a topic as slippery as risk, she allowed him to persuade her to go along with him.

For the following three months, Ryo was afflicted with vomiting as he underwent the grueling germinoma treatment. Rié quit the bank she had been working at since university graduation to remain by his bedside. But the tumor did not shrink as expected. Instead, it grew. Based on the results of another MRI, the doctor gave a new name to Ryo's tumor—glioblastoma—and pronounced that the boy had less than a year to live.

"What I'd like you to do now," he said, "is stay close to home and try to enjoy the time that remains with your son."

Rié took Ryo to another hospital, but the diagnosis was the same and he died only four months later. He had lived a mere seven months after visiting the first hospital and spent three of those tormented by the pointless treatment.

While both parents were overcome with remorse, Rié's husband tried to rally her and Yuto to move past this calamity together as a family. But Rié was firm in her refusal and said that she wanted a divorce. Not because she blamed him for their son's death. On the contrary, she agonized over the belief that it was her fault. Rather, she simply could not accept the idea of sharing her future with a person like her husband.

As much as Kido sympathized with her, he had to explain that, legally speaking, this on its own would not stand as a conclusive reason for divorce. At the same time, he felt sorry for the husband. Although it was true that he had committed an irreversible error of judgment as a father, when Kido asked his brother-in-law for his opinion as a doctor, he said that it was a difficult decision for a layman to make, that the doctor's explanation had been flawed, and that, in any case, he couldn't understand why the wife was so angry with her husband. What swayed Kido to nonetheless take on the case was something he sensed in Rié, a sort of complex but pure facet of her humanity that seemed to be seeking a deeper dimension of compassion in him.

When Kido met with her husband as Rié's attorney, he soon understood why her feelings toward him had hardened. Launching into a lengthy rant, the man emphasized his own suffering, railed against Rié's stupidity and madness for pinning the responsibility on him, appealed to Kido as a lawyer and therefore fellow rational human being, described in tears the pain of losing a child, insisted on his great love for Rié, and finally pressed Kido to persuade her to get back together with him. In keeping with Rié's appraisal of her husband, he did not appear to be a bad person. But it was heartrending for Kido to see how the man's bloated sense of self-importance had hurt his wife, had put their young child through agony during what little time had remained to him, and was now in the process of bringing his own life to ruin.

Over the yearlong divorce mediation, Kido let her husband get all his complaints off his chest while doing his best to make him realize that there was no hope of his regaining Rié's love. Oddly, the man came to treat Kido with something like reverence, repeatedly rehashing Kido's legal explanations in his own words and discovering a new salve for his wounded pride in feeling as though he properly understood them. Much as with many perpetrators of domestic violence, his efforts to show Kido that he was a respectable person reeked of desperation.

After ten months had elapsed, Rié's husband began to show signs of impatience with the mediation. Kido couldn't help noticing that he was in an uncharacteristically good mood about something and, though he had some compunctions about it, decided to hire a detective to investigate. Then, showing the husband a photograph of him with the new woman he was seeing, Kido advised that the time was ripe to conclude their negotiations. In the end, with a surprising lack of rancor, Rié's husband consented not only to divorce but also to handing over custody of Yuto, an issue he had until then refused to budge on.

Now, Rié had met with the misfortune of losing her second husband—who, moreover, had been deceiving her the whole time about his identity.

To what end, I wonder? Sitting up with a sigh, Kido glanced at the clock. It was nearly two in the morning. He tried to consider this question further, but was interrupted when a heavy yawn escaped him.

Kyoichi Taniguchi had introduced him to several people who he said might know his brother's whereabouts, but claimed that the most promising lead was Daisuké's former lover. Setting aside the question of who X truly was, Kido was confident he could find records of Daisuké Taniguchi changing his address on the attachment to his family register and decided that tracking down that document would be the best way to start looking for him.

He gulped down the final drab of vodka in his glass. Now luke-warm, it lingered sharp and bitter on his tongue, eliciting a slight sigh, the last one of the day.

CHAPTER FOUR

When Kido's work finally settled down in the new year, toward the end of January 2013, he arranged a meeting with Misuzu Goto, the woman said to be Daisuké Taniguchi's former lover.

Although the phone number Kyoichi Taniguchi gave him was out of service, he had also mentioned that she was a web designer, and Kido had used this information to track down her Facebook page. After he sent her a message explaining the situation, her reply came swiftly. She appeared to be confused and worried about Daisuké and asked Kido to come to a friend's bar in Tokyo where she worked nights on the side. Kido doubted it would be an appropriate place to talk but nonetheless agreed, supposing that she was wary of meeting him alone.

The bar was located in an area of Shinjuku called Arakicho, a short walk from Yotsuya-Sanchome Station. It was an old district of intricately connecting alleys lined with bars and restaurants. Since it was his first time visiting, Kido decided to take a brief stroll. Thankfully the cold and the light snowfall of the morning had cleared up in the afternoon when the clouds broke.

Kido quickly discovered that there was no shortage of places to drink in Arakicho, not to mention a variety of eateries that specialized in everything from German and Spanish cuisine to curry, pork cutlet, sushi, and other traditional fare. He'd already had a light meal of buckwheat noodles in the underground restaurant area of the Tokyo Bar Association Building to tide him over for his meeting with Misuzu but, seeing the mouthwatering options he might have enjoyed here, was now beginning to regret it.

In preparation for his visit, Kido had asked one of his partners at the firm, who was an avid reader, about Arakicho. Displaying meticulous knowledge of the area, this colleague had explained that it used to be a famous pleasure district. It had been featured in the 1931 novella *During the Rains* by Kafu Nagai, and there was a nearby publishing company housed in the building of what had been a love hotel during the heady days of the bubble economy. Even on this Monday evening, there was a fair number of people out and about, with taxis frequently coming and going.

On the second floor of a building full of small establishments, Kido spotted the sign for the one he was scheduled to visit. It read "Sunny" in stylized yellow lettering reminiscent of sunshine, and Kido thought it was a nifty name for a bar that only operated at night. Upon asking later, he would learn that it had been taken from a hit song by Bobby Hebb.

The interior was pleasantly dim and cozy, with just enough space for a bar accommodating six stools and two low tables with sofa seating. When Kido stepped in just after eight o'clock, an old live album of Ray Charles played on the sound system. It appeared to be a soul bar, the walls densely festooned with related paraphernalia, including a Marvin Gaye LP and a photo of a child Stevie Wonder. The sofas were taken. At the counter, a lone man with the air of a regular was drinking Guinness while practicing magic tricks with a coin.

"Welcome," called a woman behind the counter. She squinted at Kido as though trying to decide if he was indeed the man she was expecting. From beneath a studded black cap, her lightened hair draped behind her ears and hung down over slender shoulders, her features sharp and defined, with gray-colored contacts that made her pupils glisten along with her lips. Kido thought she was beautiful.

Dressed in shredded jeans and a loose black sweater that made her look more rock than soul, she sat on a stool, cradling one knee in its ripped denim as she talked with an unshaven man of about fifty in a black hoodie who turned out to be the proprietor. Unlike her, his style matched the bar's theme.

"My name is Akira Kido. I'm the lawyer who contacted you."

When Kido presented his business card, the man in the hoodie, whose name was Takagi, peered at it skeptically.

"Don't lawyers wear a badge or whatever?" he asked.

"Oh. These days we're no longer required to wear them. But I happen to be carrying mine," Kido replied, taking his badge from his bag. While Takagi still looked doubtful, Misuzu's eyebrows shot up.

"Wow. I've never seen one of those before. Can I touch it?"

"Of course. Go right ahead."

As Misuzu would later explain, she had originally been a regular patron of the bar, but a year earlier had taken up serving two nights a week for the fun of it. Kido thought she might be seeing Takagi, though her manner made it difficult to tell. Whatever their relationship, Takagi turned out to be the one who had advised her to meet there, and although he did not subject Kido to any more rude probing, it was clear he was keeping an eye on him.

"Come take a seat. You can hang your coat there," said Misuzu with a smile. "What would you like to drink?"

She spoke at a distinctive, relaxed pace, with a sort of cheerful languor. The swell of her lower eyelids contributed a certain warmth to her features that softened the distancing force of her beauty.

"Oh, right . . . ," Kido replied. It was hardly the place for a water, and he wanted something that wouldn't be too much trouble for her to make. "OK. A Chimay Triple."

After a sip of his Chimay, Kido dived immediately into the matter at hand. "So, about the issue I explained in my email."

"Daisuké still hasn't turned up?"

"I'm afraid not—do you know the man in this photo?" Kido asked, showing her a photo of X.

Misuzu held it in her hand and looked at it for a while before shaking her head and returning it to the counter.

"That's not Daisuké?"

"No. Is that the man who was impersonating Daisuké?"

"That is correct."

"They look nothing alike. And judging from his build, that man couldn't have been very tall. Daisuké was a bit taller than me so . . . about this high?" She held her hand about the height of Kido's glass above her head.

"You mean to say that you don't recognize him at all, then?"

Misuzu shook her head and passed Kido a brown envelope. "I thought I might as well bring some pictures of Daisuké, though these are from back when we were seeing each other, so they're more than ten years old."

The envelope contained three photographs, all more recent than any Kyoichi Taniguchi had been able to provide. Apparently, he was short on photos from when they were growing up, as it was before the ubiquity of digital cameras, and lacked any from when they were adults due to their falling-out. The one Kyoichi had shown him was a family photo with a tiny image of Daisuké in profile. In the pictures Kido saw now, Daisuké's expression, as he faced Misuzu behind the lens, might have been that of a different person. It was stiff and bashful in the way of someone shy being photographed by their lover, and Kido could almost see the bemused look Misuzu must have been wearing in those moments. As expected, Daisuké Taniguchi did not resemble X.

50

"Feel free to keep them if you think they'll be useful . . . I haven't been in touch with Daisuké for over a decade now, so I have no idea what's going on in his life these days."

"Really? You see, his elder brother said that you might know how to reach him."

Misuzu put some ice in a glass, poured Cinzano Rosso over it, took a sip, and frowned. "I've known Daisuké since high school. We'd date and then break up and . . . We were together for a while. I guess that's why Kyoichi thinks that."

"Then you're well acquainted with Kyoichi too?"

"Uh-huh," said Misuzu with a nod, looking off distractedly at something behind the counter. Kido thought this might be a sign of her impatience because he had asked something obvious. When she met his gaze again, her eyes seemed to urge him to get to the point.

"Were the two brothers on bad terms?"

"I think that Daisuké . . . liked Kyoichi. They were like opposites, but they got along well until high school at least." Misuzu started to say something else, then thought better of it and closed her lips. Kido noticed but said nothing, allowing her to go on to what was probably a different topic.

"I don't think it was so much a problem with the brothers as with their parents . . . It's the same old story. They went back and forth about who to leave their estate to. Kyoichi refused to take over the family business, so they made Daisuké their backup plan. They should have just given it to him, but they kept up this attitude about Kyoichi, without coming right out and saying it, like he could change his mind whenever he wanted. But that just puts Daisuké's life on hold, doesn't it?"

"Did Daisuké-san want to be next in line?"

"Yes. He liked the inn. In Ikaho Onsen, it's a pretty well-known place, with some history."

"So I hear. I took a look at the home page. The new building was done in contemporary style, but the main building is a really classy piece of architecture."

"The new building was Kyoichi's pet project." Misuzu gave Kido a sardonic smile. "All the rooms have outdoor baths that are in plain view from the bed. The layout ensures complete privacy and the interiors are chic, but there's something about them that's just obscene."

Kido burst out laughing and tipped back his glass with newfound cheer. After glugging down some of the beer, he let more laughter slip. This set off Misuzu, and soon her shoulders shook with laughter as well.

"Well, I suppose those rooms are not exactly suitable for a family vacation."

"It's a high-class love hotel, is what it is. A few years back, a reporter caught this woman announcer having an affair there."

"Oh right . . . at Ikaho Onsen . . . I remember that story . . . Now that you mention it, I saw something about it when I was searching online. I didn't take a proper look, though."

"Kyoichi has done his fair share of playing the field, so he's got the whole system fine-tuned. He knows exactly what couples are looking for when they go on trips to hot springs inns like theirs. Daisuké just doesn't understand things like that. He's a serious guy."

A wistful and somewhat piteous smile flitted across Misuzu's face.

"The new building is supposedly a big success," she continued. "I hear they were praised for taking in survivors after the earthquake."

When she was finished, Kido decided that beer wasn't cutting it anymore and ordered a vodka gimlet.

"Sure thing," Misuzu replied, and began to wield the cocktail shaker without any hint of showiness, as though she were cooking alone at home. Her attitude was laid-back and unaffected, despite the fact that they had just met, and this struck Kido as distinctive of her personality. When she was done, the vodka gimlet was so thoroughly shaken it fizzed as she poured it into the frosty glass. Kido found it well chilled and smooth and detected a mellow sparkle to the flavor.

"Mmm. This is good," he said.

He wasn't just being polite. It really was good, and Misuzu beamed a delighted white-toothed smile that made him believe what she had said about working the bar for the fun of it. Then she pinched the collar of her sweater, which had slipped down to inelegantly reveal the divot of her collarbone, and pulled it back into place. Her small diamond necklace caught the light and glittered like a grace note in a song.

Another man with "regular" written all over him arrived, sat down on a stool one removed from Kido, and launched into an animated conversation with Takagi. The music had changed to a live album of Curtis Mayfield, the voices of the audience filling the room. Kido decided he had better ask her a few more questions before the place filled up.

"I suppose it must have been after Daisuké-san's father passed away that you lost touch with him."

"I guess you could say that. We were at the funeral together. He continued living with his family for a while after that. I'd already moved to Tokyo then, so we were meeting maybe twice a week."

"At that time . . . were you, um . . ."

"Yes, we were seeing each other. But then he disappeared suddenly. No breakup talk, nothing."

"I see . . . Any emails or calls after that?"

Misuzu shook her head. "His number was disconnected."

"Would you say Daisuké-san felt hurt about the whole business with the liver transplant?"

"Who told you about that? Kyoichi?"

"No. The man in the photograph who died with Daisuké-san's name. For want of anything better, I'm calling him X. Apparently he told the woman he was married to, and I heard it from her."

"How could this guy even know about that? It's creepy."

"I don't know. My best guess is that X met with Daisuké-san. He must have heard the story from him directly. Then for whatever reason, he must have felt compelled to imitate him and to live as him, making his past his own."

"Why? It's not like Daisuké had credentials worth being jealous of. Was the guy after his inheritance or something?"

Across the crescent of Misuzu's brow under the brim of her cap flickered a faint shadow of worry.

"I don't know what X was after. The family estate is a possibility of course. Sorting out confusion around the inheritance is one of my primary goals."

"Is Daisuké OK? Has anyone contacted the police?"

"For now, they've accepted a missing person's report, but that's all."

"Shouldn't we be making a big stink about this, like, telling a TV station or something?"

"It might get to that eventually, but that's not what Kyoichi or X's wife wants."

"Why not?"

"She's still . . . bewildered. As of course she must be. And Kyoichi is concerned about the inn's clientele. He says he doesn't want media attention about a murder or whatever this turns out to be."

Misuzu looked appalled and let out a deep sigh.

"Could he have been kidnapped by North Korea or something?" interjected Takagi, who Kido hadn't realized was listening.

Kido responded with an ambiguous gesture, somewhere between a nod of agreement and a quizzical crooking of his neck, as he pressed his tongue to the roof of his mouth to kill the tang of the gimlet's lime. The idea that there might be even the faintest possibility of such a kidnapping struck him as patently ludicrous. Maybe in the late seventies or early eighties but certainly not now. And he looked away almost before he realized what he was doing, afraid that Misuzu, who he'd been growing to like more and more since the moment they met, might be led by the flow of the conversation to let slip some slur about Zainichi.

Although Kido was third-generation Zainichi, neither of his parents had drilled him on the importance of his heritage, and as he had been born and raised in a typical area of Kanazawa rather than a Korean enclave in one of the bigger cities, he managed to reach adulthood without, for the most part, experiencing racism. This was true both when he went by the family name Lee and after he began to introduce himself as Kido around the start of middle school. But since his parents never told him their reason for switching to this Japanese name, he suspected that there may have been some sort of incident that he was unaware of.

The family business was a regular *izakaya* with no specialization in Korean cuisine. Since the teachers at his elementary school would frequently visit to drink themselves under the table, Kido became well known among them, even the ones in charge of classes in other years.

In high school, he'd become a Japanese citizen together with his parents, throwing away his claim to Korean citizenship, which dated to before the end of World War II. His parents had viewed this choice as inevitable for him, given that he was completely illiterate in Korean and could never see his father's relatives who visited from South Korea as anything other than foreigners, while Kido was indifferent about his citizenship.

The catalyst for his change of heart was a piece of advice he received from his father when he was set to go on a school trip to Australia. The gist of it was that Kido ought to naturalize so as to avoid any issues involving his passport, and Kido would never forget his words. In the event that something happened while he was travelling, his father had warned, he could only hope for protection from the government of

Japan, since the nation of South Korea did not have any "sense" for him and its government wasn't even aware that he existed.

Although his father only ever said "sense" once and didn't elaborate, Kido thought that he had chosen the wrong word and guessed that he had wanted to say "reality." It was true that South Korea didn't have any reality for Kido, at least not in any immediate way. But even now, more than two decades later, this seemingly out-of-place usage remained stuck in Kido's mind, giving rise to a strange image of the personified nation of South Korea lacking any "sense" of his existence, while, conversely, allowing him to "sense" the nation of South Korea for the first time. So he sometimes wondered if it had been intentional after all, rather than a slip of the tongue.

Kido's father took him aside for talks that touched on his ethnicity on only two other occasions. The first was when Kido was wavering about what to do after high school, and he advised him that, due to discriminatory hiring practices, he should get some sort of national license. Kido had been taken aback—as if there were such problems in this day and age, let alone for a naturalized citizen like himself!—and had wanted to dismiss the suggestion as a bad joke, but his father's expression had been dead serious. In the end, although Kido would only drift to law school in the grips of the fuzzy thinking that plagues many students of the humanities, his father's words would contribute to his firm decision, while enrolled there, to try to see things through and become a lawyer.

The last time his father showed concern about Kido's ethnicity was when he got married. While not opposing the marriage, he had joined Kido's mother in proposing that he have the ceremony overseas, since Kido's maternal grandmother wanted desperately to attend wearing a *jeogori*. Kido couldn't see the point and refused, insisting it would be too much trouble. Nevertheless, after learning that his wife's parents were worried on his behalf about the same issue, he thought it over and decided to hold the wedding in Hawaii with only relatives in attendance, incorporating their honeymoon into the same trip. He and Kaori then held a modest party at a restaurant to celebrate with everyone else upon their return to Japan. Over the course of all this, Kido's parents met his in-laws twice—once at Kaori's family home for the obligatory prewedding introduction and once at the wedding—and he observed their almost groveling degree of nervousness on both occasions with a feeling somewhere between shame and pity.

※

Until very recently, this was the extent of Kido's awareness of his roots, and while he might have been simply oblivious, he truly could not recall any discrimination to speak of. He even felt somewhat embarrassed when, upon moving to Tokyo for university, he heard the stories of other third-generation Zainichi who had experienced more profound bigotry and discovered that he did not share their pain. Regarding the political situation—including the surge in historical revisionism and the domestic backlash after the Murayama Statement on the fiftieth anniversary of the end of World War II, in which the prime minister apologized for Japanese atrocities in Asia—Kido could only be described as obtuse.

It wasn't until after the Great East Japan Earthquake, when he started thinking about the massacre of Koreans all too close to home in Yokohama, that Kido first became uncomfortable with what it meant to be perceived as someone of the so-called "Korean race." Aggravating this discomfort were reports the previous summer of Japan's rising nationalism and xenophobic far-right demonstrations provoked by the landing of President Lee Myung-bak on the disputed island of Takeshima. Such developments forced Kido to acknowledge that there were some people in the country he lived in that he did not wish to meet and some places that he did not wish to visit. This was not an experience that every individual—every citizen—necessarily had to come to terms with.

Sometime later, an old university pal got in touch with Kido for the first time in years with the express purpose of informing him— perhaps out of the misguided belief he was doing him a favor—that Kido's picture from one of his elementary school yearbooks had been posted online with the caption "Zainichi Minted as Lawyer!" Visiting the webpage, Kido discovered that someone had dug up an assault-and-robbery case he'd overseen so long ago, even before he was married, that he could barely remember it. Because the suspect Kido had defended happened to have been Zainichi, the author had taken it upon themselves to fulminate over a muddle of fact and spurious distortion. At this barrage of grotesque racial slurs so outmoded that even Kido, one of their intended targets, had never heard them, he felt not so much hurt as dumbfounded. What ultimately got to him was seeing his name and an image of himself as a boy alongside insults such as "spy" and "North Korean agent." And the post wasn't only about him; it also mentioned that he was married and had one child. This made him so incensed that his hand shook on the mouse, while the uncanny perception came over him that the energy in the core of his body was draining away, as though his capacity to persist across time were breaking down. Into the gap left behind surged a cold, gunky dissonance that Kido didn't think he could ever completely clean out. Never before had he experienced his mood as a liquid like this.

To this day, Kido still hadn't told his wife about this episode. Part of him thought he should, but he didn't want to and he couldn't. It wasn't simply that Kaori had been concerned about growing reports of hate speech, as had her mother, who had at one point watched Korean Wave soap operas with such carefree absorption. The truth was, Kido had grown tired of his own hypersensitivity to prejudice. In the past, he had always shrugged off the occasional intolerant sentiments expressed by those around him as some kind of mistake. Now he almost wished he could still be so blithe.

On the topic of North Korea, Kido lined up with common opinion in being critical of the authoritarian regime and appalled by the abduction of Japanese citizens, feeling sincere pity for both the victims and their families. He grasped well enough—albeit from a somewhat distant perspective—the impact this issue had on the Zainichi community and the deep wounds that still lingered. He was also angry at the Japanese government's inaction.

Yet when he considered this problem in the light of his ethnicity, it became something altogether different. Often he would imagine a hypothetical blood relative of the same generation as him but living under that regime and find himself drawn inevitably into a kind of fatalistic speculation. If asked whether he wished for the unification of North and South on the Korean Peninsula, he probably would have nodded soberly without being able to articulate why. Likewise regarding whether Japan should one day pay war reparations and normalize diplomatic relations with the North. He had no clue, of course, when any of this might happen.

✳

Kido had been hoping to let Takagi's remark pass without comment, but the silence stretched out and grew altogether too heavy, so he decided to speak up.

"An abduction of that sort happened in the eighties. I looked into it a bit in light of Daisuké's disappearance. The case involved a bachelor who worked as a cook at a Chinese restaurant in Osaka. After being invited to a supposed job interview, he was kidnapped from Miyazaki to North Korea. A spy who had perfectly adopted the man's past and career then came to Japan in order to masquerade as him. It seems that he was active for several years, acquiring a driver's license, a health insurance card, and so on, though he was eventually apprehended upon visiting South Korea."

In the course of researching the case, Kido had learned the word "piggybacker," a piece of Japanese police jargon for a foreign spy who steals the family register of a local and poses as them.

"What did I tell you? That X guy died in Miyazaki too!" said Takagi, his eyes wide with amazement at the belief that his idea had unexpectedly hit the mark. With the two barflies now seeming to perk up their ears also, Kido noted reluctantly that the time for discussing anything concerning his client had passed.

"Yes. But that was in another era," he said. "I'm sure it's just a coincidence."

"But, like, that area is still full of North Korean agents or whatever, you know."

"Do you think? Well, I suppose there are intelligence people gathering information in every country, but I wouldn't say that area is full of them."

"But, like, anti-Japanese education in South Korea is messed up, you know."

By this point Kido was annoyed, and his jaw stiffened even as he put on a sour smile. "We are talking about North Korea, correct? Not South?"

"No . . . I mean both."

"They're completely different. In South Korea, students learn about Japan's former imperialism in history class, sure, but it's not 'anti-Japanese' propaganda or anything of the sort. After all, they don't allot very much time for modern history, any more than we do in Japan."

"Then why do they hate our country?"

"Are you referring to someone you know personally?"

"No. All you've got to do is flick on a TV or whatever."

"Well . . . I'd recommend you take a trip to Seoul and get to know some of the young people in the nightclubs before you let the TV tell you what 'they' think."

Not wanting to steer the conversation down any darker turns, Kido concluded with a genial smile and ordered another gimlet from Misuzu. Takagi, seeming to pick up on how upset the lawyer actually was from his crisp manner, said nothing more.

Misuzu looked as though her mind was elsewhere, perhaps on Daisuké Taniguchi, and Kido took solace in her indifference to the exchange that had just unfolded. While waiting for his cocktail, he picked up the case for the CD that was playing, Billy Preston's *The Kids & Me,* and looked it over. Despite the album's upbeat grooves, the silence between Misuzu and him lingered, forlorn.

"It would be a serious problem if it turned out that Daisuké Taniguchi had indeed been abducted by North Korea," Kido began matter-of-factly, lowering his voice so as not to include Takagi, "but I really can't imagine it. Those abductions happened decades ago. Plus, X was working for a logging company in a small town. What would a secret agent possibly achieve by doing dangerous labor out in the sticks?"

As Kido leaned forward speaking confidentially to Misuzu, he suddenly became aware of a psychological passageway connecting him and X. It had been opened by their commonality, namely, the respective circumstances that led others to question their Japanese identity.

"Here you are, gimlet number two." Misuzu gave Kido a faint smile as she handed him the glass and, without acknowledging his question, said, "Poor Daisuké. He really did have it rough. Do you know about the risks of being a live liver donor?"

"No, not in detail."

"Well, from what I heard back then, about one in fifty-five hundred in Japan dies."

"You mean the donors?"

"Yes. Almost all of them survive, but as many as one or two in ten have problems with fatigue, or they feel chronic pain in the wound.

They say there are all kinds of complications that can stay with you. Depression, you name it."

"Did Daisuké-san's father ask him directly to be his donor?"

"I can tell you that Daisuké would never have said that, not in a million years. But wouldn't you deny being asked if the doctor and your father wanted you to keep quiet about it?"

"But Kyoichi-san claims that Daisuké-san offered entirely on his own initiative."

"I bet that's what Daisuké said. Because he was starving for his family's love." On this hackneyed phrase, Misuzu's voice filled with pity. "Not only that. I think he felt obligated. I mean, Daisuké was the only one who could save his father . . . It's not like risk is black-and-white. He really beat himself up for not believing that he wouldn't be that one in fifty-five hundred. Like, why did he have to be so afraid when other donors did it for family without question? When the doctor explained that most people get up from the operating table to lead healthy lives without any kind of disability, how come he only thought about the handful who suffered?"

"I can relate to that, I think."

"Right? But Daisuké was really hard on himself, and in the end he decided to go through with it. I felt so bad for him, watching from the sidelines . . . But there wasn't anything I could do."

Kido kept bobbing his head to indicate both his solidarity with Misuzu and sympathy for Daisuké Taniguchi. The sweet notes of the classic ballad, "You Are So Beautiful," hummed from the speakers. The piano and strings rose to an overwhelmingly dramatic crescendo that led into the chorus. Glancing over, Kido noticed that Misuzu was tearing up. He thought it was about Daisuké Taniguchi until she spoke.

"This song is always too much for me," Misuzu explained, shaking her head as she wiped her eyes, smiling. "I'm turning into such a crybaby as I get older."

Kido, spellbound by the tender expression on Misuzu's face, echoed her sad smile.

"I only know Joe Cocker's schmaltzy version," he said. "Is this the original?"

"Uh-huh. Personally, I like this guy better."

"It's my first time hearing Preston, but I think I might agree with you. Not bad at all."

"Right?"

"When I was younger, lyrics that praised a lover directly used to make me squeamish. I must be getting old too."

"Ahhh." Misuzu let out a breath, wiping her eyes once more as she looked upward, and appeared to have herself under control.

"Kyoichi always called Daisuké a little shit," she said after a brief pause. "He never appreciated anything he did. He could never understand why I would date him, or maybe I should say he could never accept it . . . He had complicated feelings about his loser brother being in a position to save their father's life, and when Daisuké couldn't make up his mind, he got irritated with him."

"I see."

"He told him that the risk was no big deal and he should stop being such a drama queen, like he was doing their father a big favor. Said that if his own liver was up to scratch, he would have shut his trap and bitten the bullet."

"He said this to Daisuké-san's face?"

"To their mom. Daisuké overheard it."

"Ah . . ."

"Who wouldn't want to run away after that? And then to find yourself with no one to depend on and get murdered or abducted or . . ." Trailing off, Misuzu shook her head and seemed to lose herself in thought again. The hair hanging over her shoulders swayed, and she brushed it back behind her ears before bringing her glass to her lips.

"I think he's still alive," said Kido. "I'll do what I can to track him down."

He was willing to bet that Daisuké Taniguchi was a good man. Anyone who could appreciate such a fine woman and who she could love deeply had to be. The same could be said of X, in having loved Rié and been loved by her. Of course, this line of reasoning only went so far. While he hated to think badly of people, Kido did not, for example, think much at all of Rié's previous husband.

Misuzu gazed at the picture of Daisuké Taniguchi that she'd brought and then at the picture of X again. Strangely, Kido suddenly felt like he'd seen X's face somewhere before. But as he was somewhat drunk, he let the hint of a memory slip away. And checking his watch, he asked Misuzu for the bill, sad to have to go.

CHAPTER FIVE

On the day that Kyoichi visited Rié's home, she went with him to the police, still in shock about the revelation he'd thrust upon her. As distrustful as she was of him, she nonetheless felt it incumbent upon her to report the alarming situation.

Although the police station was directly in front of the bus terminal she had always used when commuting to high school, it was her first time stepping inside. She was hurriedly relating everything to the detective just as it happened when she began to worry about word of this bizarre event getting out. Once the investigation kicked off, Yuto and Hana would inevitably be drawn into it. Rumors spread instantly in a small town like this. The story might even get picked up by the newspapers . . .

But to her surprise, such concerns turned out to have been misplaced. For starters, the detective who saw to her was for some reason already in a bad mood and, throughout her and Kyoichi's scattered explanation, kept tilting his head to the side in befuddlement.

"Huh? Then the one that died was who?" he asked when they were finished. Without bothering to seek advice from anyone else in the station, the only action he took was to have Kyoichi submit Daisuké's missing person's report. When Rié asked how she might find out who her late husband had been, the detective neglected to give her an answer, claiming that the search for Daisuké had to come first.

After that, she heard nothing from the police. When she finally broke down and called the station two weeks later, she was brusquely informed that they had found no one matching Daisuké Taniguchi on the missing person's list. She tried to push them on the identity of her husband but was told that there was "no way to investigate at the present time" and bluntly dismissed.

※

With nowhere else to turn, Rié soon hit upon the idea of consulting with Kido. This was not merely because she trusted him as a lawyer. Now that the seven years since she returned home had suddenly lost all sense of reality, her time in Yokohama when she lost Ryo had become the most distinct period in her memory. And Kido had, after all, been her lone bedrock in those days.

When Rié told him on the phone what little faith she had in the police response, he replied in the same calm voice that she remembered.

"I doubt the police will do anything," he said. "They already have thousands of missing persons cases to deal with each year, so they'll be trying to avoid any additional headaches stemming from your late husband's identity. They're basically just bureaucrats."

Rié found this explanation flabbergasting, but she was relieved to have someone sensible with whom she could discuss her predicament and raised a worry that she never would have mentioned to the police. "Could my husband have been . . . involved in some kind of crime?"

After a pause, Kido cautiously agreed that was a possibility, asked her for more time to look into it, and left it at that.

※

Toward the end of February, Kido came to visit Rié in Miyazaki. They talked in the shop's waiting area, and when he told her he hadn't eaten, she took him to the local eel restaurant. It was the very same restaurant where X had once divulged the story of Daisuké Taniguchi, but she didn't pick it for that reason; it was simply one of the only suitable places within walking distance that hadn't gone out of business. Although Rié felt she was hardly one to talk, she observed that Kido had aged in the past seven years, with plenty of white appearing at his temples.

"You seem busy," she said.

"Yes, February was quite hectic," said Kido, smiling as he inserted his middle fingers below his glasses and pressed the corners of his eyes. "But it's calmed down now."

As they had always met at his firm in Yokohama, Rié felt strange to have Kido in Miyazaki with her. Whenever there was a break in the conversation, he would gaze out the window at the desolate mountain-ringed town as though he might remain absorbed in the scene ever after. And complimenting the food, he tidily devoured his high-grade eel along with its bed of rice, as well as the *gojiru*, a hearty local soup of mashed soybeans and miso served in place of the usual eel entrails in clear broth.

During the divorce mediation after her son's death, Kido's gentle smile had soothed Rié's heart on more than one occasion. He was a kind, collected lawyer, and just as much the gentleman this day as all those years ago. But she detected a subtle hint of loneliness that sometimes crept into his expression now. He did not appear to be aware of it himself.

Kido's first proposal was that they sort out the link between the family registers of Rié and the Taniguchis. If X was not "Daisuké Taniguchi," he told her, then there was no reason for her to continue going by her married name, and Rié quickly agreed. While she still felt somewhat sentimental about the name Taniguchi when she thought of her late husband, she'd felt guilty about continuing to use it ever since she met Kyoichi, as though she were brazenly introducing herself by the name of a total stranger.

Her bigger concern was the life insurance X had taken out, but Kido was quick to explain that there was no need to pay it back.

"Although the name 'Daisuké Taniguchi' is listed on the documents, it was X who was the contracting entity from the start and X who paid the premiums. Therefore, you can hold on to the sum you collected. There's no need to revise the name of the subscriber or make any changes of that kind. And if you run into any problems, please rest assured that I'll take care of them."

Since the family register that included Rié and "Daisuké Taniguchi" listed their legal residence as Rié's family home, Kido filed a petition for two revisions at the Miyazaki Family Court, which had jurisdiction over the registers of families residing in Town S. The first revision was to cancel the removal of "Daisuké Taniguchi" due to death. This would make the census records show him to be alive again and thereby ensure that the police were no longer stuck with a missing person's report for someone who was technically dead. The second revision was to then remove all record of "Daisuké Taniguchi" from her family register and reinstate the register under her maiden name, Takemoto. In other words, their marriage was to be annulled on the basis of error. The upshot of these changes would be the complete erasure of Rié's second marriage from her family register, thereby making Hana, her child with X, illegitimate.

Although Kido would have usually been able to handle this procedure on his own, given the complexity of the situation, the court asked Rié to present herself in person and requested a DNA test to prove that X was not Daisuké Taniguchi. So Kido collected various samples from X's personal effects—hair from his clothes, nails from his clippers, his electric razor, his toothbrush—and returned home with them to Yokohama.

During the nearly half a day that Rié spent with Kido, their conversations were wide ranging. When she asked if he had children, remembering that he and his wife had been childless before, and learned that he now had a son around Hana's age, the two of them chatted at length about parenting. When she then brought up the topic of what he had been doing when the earthquake struck, he told her about the streets bursting with cars and the crowds trekking home after the transportation system was paralyzed, about the cracked buildings, about enduring the blackouts and water stoppages, about the lull in Chinatown after its foreign workers returned home and customers grew scarce. Rié imagined herself going through the same ordeals in Yokohama, in a world where she'd never lost Ryo or divorced his father. Of course, then she would never have come to know a man who died in a logging accident in her hometown.

Kido was a good listener and this naturally led Rié to confide. As she was gathering X's things, she told Kido about their first meeting and described the sort of person X had been, details that she had not gone into on the phone. Kido studied the drawings on each page of X's sketchbook collection, taking pictures now and then with his phone, as he did with X's other personal effects—just in case, he explained. Rié watched Kido sitting in profile and couldn't remember the last time she had seen someone so tranquilly lost in thought.

"These really give you a sense of his character," said Kido. "They're like the work of a boy who became an adult without growing up."

"I know exactly what you mean. They definitely aren't good enough to show off. But they're like a mirror for his heart and mind . . . They're exactly like him. Incredibly pure, and serious, and giving. Not the sort of person who could ever tell lies or deceive anyone."

Kido listened attentively, offering words of encouragement. He then agreed to take on the investigation into X's background for a fee so low that Rié felt guilty.

"You're a good person, Kido-sensei, I mean it," Rié said quietly and then immediately regretted being so familiar.

"It's my job," said Kido with a smile, leaning away from her slightly with wide eyes.

Rié looked down, embarrassed. She had thought that Kido seemed lonely, but now she was the one letting herself get carried away by the intense loneliness of middle age.

※

Though Kido's time in Miyazaki had been brief, Rié did in fact feel lonely once he was gone. Not wishing he had stayed longer. Just generally wanting to have company.

She found herself replaying what the detective had said to her in her mind.

The one that died was who?

She would imagine replying, *Who died?*, and although this amounted to the same question, she felt as though the meaning changed a little.

A life is something that you can exchange with someone else—Rié would never have dreamed such a thing if her husband hadn't demonstrated it was true. He had actually led the life of another. But what about death? Death, she felt certain, was the only thing you could never exchange with anyone. Losing Ryo had taught her that.

Ryo had been a cheerful, energetic child, and partly thanks to all the time he spent playing with his elder brother, Yuto, he had picked up words at an astonishing pace. When he graduated from diapers at twenty-two months, Rié had been just as amazed as his day care teachers, though her husband chalked it up boastfully to his application of an early education method he had found online.

But just before Ryo reached his second birthday, he began to frequently wet his bed and to pee his pants at day care. While Rié and the teachers agreed that ending his potty training may have been a bit premature after all and returned him to diapers without further ado, her husband denounced Ryo's behavior as an attention-seeking regression and began to scold him for it, most vociferously before bed.

70

"This is why you piss yourself, boy!" he would say when Ryo cried and shrieked for water at night. This became the source of repeated arguments with Rié.

Soon, Ryo no longer seemed his usual bouncy self and began to occasionally throw up. At first Rié suspected it was a psychological reaction to her husband's overbearing attitude, and his teachers arrived at the same conclusion. But she could never tell what exactly was wrong with her son. She would try asking him if his tummy ached. Then she would try asking him if it didn't. Either way, he invariably gave her the same vague "uh-huh" in reply. All that seemed certain was that his head hurt when he woke up in the morning.

Rié's husband took her worries about Ryo as passive aggression directed at him and was often in a foul mood about it. Then one day, he uncharacteristically volunteered to pick up Ryo from day care by himself, and on the way back, brought him to a local pediatrician without telling Rié.

"It's just a cold," he said when he returned, tossing the medicine he had received with a clack onto the kitchen counter.

Reflecting back on all this, Rié remembered how her husband would come to regret his behavior during this period. It seemed to mark a turning point in their marriage, after which everything went wrong.

When Ryo had taken the medicine for a week and his condition failed to improve, Rié decided to bring him to another pediatrician, this time their usual one, but her husband did not approve.

"With you asking him, 'Does your head hurt, does your head hurt?' all the time, the boy's bound to start believing it. So if you want to call it something psychological, well, then it's your fault."

Upon examining Ryo, the doctor advised them to take him immediately to a bigger hospital and wrote them a letter of referral. This was the first time that the possibility of a brain tumor was brought to their attention; an MRI the following week confirmed it. The tumor was located in Ryo's basal ganglia, and he was diagnosed with "a typical case of germinoma." His bedwetting and thirst, the doctor told them, both stemmed from the diabetes insipidus that was concomitant with this condition, but with treatment, he could make a full recovery.

To this day, Rié regretted the way she clung with faith from then on to that word. Recovery. Not that it was entirely her fault. The doctor had seemed confident of his diagnosis and hadn't explained the possibility of glioblastoma as thoroughly as he would later claim.

It was a difficult reality to face, and Rié was surprised to find that her husband was quicker than she was to accept it. Bravely confronting their grim destiny was where he had located the grounding for his self-respect, and he began to display a peculiar elation. This was his way of compensating for all the hurt his pride had suffered at the hands of his wife throughout their disagreements. He almost seemed invigorated.

But Rié was the one who quit her job, brought a folding cot to Ryo's ward, and stayed by his side, caring for him during his three months in the hospital. Her husband did no such thing. Like her, he had been seduced by the word "recovery."

"Giving it a go with radiation and chemotherapy is rational," he told her, repeatedly insisting she didn't understand because she was a woman and had studied the humanities, all the while lacking the faintest inkling of just how awful the treatment actually was.

Rié tried her best not to call up her memories of Ryo racked by relentless vomiting. His oral inflammation had been so bad that the pain of swallowing his own saliva was enough to make him cry, and she watched as he grew skinnier and skinnier. Rié herself could hardly sleep or get food down. A small woman to begin with, she lost a fifth of her body weight in just three months. Undeterred, she went on hugging Ryo as he thrashed about in misery, making him go through with the treatment, for she never stopped believing in that word: "recovery."

"Hang in there," the doctor would say. "You are a big boy, aren't you?"

"Yes, sir . . . Yes, sir . . . ," tiny Ryo would reply, sitting on the edge of his bed with his hands in his lap, nodding earnestly. It was Ryo's expression of tender innocence in these moments rather than his crying scowl that Rié remembered now, his hair fallen out, his face swollen almost beyond recognition. He always replied this way instead of saying "yes" or "yeah" because his father had drilled it into him. How many times had Ryo appeared in Rié's dreams since his death, nodding to those paternal instructions with a "Yes, sir. Yes, sir. Yes, sir"?

And the despair that set in when they learned that all the suffering they'd forced upon him was utterly pointless. If that's how it was going to turn out, they should have set aside the days that remained in his short life to serve him his favorite foods, to take him to the zoo he so enjoyed, to spoil him with whatever he asked for, to teach him the joy of living if only briefly. Like there was ever any need for such harsh rearing. If only she could have known! When Rié learned that "recovery" was never coming, that Ryo would not be saved, she couldn't breathe. It was as though a savage, invisible hand covered her mouth and held her tight in its grasp. The inside of her body blazed with heat and then filled with glacial cold, and rubbing her arms and legs together erratically, all she could do was cry.

Now Rié thought she finally understood her body's intention: to fly into such a frenzy that all feeling ceased.

※

Rié could not die in Ryo's place. While expressing the wish to die for the sake of a sick child is something of a platitude, Rié's desire to do so was genuine and came upon her with excruciating force. All she could do was pray to nothing and no one in particular for some kind of miracle. But in the end, only Ryo could die his own death. And for Rié, there would be no other death than the one that awaited her.

Who died? she kept asking herself in her head. According to the family register census records, it had been a man named "Daisuké Taniguchi." Yet Daisuké Taniguchi should have had a death reserved for him alone. So Rié had to wonder who her late husband had been. Or in other words, whose death he had died.

Rié had never made a habit of such abstract philosophizing. But thinking was essential for her now, if she was to go on living and stop herself from going mad as her body almost had when she realized that Ryo was gone.

Kido called her late husband X, but Rié, even for the sake of convenience, refused to do the same. Referring to someone by a code you have chosen without their permission rather than by their name seemed to her a fundamental insult to the dignity of the human being. Whenever she heard Kido say X, it made her feel like they were discussing a stranger, and words would slip away from her. Faltering in the middle of the conversation, she would reflect on the sound that had just passed her by. And she would feel fairly certain that it was supposed to refer to her husband. But without knowing his real name, she had nothing to call him as he receded with his back turned into the distance.

The dead cannot call out to us. All they can do is wait for us to call to them. Except for the dead whose names are unknown. Uncalled by anyone, they sink ever deeper into solitude.

Rié knelt facing the photo of her husband on the altar in her home, not knowing what to say to make him turn around. During his life, she had called him "Papa" or "Father" whenever the children were present, but had been accustomed to calling him Daisuké-kun as soon as they were alone. Usually she would have only used the suffix *"kun"* with the name of a child or at least someone younger than her. But there was something about him, in keeping with the juvenile vibe of his sketchbooks, that compelled her to attach "kun" to his name, as though he were one of her classmates in elementary school. For some reason, she also felt that the *"suké"* sound at the end was just asking for it. And yet "Daisuké" was the name of a complete stranger.

Rié tried to recall the times she had said "Daisuké-kun" when the love for her husband had been deepest, the distance between them smallest. With no one else there, no room for mistaking the other, no need to distinguish them from anyone else, even then—especially then!—we call out to the beloved by name. She wondered how he might have felt in such moments to have his wife speak the name of another, to have her affection permeate every nook and cranny of that name and envelop him forever in its lingering resonance.

)(

His name wasn't the only problem. Rié's late husband had also told her the story of the man who bore it, and she had empathized deeply with the life it bespoke.

Her husband had never wanted to talk about his childhood, and she used to enjoy imagining what it might have been like. Suppose they had been the same age and went to the same school. Would it have taken a whole year, until they moved up to the next grade, for them to have a proper conversation? After all, he would have been the quiet, serious type who went off during lunch to a secluded spot removed from the main class clique to play contentedly. The type who, in later years, was excluded by default from talk of crushes and other gossip but who had no qualms whatsoever about being left out. The type who, in spite of this inconspicuousness, appears out of the blue in the reminiscing mind's eye of former classmates, even more vivid somehow than the kids they played with on a daily basis, summoned by the nostalgia clinging to their memory.

Even after they were married, he remained gentle and generous. Although he spoke little, his expression was always mild and he never raised his voice to Rié or the children. The exact opposite of her previous husband, who tended to be irritable after Yuto's birth and consequently overlooked the odd changes that eventually afflicted Ryo.

Rié thought she had never been happier than during the three years and nine months of married life with him. But when she looked back on her memories of that time, they spun precariously like a top, falling over with his abrupt end and moving no more. If he had remained alive, Rié might never have noticed the contradictions that arose from the false story he had told, just as a blot of dirt on a top looks like a perfect circle as long as it keeps spinning. Those years had left their mark in every part of her body, and it terrified her to think that lurking inside she might find an uncanny face that actually matched the barren moniker, X.

There had to be a good reason he had done this. That's what she wanted to believe. But why didn't he tell her? He'd had four and a half years from the time they met to do it. They had trusted each other enough. It wasn't as if he hadn't had the opportunity.

Facing his photo, Rié always stared into his eyes and wished there was a name by which she could call him. Could mendacious sincerity, consummately performed, be the ultimate deception?

CHAPTER SIX

Kido had warned Rié that the court ruling on their petition to annul Daisuké Taniguchi's death and restore Rié's maiden name to her family register could take anywhere from two months to a year. If the latter was rejected, they would have to sue for a declaratory judgment of the invalidation of her marriage. But as it turned out, both petitions were approved five months later, around the first week of August.

With the DNA test providing definitive evidence that X was not Daisuké Taniguchi, Rié's second marriage was erased from the records. Her past now corrected, she was no longer a widow and had only been married once.

The error hadn't simply been one of bureaucratic procedure. It was her actions that had been in error. She had come to the false belief that she had married someone named Daisuké Taniguchi, who she had never even met, publicly declared this to everyone around her, and illegitimately notified the government of his death despite having no idea what this person might be doing or where. When she thought about this, she felt a sort of mystified harrowing sadness, and lost all concrete sense of whose life she herself was leading.

"Mama," said Hana in her still-babyish voice. "I kept trying to wake Yuto. But he won't get up!"

"Oh," said Rié, looking over her shoulder at Hana as she fried eggs sunny-side up. "He's not up yet?"

It was the morning of the opening ceremony for Yuto's fall semester, and Rié was making breakfast.

"This I think," said Hana. She had developed the habit of prefacing her opinions with this phrase, a sort of anastrophe that mixed up the word order of Japanese. As she invariably did after saying this, Hana paused for a moment, swallowed, and glanced obliquely upward to gather her thoughts. Rié found this quirk hilarious and always broke into a smile as she waited for her daughter to continue.

"Yuto is still sleepy because he slept in every morning over summer break," Hana conjectured, her eyes crescents of amusement.

Next month Hana would be five. Until recently, she had been known to everyone as "the Puffy Tot." Although Hana had never been fat on the whole, her arms and legs had been so plump ever since she was born that people found touching them irresistible and immediately discovered that they had a certain "puffy" feel to them for which there was no comparison on earth. But she had since learned to walk, and with all the scampering around that she did at day care each day, her infantile physique had gradually tightened up until, within the past year, that extra padding had disappeared altogether. Now that the nickname no longer stuck, Rié doubted that Hana even remembered it.

Children developed entirely too fast, immediately outgrowing whatever seemed to define them as individuals. Rié had come to know Ryo's personality traits—his quick comprehension, his perseverance, his charm, his timidity—and now that he was gone, she was painfully uncertain what they might have signified. Looking at Hana now, Rié could see that she was becoming more and more like her father by the day, at least on the outside. While her nose showed signs of growing long unlike the nose of either of her parents, her eyes were very much like his—but these were the features of a man whose identity was still unknown. And suddenly Rié felt the warmth drain out of her cheeks as a sort of foreboding came over her.

Putting the eggs on a plate and spreading jam and butter on Hana's toast, she said, "Hana, I'm just going to go wake him up. Can you go ahead and start eating? Grandma should be crawling out of bed soon to join you."

"OK!" said Hana.

When Rié entered Yuto's room on the second floor, she found him in bed, wrapped up in a light cotton blanket with the air-conditioning on.

"What's the matter?" she asked. "Have you caught a cold?"

Too worried to wait for his reply, Rié sat down on the edge of his bed and put her hand on his back. Yuto was facing the wall and now curled his body up even tighter. When Rié reached out to touch his forehead, he buried his face in his pillow, but she found enough of it to tell that he didn't have a fever.

"You need to tell your mother if you're not feeling well. We've got to take you to the doctor."

". . . I'm fine."

"Oh yeah?"

After a pause, Yuto roused himself and sat up slowly.

"Mom, you worry too much," he said, scratching his tousled head, eyes downcast. "I'm not Ryo. You freak out every time I have a bit of a headache or a cold. I'm me. My brother was my brother."

Rié let out a small sigh and nodded.

"You're completely right, Yuto, but can you expect me to behave any differently after what I went through? You're just going to have to accept that my anxiety isn't going anywhere and learn how to handle it."

Lifting his head, Yuto gave her an exasperated smile. Rié reminded herself that, already at his age, he had lost three close family members. On the surface, the aloofness toward death typical of someone so young seemed to have protected him from deep psychological scarring. But even if that were true, his childhood was a far cry from Rié's happy one.

The idea that he might reach adulthood without having any issues suddenly struck her as naive.

"Are you really OK?"

"Yeah . . . There's nothing wrong with my body, anyway."

"What is it then? Your mood?"

Yuto remained still as though in thought. Already he was taller than her and had pimples on his cheeks.

"Go on."

Yuto scratched his head again, brushed his hands over his face, bit his lip, and searched for words. "I . . . I've decided that I don't want to change my name . . . Can't we stick with Taniguchi?"

Why didn't I realize what was behind his sulking sooner? she thought. *How foolish of me.* Not long ago, she had announced without explanation that she would be switching back to her maiden name, and should have noticed something was up when Yuto merely nodded, acknowledging the news with seeming indifference.

"When I was born, we were the Yonedas. Then you got divorced and we became the Takemotos. When I started elementary school, we became the Taniguchis . . . Now I'm in middle school. All my friends, the older students, the younger students, everyone calls me Taniguchi, and you're telling me we're going back to Takemoto again? Like, maybe you're used to Takemoto, Mother, but for me it just feels like Grandma and Grandpa's name. So, like, it's weird, OK . . . Having to go around being like, 'No, it's Takemoto' every time someone calls me Taniguchi would just suck . . ."

"I see what you mean."

"And if you marry someone else, my last name is going to change again! I don't even want a last name anymore." Yuto made a show of slapping his knees, wearing a histrionic, fed-up smile.

"I'm done marrying. I'm all married out."

The first time Rié got married, she didn't think twice about the fact that her name would change, at least insofar as it was her husband's name. But she remembered the intense dissonance she had felt the moment it dawned on her, while surrounded by in-laws at her husband's family home, that she shared that name with these other people too. And every time she returned to her hometown during that period, she would think longingly of the name Takemoto that lay dormant inside her. Although the situation with her second husband had been completely different, a similar discomfort had probably contributed to her knee-jerk aversion to Kyoichi. Such experiences made her wonder if there might even be people out there who, unable to love their biological parents, could not feel that the name they were born with was their own . . .

"Mom, have you already forgotten Dad?"

"Of course not."

"Then when are you going to make a grave for him? His ashes have been in the urn forever. You hardly even talk about him anymore. It's messed up, Mom."

Rié didn't know what to say.

"When you go back to Takemoto, you'll let me stay Yuto Taniguchi, won't you? It's . . . it's just not right to do this to Dad. His family turned their backs on him and now what if we forget him too?"

The whir of the decrepit air conditioner accentuated the charged stillness of the morning, and suddenly Yuto seemed grown-up to her. His voice had begun to change a few weeks earlier, after growing hoarse on their family trip to Beppu during the Obon Festival. Over the course of their brief conversation, the sun shining in through the seam in the curtains had grown noticeably brighter, spurring on the rising pitch of the cicadas. Relaxing her firmly pursed lips, Rié sighed feebly.

"Yuto, what sort of person would you say your father was?" she asked.

"Huh?" said Yuto, caught off guard. "A really nice guy, I guess. You don't think so?"

"No. I agree."

"Even when he scolded me, he'd sit me down to explain what I did wrong and listen to what I had to say . . . I think he was a better person than my old dad. I know I'm related to him. But I just wish my second dad was my real dad. Hana is so lucky."

After Rié remarried, Yuto never used the phrase "real dad." Still only eight at the time, he instead parroted Rié in calling his biological father his "old dad." But eventually, out of affection for his "second dad," or perhaps out of consideration for Rié, he seemed to come to the resolution never to use the phrase. For to do otherwise would be to implicitly deny that his second dad was his real dad.

When Rié intuited her son's thought process about this, she adored him even more. It demonstrated a thoughtfulness beyond his years. How fitting that he seemed to have picked up this strength of character not through heredity from his old dad but through the influence of his second.

"Your father took great care of you, didn't he, Yuto?"

"I . . . Since Dad died, I . . . I'm not sad anymore. Grandma has been so nice to me. But, like, . . ." Yuto smiled in embarrassment. "I come home every day with all these things I want to ask him and . . . I miss him . . ."

At last Yuto burst out crying. While sobs racked his shoulders, Rié gently stroked his back, growing teary-eyed along with him.

"You really loved your father, huh, Yuto."

"Mom . . . Mom, I know there has to be some reason you're doing this, but if I stop being Taniguchi . . . it's like he'll no longer be my dad anymore . . . I'll be nothing but the child of my old dad . . . and my second dad will be nothing but the husband from your second marriage . . . and Hana will be his child, and her dad will be different from mine . . ."

Bent over as he was, Rié could only see his flushed cheeks as tears went on pattering into his lap. She hadn't seen him cry so much since his dad's funeral.

"Oh, look. Now what do we have here? It's little Hana all by her lonesome." Rié heard her mother's voice coming from the first floor. "Where's Mommy? Upstairs? . . . Riééé. You've left Hana to eat alone?"

"I'll be right there!"

Yuto kept wiping his bloodshot eyes as he stifled the spasms in his chest.

"You can keep Taniguchi, Yuto—alright? But a bunch of things happened and for legal reasons I had to go back to Takemoto . . . I'll explain everything. I'm sorry I haven't been clear with you, sweetheart. It's just that it's kind of complicated . . ."

Rié realized that she had to fill him in sooner rather than later. While she had been planning to wait until the truth had at least become clear, there was no telling when that might happen. But how would he react when he learned about his beloved father's lies?

Yuto had already intuited that his mother was hiding something. So when she said that the situation was "complicated," he decided that his vague premonition about her getting married for the third time had to be true as well. When Yuto told Rié about this later, she would be taken aback that he would leap to such a conclusion. It only made sense when he explained that her recent outing with Kido and her furtive conversations with him on the phone had set off his alarm bells.

The outline of Yuto's flushed face gently warped and swelled in Rié's moist eyes. Without a word, he nodded, rose from the bed, and went to open the curtains. Then, gazing outside, he roughly brushed away his tears once again. At such moments as these, when Rié saw that one of her surviving children was growing up, she always reminded herself to be strong and keep moving forward.

CHAPTER SEVEN

"So you bought that ring for yourself?"

"Yes."

"Not for your daughter?"

"For me . . . yes."

"But you gave it to her to hold on to?"

"Only because when I let her hold it, she looked really cute and happy and stopped crying. It was just that one time."

"In other words, you knew that your daughter was holding the ring in her hand and you let her, is that right?"

"Just that one time, like I said. Only when I was watching her . . . yes."

"You didn't use the ring as a soother to make your daughter stop crying?"

"I would never! Nope. The person who made it should have warned me to be careful that small children might put it in their mouths. It doesn't matter if the ring was meant for adults. If a young woman buys it, it's common she'll have kids in the house. For a university student to think he can go making and selling something like that is just irresponsible!"

"I present to the plaintiff exhibit five, a photograph taken inside her residence. Are those magnets in your living room?"

"Yes."

"They're not your daughter's toys?"

"What? No, they're not . . ."

"And the magnets are placed out of your child's reach?"

". . . Yes."

"Are there other rings in your house besides the one at issue?"

". . . Yes . . ."

"And earrings as well?"

". . . Yes."

"And you always keep those rings and earrings out of your child's reach?"

". . ."

"What is your answer?"

"Yes."

"So that your daughter won't swallow them by mistake, correct?"

". . . Well, that's . . ."

"But you placed the ring at issue within your child's reach?"

". . ."

"And you didn't just place it there, you gave it to her to hold on to, correct?"

". . . Like I . . . Yes, that's right . . ."

"That's all."

※

Having completed his oral argument for a civil suit at the Yokohama District Court that morning, Kido was having lunch in Chinatown with Nakakita, one of his partners at the firm. A freshly stir-fried plate of sweet-and-sour black vinegar pork rested on the table in front of him. His tongue hurt, as he seemed to have burned it when absentmindedly shoveling the food in.

"I was already amazed that that lawyer would get her to sue for that, but boy, did he ever look like a villain," said Nakakita. "What year do you think he got his license? I've never seen him before."

"The media turnout was quite something," said Kido. "And the internet is in an uproar with the hashtag 'parental mishap,' the poor plaintiff. She absolutely refuses to settle and she's bound to lose her case. When I think about the prospects of a single mother like her looking after a kid with brain damage . . . well, it really brings me down."

The lawsuit was filed after a baby girl choked on a ring that her mother had purchased online from a graduate student, who had been selling accessories he produced with a 3D printer in the lab at his school in Fujisawa. Although the girl's life had been saved, she was left with severe brain damage, and the mother was suing for millions.

The chic, vibrant rings, studs, chokers, and other items that the defendant made had impressed Kido when he first saw them. Recently, the young man had branched out into promotional novelties for events, and over the past year his sales had grown steadily. Considering the time and effort he put into his work, his profits had been modest, but he had had a long-term vision of becoming a designer and making a living off his creations. Meanwhile, he had neglected to take out product liability insurance, a no-brainer for any corporation in the same industry. He didn't even know he was required to file a tax return for business earnings over a set amount.

Kido felt sorry for the defendant. Every time they met, he burst into tears at the thought of the asphyxiated child. Like the plaintiff, he had been doxed and was now mentally unstable, claiming that he would never sell accessories again. It seemed a shame to Kido that he would lose the outlet for his talents in this way. Such a legal outcome also struck him as unfair.

In court, Kido had challenged the plaintiff, arguing that the design of the accessories was not lacking in the level of safety one could reasonably expect as the student had not originally envisaged them being used as children's toys, and pointing out that the plaintiff had a number of other knickknacks at home of comparable size and shape. The plaintiff's lawyer insisted that failing to attach a detailed written warning counted as a defect, but Kido didn't believe that the student's labelling requirements were that onerous. While he conceded a certain degree of persuasiveness to the general position that responsibility for such hobbyist products should be interrogated for the sake of security in society going forward, there was a limit to how far such an inquisition could be taken in court.

Nakakita had decided to try the twice-cooked pork curry, an unusual specialty said to be a recent hit at the restaurant, and did not look disappointed as he devoured it with gusto, sweat beading his forehead.

"By the by," he said, "that Supreme Court ruling about the inheritance disparity for extramarital children reminded me, how's the case in Miyazaki going?"

Some years Kido's senior, Nakakita was the sort of man who seemed like everyone's elder brother, at once inspiring reverence and fondness. With a sparse, downy five o'clock shadow on sunken cheeks that endowed him with an unlawyerly allure, he played drums in a band in his spare time. Although this and his family duties seemed to keep him busy, he liked criminal cases and continued to take on plenty even at his advancing age, sticking obstinately to the letter of the law no matter how tragic the circumstances. His band played in the style of The Gadd Gang, and on the several occasions that Kido had gone out to hear them, Nakakita's steady rhythm had felt rife with personality. As Kido himself had played bass in a band back in university, they had hit it off as soon as they'd met. So when Kido had been establishing the firm, Nakakita was the first person he reached out to.

"The notifications of death and marriage for the man who was impersonated have been annulled," Kido replied.

"Oh yeah? Well, I guess that's about all you can do, huh?"

"Yes, though partly out of personal interest, I'm continuing to investigate his whereabouts as well as the identity of X."

"It sure makes you curious—hey, what kind of music did they listen to? You can't fake taste in music."

"Oh . . . I wonder about X. I know he was into drawing pictures. Apparently Daisuké Taniguchi liked Michael Schenker. Thought he was God, according to his ex."

"Then I can guarantee you he's a good dude," said Nakakita with a laugh.

"What makes you so sure?"

"No one living in the boonies in that era who cried to the wicked guitar licks of Schenker could have been bad. Trust me."

"You used to listen to that kind of music too? I never would have guessed."

"Come on. It was the eighties—you know those bands are still at it, coming on tour to Japan and everything? Our guitarist went to a show in a fit of nostalgia and said it was a real blast from the past. Though it sounds like the audience was all hags and geezers. If you go to the concert halls, who knows, maybe you'll find that Taniguchi guy."

"Huh . . . I never would have thought of that."

"Well, taste in music changes like everything else, but good memories stick with you. You could try checking one of the fan pages. You never know. Maybe he'll be hanging around."

Kido crossed his arms and thought about this for a while. Nakakita had finished his curry and soon asked the server for more water.

"How about the other case?" he said. "That death-by-overwork suit."

"The first hearing is in October so I'm taking down the accounts of the parties involved and, well, various things . . ."

The family of a twenty-seven-year-old restaurant employee who killed himself after being forced to work an unconscionably long shift was suing the company and the management. Although Kido had been regularly handling approximately fifty cases of late, he found this to be one of the most emotionally taxing.

"Sounds like the case is tiring you out."

"Is it ever . . . I'm only able to cope because it doesn't involve me personally. I still have to tell myself that after all these years."

"It's a basic truth about the job. Remind me—did you end up going anywhere last summer?"

Kido shook his head. He meant to keep his lips sealed, but words spilled out that even he didn't expect. "Things are not going well at home at the moment."

As Kido hardly ever discussed his personal life, this abrupt confession left Nakakita wide-eyed, his lips protruding.

From the outside looking in, the lack of conversation between Kido and Kaori that had imperceptibly established itself as a fixture of their daily routine was the very picture of a typical marriage slump and nothing more. To Kido on the inside, it felt transparent and tranquil, like water in a glass. A single sip should have been all it took for either of them to bring the awkwardness to an end, except that the water had been left out for too long and was no longer drinkable. Now, a sliver of ice had fallen in with the slightest splash and disturbance on the surface—nothing toxic, just ice that quickly melted, spreading a new chill through the silence and sustaining the memory of it forever.

The problem owed its origin to Kaori's suspicions about Kido's trip to Miyazaki. In part because he was required to maintain the confidentiality of his clients, Kido rarely talked about work at home, and Kaori, in any case, showed zero interest. So until then, when either of them had to stay overnight in another city, all they had to do was say "work" and the matter was settled. But for no reason Kido could discern, something about this trip had seemed fishy to her.

At first, Kido had laughed and dismissed it as paranoia. Later, he began to worry that she might be stressed out about something else. When he suggested this to her, Kaori denied it, but there was a shift in her after that. Instead of directing her thorny silence unrelentingly at Kido, she began to come down with unusual harshness on their son.

This Kido could not abide, and he eventually lost his temper, dragged by feeble anger over the bounds of his self-control without even the impetus for a full-blown outburst. The lesson he took away was that he wasn't his usual collected self when confronting his wife.

He knew Kaori had no justification for thinking anything had happened with Rié. Even supposing she had taken a peek at his cell phone, there was nothing in their exchanges to invite misunderstanding. So her concern about his trip could only mean she had a hunch that something might happen between them. The very idea was foolish on too many levels to count.

"If I were to get involved with a client, I would be reprimanded," he had said, trying his best to maintain a light tone and keep from looking stern. He had wanted to tell her that she lacked respect for his work but decided not to go that far.

Even with his marital troubles flashing through his mind, Kido was reluctant to describe them to Nakakita. But as Nakakita appeared to be waiting patiently for him to follow up on his confession, Kido decided to approach the topic from a different angle.

"My wife seems to have this vague notion that problems between a husband and wife can be traced to disagreements in their fundamental philosophy, though I doubt she's used that word with any seriousness in her entire life."

Nakakita frowned. "You mean in a political sense?"

"No . . . That might be what it boils down to, but I'm referring to something more basic than that. I mean, she didn't vote in the upper house election in July. I can't convince her to vote at all."

"I hear you."

"As a Zainichi, I'm aware of the importance of the right to political participation, but if I try to tell her that . . . well, she thinks I'm being self-righteous. Ever since our child was born, she doesn't seem to want to acknowledge my heritage—if I'd dragged her kicking and screaming to the polls, I bet she'd have voted for the LDP without blinking in any case, even in the last election."

"What does her family do, again?"

"Her father is a dentist. Her brother is a physician."

"Oh yeah. You told me."

"I felt really bad about having to cut short my volunteer work after the earthquake. That was the first time my wife and I had a serious fight. She said it was hypocritical to leave your wife and child alone to go help other mothers and children, even if they were voluntary evacuees. As if I had the time for that when my hands should have been full already taking care of my own family. But I got absolutely nowhere when I suggested she go volunteer while I looked after our son. She has no interest in volunteering. She claimed that she'd be too worried if she was apart from him."

"Your boy is still pretty young."

"Sure. And I can understand her concern. The buildings around here took a lot of damage, and with the power shortages and aftershocks, we were psychologically exhausted. On the city's new hazard map, our building is directly in the tsunami zone. When I consider the earthquake they're predicting here, the Nankai Trough earthquake, and all the rest, it makes me wonder if it's OK for us to stay in our condo."

"Same with us. There's something about earthquake risk that just doesn't stir you to act. We stock up on disaster goods, but I don't think we'd actually move."

"So I conceded her point. You can never know when an earthquake might come. I was offering pro bono legal advice once or twice a month, but I had to call it off."

"You did plenty. With a young child like yours, the timing just wasn't right."

"Well, maybe it's wrong of me to label what she says in an emergency situation her philosophy. The idea that there might be a connection between loving someone and their philosophy never even crossed my mind when I was young. It's hard to say if I was overvaluing love or undervaluing philosophy."

"Love and philosophy . . . I wouldn't be surprised if there were more youngsters nowadays who make that connection right from the start."

"Indeed," Kido said with a nod and took the shift in topic as an opportunity to speak no further. He had wanted to conclude by wryly mentioning that his marriage had been sexless ever since, but was dismayed to find the words catching in his throat. Ashamed of himself and jealous of happier couples, he imagined living out his days with an unsatiated sex drive and felt vaguely sad.

As Nakakita needed to return to court in the afternoon, Kido parted with him in Chinatown and began to walk toward the Kannai Station area, where the firm was located. He was surprised to find that his forehead wasn't sweaty, his dry hairline a sign that the summer was fading.

In the park by Yokohama Stadium, he saw mothers pushing strollers and salarymen eating baked goods on a bench. With the firm, the court, and his home all too close together for comfort, he viewed this local scenery regularly—the clusters of stubby high-rises, the restaurant stretch, the gingko trees—from multiple perspectives: as a lawyer, as a husband, as a father. At that moment he looked around with an indeterminate gaze that was none of these. And as he turned over the conversation with Nakakita in his mind, his thoughts turned to the day he had first gone to Miyazaki to meet Rié.

As it had been baseball spring training season, the only vacant room he could find was a double at the Sheraton Grande Ocean Resort, which had been one of the factors that made Kaori suspicious. The room was indeed too good for a regular business trip, and as he was looking down from his window onto the golf course, absorbed in the sea and sky beyond, the idea of spending the night there alone began to feel empty.

For a time, he lounged on the bed. The stark white sheets stiffly wrapping the mattress like a uniform on a body seemed to be waiting for someone to tear them off with reckless, scrabbling hands. Eventually he took off his glasses and stretched out on his back. He tried to recall all the ceilings he'd ever looked up at with his heart pounding, his breath deep and pleasant, his skin naked and sweaty, and obscene images rose in his mind's eye. The bridled tranquility seemed to demand someone by his side with whom to exchange the feeling of heat from their unclothed flesh.

Presently he shook off these pointless fantasies with a sigh, went down to the ground-floor restaurant for their specialty—fried chicken with tartar sauce—and took a taxi into the city center for a drink. Although the night was slightly chilly, he strolled in only jeans and a light jacket. Kido was hardly new to travelling for work. And yet this time, his being not even a tourist steeped him in the sense that he was no one. To everyone in this city, he was a complete stranger. Not that Yokohama was all that different in this regard, but there was something even more unfamiliar about here. And this state of anonymity felt simply wonderful.

As he walked through a shopping arcade, several parlors of the sort he had sampled in his twenties passed along the edges of his vision. Although he'd never developed a hankering for them and had eventually lost interest, he began to slow down in front of one of their tacky lit-up signs. Suddenly—as though, yes, he were someone other than himself—Kido felt that he was meant to go inside. He read the description on the sign and looked over the pictures of girls with lightened hair. Then, with the idea still smoldering inside him, he coasted onward and arrived at the bar he had looked up in advance.

The décor was classy, with illuminated exotic plants on display beneath the see-through counter, and a multiplicity of whiskey and liqueur bottles magnificent in the lush green glow. Already tired, Kido had been planning to show up around eight o'clock and return to the hotel after one or two drinks. But he would later be surprised to find himself drinking alone past midnight.

During the entire time he was there, the counter was devoid of other patrons. While the tables were only sparsely occupied, he could hear a buzz of rowdy voices spilling from the door to the private room at the back every time it opened. This party kept the server busy rushing back and forth with beer and snacks. When several huge men lumbered in late, Kido realized they were professional baseball players in the midst of training. As he had no interest in baseball and couldn't name even the players on the Yokohama BayStars, he had no idea what team they were on, but from the suggestive looks the server shot him, he gathered that they were famous.

Classic jazz albums like *Kind of Blue* and *Portrait in Jazz* played at a subdued volume. For his first drink, Kido ordered a vodka gimlet, remembering Misuzu. His drink of choice for a long time had been a balalaika, but he'd ordered a gimlet on impulse that night in Arakicho and found himself unable to go back to the sweetness of Cointreau ever since, even though he'd sworn by it since he was a young man.

The bartender was a man who looked to be a few years older than Kido. Although he brandished his shaker with flair, preposterously, he used store-bought lime juice rather than squeezing it fresh, resulting in a superlatively foul cocktail. With this, Kido's impression of Misuzu as a mean mixer of gimlets synergized in his mind with her languid carefree vibe, casting her in an even more beguiling light.

For his second drink, he ordered Stalinskaya, a rare offering, and took it straight. Well chilled and refreshing, it spread more fully across the palate than expected and he wished he had started with it. With one more exhalation, he was fully immersed in the pleasant strangeness of being in Miyazaki alone.

"Are you visiting from outside the prefecture?" asked the bartender, when the orders from the back room had finally slowed down.

"Yes. Can you guess?"

"I sure can. Near Tokyo?"

Kido nodded and drained his glass, his gaze pausing on the smattering of droplets at the bottom that would no doubt fail to reach his tongue even if he tilted it back. Then, not feeling particularly drunk, he began to say at a slow and steady pace, "I'm from Gunma originally. Ikaho Onsen."

"Huh. Is that right. Supposed to be a famous hot springs area, I hear. Can't say I've ever been there myself."

"I'm not surprised. Why go all that way with so many great hot springs right here in Kyushu? My elder brother inherited the family inn. I left home because I'm the second son. I never got along well with my family anyway."

This abrupt outpouring of personal information seemed to throw the bartender off for a moment, so Kido gave him a smile. He wondered if X had arrived in this town as Daisuké Taniguchi and related this past like it was his own in the same way, feeling out the comfort of his new life as though trying on a garment or test-driving a car.

"Same with my folks," said the bartender with a gentle, understanding look as he dried a glass. "I don't talk about this much with first-time customers, but they were in construction. Just like with you, my elder brother took over the business."

The bartender explained that he was the manager of the bar and passed Kido his card.

"Sorry, I just ran out of mine," said Kido. "My name is Taniguchi. Daisuké Taniguchi."

The bartender, of course, didn't doubt him for a second. Already, Kido felt a kind of special relationship budding between him and this man he'd just met. He was no longer a complete stranger in the town. Now, if he were walking around and crossed paths with this bartender, they would probably nod to each other in startled recognition.

Kido ordered another glass of Stalinskaya and continued to relate Daisuké Taniguchi's past as though it were his own. Just like X that afternoon with Rié, he talked in a detached tone as though of events long ago, mixing in a woeful grin now and again as he described how his agreement to be the organ donor had finally led to an irreparable break with his family. With hardly any awareness that this was a performance, Kido felt, to the contrary, that in speaking these words he drew ever closer to unity with them.

"That's tough, my friend," the bartender would say occasionally, showing empathy but not overdoing it—a true professional. That night, Kido felt as though he could have kept on going like this until he'd drunk himself under the table in tears.

While waiting for a stoplight, Kido gazed at the cars passing in front of him. Suddenly he found himself wondering what would happen if he was fatally hit by one of them as Daisuké Taniguchi. In the deep, secluded recesses of that mountain forest, at the instant the cryptomeria fell to take X's life, what thoughts might have crossed his mind?

Even after returning to Yokohama, Kido's memory of his inexpressible joy during those two hours impersonating X stayed with him. He had felt nervous and excited and dizzy. It was an experience most people know as the effect of tragedy, but in place of watching tragic movies or reading tragic books, Kido now saw the potential for a new sort of hobby in synchronizing himself with the life story of another so as to vicariously inhabit their inner world. Admittedly, a shameless game with a bitter aftertaste.

And yet, upon his recent return to Miyazaki, though he quietly nurtured the wish to become the self he had left downtown that night— the continuation of the life of X impersonating Daisuké Taniguchi—he couldn't bring himself to return to the bar. For he'd met Rié the next day and, seeing her distress over the truth of X's identity again, felt guilty for taking pleasure in his little masquerade. It seemed unlikely that he'd get the same kick out of it if he went back now. And besides, there was almost nothing left that he needed to say as Daisuké Taniguchi.

Kido had no idea what X's reasons might have been, but it seemed that he had, in his one and only life, led the lives of two people, resolving to wash his hands of the first and kick off a completely new phase as the second.

There were two things about X that Kido was unable to fathom. First was his ability to throw everything away. Of this, Kido was vaguely jealous, for no matter how weary he grew of his current life, it was simply not in him to do the same. Again and again, while bathing in an outdoor hot spring bath at the Sheraton, he had thought about how much his son would enjoy it there. Had X possessed no comparable joy in his former life that would have made it worth sustaining? If not, then he was of a kind with Daisuké Taniguchi, who had sloughed off his past to be rid of the family inseparably bound to it, choosing to give up on hating them in order to dissociate from them out of an even more consuming hatred. Could X, in adopting this past and tracing its course into the future, have found some sort of redemption?

The second thing that Kido could not fathom was the way that X went on deceiving Rié to the last. For the love between them seemed to Kido far more beautiful and pure than any he had known. If death had not found X suddenly, was he planning to one day own up? Was it not that very mendacious past that made Rié fall for him in commiseration after all the pain she herself had borne? Even supposing everything else X had said was false, if there was one moment in which he was going to be absolutely honest, shouldn't it have been when he opened his lips to speak in that restaurant? Could his lie have been absolved by the true love they eventually shared?

True love?

CHAPTER EIGHT

Kido received word that a lawyer friend had died suddenly of ischemic heart failure, and in mid-September, just after Respect for the Aged Day, he went to Osaka to attend the wake.

Now, riding the final Nozomi back to Tokyo that night, Kido gazed from his window and zoned out on the passing scenery. The interior of the bullet train had looked somehow grotesque under the weight of his exhaustion and the sharp fluorescent lights. While many passengers dozed, several drunken groups chattered incessantly. The air in the car was stagnant and heavy, laced with the stench of workday sweat, beer, and some pungent junk food, perhaps dried squid. Kido's suit was tinged with the added scent of the incense he had burned for his friend.

He and the deceased had been legal apprentices together in Kyoto, starting at the same time. Kido was now at the age where relatives and acquaintances passed away with some frequency, but as most of those were seniors, he was accustomed to wakes for those who had slipped away quietly. The ceremony for his all-too-young friend had taken a toll on him. The man should have had so much more life ahead. His surviving wife and two elementary-age daughters had wept all the way through, and Kido regretted his failure to give them any meaningful words of condolence. In retrospect, his friend had probably verged on obese, but had treated the issue lightly, sometimes rubbing his belly and swearing with a laugh that he would diet. No one had thought his weight anything to be concerned about. As soon as Kido left the funeral home, the reality of his friend's death seemed to dissolve back into the dizzying incredulity he'd felt the moment he first heard the news.

What would happen if I died? Kido wondered, and imagined the shock on his son's face when his mother told him the news.

"Daddy is dead?" he saw Sota say, not even understanding his question.

"That's right, son," Kido would be unable to reply. In his own absence, he could not very well teach his child the meaning of death, breaking it down as he would have with any other difficult topic. Kido really didn't want to die. He simply couldn't. And suddenly he found words for the nebulous mood that had permeated his mind ever since the earthquake: existential anxiety.

I'm afraid to die, he thought. The instant he died—and not a moment later!—his consciousness would cease, and he would be incapable of thinking or feeling anything ever again, leaving time to proceed with no connection to him, passing solely for the sake of the living. Trying to imagine this pushed Kido's mind to its limit. Here he was, alive today, with a world persisting for him, when the more than fifteen thousand people who'd lost their lives in the tsunami two years earlier could perceive nothing of what was occurring in the present. They had left no trace of anything substantial with which they might participate in it. Not in this world, and probably not in the afterlife or anywhere else . . . Kido's fear of the same thing happening to him made him painfully sensitive to the minutiae of life.

This was not the first time he had pondered such issues. Why were they resurfacing now after all these years, when his former attempts to think them through had all but faded from memory? The last time had been when he was a teenager. As was typical of someone that age, in the process of trying to decide what he wanted to be, he had thought long and hard about what kind of person he was. In the end he had drifted along and become a lawyer in accordance with his father's advice. His doubts about whether this was truly the right path had never completely left him, but he went on looking to the future, telling himself that the person he was meant to be would be realized through the profession he had chosen. In other words, he had asked who he was in order to live, and on the basis of what he discovered had found hope as well as fear.

For fifteen years now, Kido had left it at that. Whenever he reflected on those former days of philosophizing, he saw them as a developmental stage that he had, thankfully, already overcome. "Thankfully" because steady work was no longer as common as it once had been, and many in his generation were denied the opportunity. He understood the struggles such people faced all too well because he dealt with many of them as clients. Forced to accept a life in which their social position and income were always unstable, they could never hope to self-actualize through their profession as he had.

But what had he really found? It was no longer clear to him. For the trauma of the earthquake had thrown him back into uncertainty and reawakened the question that he had thought long resolved. *Who am I?* Except it was not a simple repeat of the words that had perplexed him in his youth. Although the meaning of the question had hardly changed, its form had evolved in keeping with his age. Now he asked, *Did I make the right choice?*

As was typical of someone in middle age, Kido saw his life as composed of several stages linked together by a shared name, with himself as their culmination. A significant portion of the life given continuity by the label "Akira Kido" that had once lain ahead had already been relegated to the past, and so his identity was in large part already determined. Of course there might have been other paths he could have taken and therefore other people he might have been. Perhaps an infinite number. It was in the light of such considerations that he confronted his former question anew. The problem now was not who he was in the present but who he'd been in the past, and the solution he sought was no longer supposed to help him live but to help him figure out what sort of person to die as.

Someday Sota would live in a world from which Kido had vanished. Would Kido even exist when Sota was thirty-eight, Kido's age now? That would be in thirty-three years. Kido would be seventy-one. Assuming he was around. He hoped to be around. If he wasn't, he wondered how Sota would remember his father as he was in the present. What sort of person might Kido carry on as in his son's recollection? Old age was not the only thing that could take him. In the next instant, the Nankai Trough earthquake could strike, sending the bullet train off its track. Then Kido would die in utter stupefaction. They had all heard ad nauseum since the quake how great the risk was.

⋊⋉

It was in the midst of his reignited existential anxiety that two new worries made their presence felt: the return to cultural memory of the massacre of Koreans and the ultraright xenophobic displays of the previous year.

The judicial order that Kido worked hard as a lawyer to preserve propped up his quotidian life. It protected his and his family's human rights and maintained their status as sovereign citizens. But what if an apocalyptic anomaly were to temporarily override this order in some limited area of time and space? To the rabble-rousers who took to the streets in broad daylight screaming, "Death to Koreans!" Kido's subtle, intricate questioning, his contemplations about his own life, would be meaningless. Forget the need for such an anomaly. All it might take to stir someone up in the midst of the everyday was the voice of fake news. Overflowing with lies, they would then be capable of murdering members of the "Korean race" as soon as they felt the urge.

This was the first time that Kido had fully articulated this to himself, and a weakness suddenly washed over him. The overhead lights on the train turned clamorously bright, taking on a blackish-red haze, and a nauseating force seemed to press in from all sides. He lowered his head and closed his eyes, took off his glasses, rubbed his face so hard it hurt, scraped one foot against the other as he planted it hard into the floor. The woman in the neighboring seat had been fiddling with her cell phone before, but now, when Kido opened his eyes for a moment, she was leaning away and observing him with discrete glances. Lacking even the peace of mind to smile reassuringly, Kido could do nothing but hold his face in his hands and rub his eyes, palms squeezed together, as he rode the feeling out.

I'm having a fit, he thought, disturbed by the way his body was reacting. As dizziness crept up on him, Kido wrenched his already loose necktie even looser and reclined his seat. Only when he started to take deep, slow breaths did the discomfort finally begin to subside. *You're a good person, Kido-sensei, I mean it.* Wasn't that what Rié had said? Kido mulled over her words as though they might have the power to heal him. Would Rié testify to that if he was accused of being a spy, or if he was given a shibboleth like "Pronounce 'fifteen yen and fifty sen!'" to test whether he ought to be killed, as some had done during the massacre of Koreans? Would her statement on his behalf have any meaning for his would-be murderers? Or would their animosity, instead, extend to her . . . ?

Still unable to relax the furrow of distress in his brow, Kido thought about his relationship with his wife since the Great East Japan Earthquake.

Although the ensuing tsunami had not harmed anyone that Kido knew personally, he was nonetheless profoundly disturbed by the unimaginable news footage of whole cities being washed away and could not bear to sit idly by. So, in coordination with Nakakita and his other partners at the firm, he had volunteered for an initiative providing legal support to those affected by the disaster.

The problem he grappled with was that of the so-called "voluntary evacuees" who had fled areas with elevated radiation levels due to the Fukushima Daiichi Nuclear Power Plant meltdown, even though the government had not designated them as mandatory evacuation zones. In particular, Kido offered consultation to those who sought to switch the "denominated temporary housing" they'd been allotted free of charge as per the Disaster Relief Act. Many subsidized apartments chosen for this purpose during the postdisaster pandemonium were dilapidated, the local residents were noisy, or there were incidents of harassment directed at evacuees. But those who moved without meeting such strict conditions as "presence of remarkable danger" or "at landlord's behest" would lose their coverage. It was because of such bureaucratic defects in the system that the assistance of lawyers like Kido was required.

Voluntary evacuees often ended up isolated, and Kido dealt with some of the more extreme cases. Many were mothers who had left their husbands behind due to disagreements over the true impact of radiation and whether or not it necessitated abandoning their jobs, and who consequently settled into the austere disaster relief lifestyle alone with their children. All of them kept alive hope of reuniting as a family, with either the husband joining them in the shelter or the wife returning home with the kids, but Kido was involved in a number of tragic cases where the end result was divorce.

Kaori could not understand these efforts of Kido's, and he was reminded of the clean lines along which her kindness divided: family and friends on one side, everyone else on the other. A good and caring mother, she remembered the names of Sota's playmates from day care far better than Kido ever could and had made friends with several of their mothers, with whom she sometimes went for tea and other outings. And yet she took it as self-evident that she would be indifferent to the lot of children starving under some unfamiliar sky.

Kido donated regularly to Doctors Without Borders and UNICEF, and Kaori used to observe such societal generosity with bemusement, writing it off as one of his professional quirks. But recently, they had both begun to sense something troubling in this difference of outlook and avoided bringing it up in conversation.

Kido wasn't such a bleeding heart as to get upset about each and every one of the numerous deaths happening all over the world at any given instant. His own death terrified him. The death of an acquaintance was sad. The death of someone he hated might be welcome news. When it came to the death of complete strangers, the truth was that Kido felt nothing. And yet by imagining them as himself, as people that he knew, he felt terrified, sad.

Some people might conceivably read a news report about a random parent and child dying in a car accident and mourn them as they would their own family, but it would be weird if this entailed, conversely, that they could only grieve the death of their family to the same degree as that of strangers. Kido had a normal disparity in his empathy and knew that it was only thanks to this fact that he was capable of being a lawyer.

He and his wife should have had no trouble sharing in their guilt and detachment within this range. It wasn't as though Kaori was exceptionally heartless. Take the Great East Japan Earthquake. By the time Kido suggested she donate, she had already given generously to the Red Cross.

What Kaori just couldn't wrap her head around was Kido's motive for giving his blood, sweat, and tears for strangers when all the while his feelings did not sincerely go out to them. Was it concern about keeping up face professionally? Was it naive shame at being unmoved by their suffering? She insisted that, if either of them had changed, it was Kido, not her, and when Kido thought about what he'd been like when they met, he had to concede the point.

If there had been two or three Kidos with a never-ending supply of time and money, while Kaori might have upbraided him for his shallow compassion, she would have probably left him to do as he wished. But in reality, volunteering required Kido to apportion the time and money he had for their son, not merely for himself. When the earthquake struck, Sota was still two and a half. Aftershocks came one after the next and it was anyone's guess when the next big tremor might hit. Kaori didn't see anything commendable in Kido's leaving behind his wife and child to go off and take care of other wives and children at a time like that, evacuees or not, and none of her friends spoke up in Kido's defense either.

In all of this, Kido respected his wife for what he perceived as her straightforwardness, honesty, and intelligence. Whenever he tried to explain himself using phrases like "social presence" and "public good," she accepted everything, understanding his activities in the name of these ideas as roundabout ways of benefitting them. But at the same time, Kaori sensed a kind of empty indulgence in his attitude toward charity and treated his good works as nothing more than a sort of hobby.

Once she had begun to see his humanitarian tendencies this way, they became all the more difficult for her to tolerate, as Kaori no longer had any hobbies of her own. With each passing year, she found less and less that called to her in the world and had already lost nearly all interest in anything besides family. When Kido grew concerned about this and urged her to go out and have a good time while he looked after their son, she just ended up discussing the finer details of child rearing over a meal with one of her university classmates. Somewhere along the way, her single friends, who could not join her in such talk, had all drifted away.

Her single-minded focus on family had begun after she gave birth and become more pronounced since the earthquake. Now she demanded to know why it was so important to Kido that she do other things. On the contrary, why wasn't going back and forth between work and home enough to fulfill him?

Hearing the announcement that the train had passed Odawara on schedule, Kido opened his eyes and sat up. He must have drifted off at some point, as the woman in the neighboring seat was gone. With eyes unfocused, he crossed his legs and recalled again what Rié had said. *You're a good person, Kido-sensei, I mean it.* Had he gone out of his way to be kind to her in order to fish for such compliments? Perhaps as proof that he was a good, harmless, in-no-way-suspicious Normal Japanese Person?

What a silly idea, Kido thought with a shake of his head and, rubbing his eyes vigorously again, told himself that the answer on both accounts had to be no. He was blowing his insecurity about being Zainichi way out of proportion. Yes, the postearthquake spike in nationalism had unsettled him, but that wasn't only because of his ethnicity. His colleagues at the firm were just as upset. It would have been one thing if the problem had been limited to the far right, but even putatively serious publishers were complicit. Kido and the other lawyers had watched, crestfallen, as imprints they'd revered suddenly began to fill the bookstores with titles like *Hating China* and *Hating Korea*. Under such circumstances, it would have been crazy *not* to become pessimistic.

. . . I admit that my concern for society is in some sense hollow and reminiscent of some goody-two-shoes A-student trying to show off to his teacher, just as you impugn it to be. But part of it also derives from innate compassion that your point fails to take account of. Trying to work out the degree to which my actions arise from sincerity and the degree to which they are merely a pretense to virtue would be a fruitless exercise.

Kido was indeed experiencing a kind of existential anxiety, but Japan's dark prospects were no doubt a far bigger factor than his own identity. Might it not be merely the banal, petit bourgeois anxiety of an age in which even lawyers struggled to put food on the table?

Kido decided that perhaps he should talk with Kaori after all. She too had to be feeling discombobulated by the earthquake. And wishing to restore the situation at home to the way it had once been, he finally took hold of the one thought that had seemed too troublesome to attend to. The situation might be much simpler and more clear-cut than he was making it out to be. In a word, maybe his wife didn't love him anymore.

If so, was there anything he could do about it? Their relationship was already in the process of gradually falling apart. And he had good reason to think so. For their dynamic was almost indistinguishable from that of the couples he advised almost daily and whose negotiations ended in divorce.

CHAPTER NINE

When October rolled around, Kido received an unexpected message from Misuzu. She was planning to visit the Yokohama Museum of Art in Minato Mirai for an exhibit called "New Visions in the Twenty-First Century" and was wondering if he had time to join her. As she also mentioned that she wanted to consult with him about the search for Daisuké Taniguchi, Kido rejiggered his schedule and arranged for them to have lunch as well.

Since Kido had been following her Instagram-linked Facebook feed, he had a general sense of her recent activities. While she wasn't the most prolific poster, she had a knack for capturing unassuming everyday scenes, whether it was a display window mannequin in fall and winter apparel or a cake she'd enjoyed, and her captions were breezy and concise, in keeping with her personality. She seemed to go out regularly on her own to the movies or to art museums, and rarely posted selfies, appearing mostly when tagged now and then in photos taken by her friends. In all such shots, she remained colored for Kido by his impression of her as a "mean mixer of gimlets," even when she appeared in the light of day.

In the comment section, Kido observed the playful back-and-forth between her friends and work associates. Among them were a few male admirers who found opportunities to compliment her on her looks. The manager of Sunny often popped up, and there were several pictures of Misuzu and him smiling together, surrounded by drunken people.

The main reason Kido had made a Facebook account in the first place was to contact Misuzu, and he still wasn't exactly an avid user. For the most part, he shared other people's posts and uploaded the occasional batch of photos, including a few from his trip to Miyazaki. As he hadn't told his friends about his account, his newsfeed was fairly deserted, but Misuzu liked almost anything he put up. At first, Kido took this for a standard courtesy of the social network, until he realized that not all his "friends" did this nor did it appear that Misuzu did the same for just anyone. He liked her posts in return, unsure what this signalled, and felt slight thrills at these fleeting interactions.

And yet, over the past two months or so, their exchanges over Facebook had been complicated by the fact that Misuzu had created an account under Daisuké Taniguchi's name and started posting as though she were him in the hopes of tracking him down. The idea was that he would be sure to send a message once the impersonation came to his attention. Kido most definitely did not approve of this ploy, but he didn't entirely blame Misuzu, as it had apparently been Kyoichi who cooked it up.

Now that it had become clear that the police had dropped the search for his brother, Kyoichi displayed outrage at any opportunity. In part, this was his way of venting about the detective in charge, who he held a grudge against for being snooty. But more than anything, it was a sign of his relief that there was no imminent possibility of the search turning into a big enough deal to attract attention. While a person going missing might be of profound importance to the family, it was an everyday occurrence to the police. Kyoichi's realization of this put his mind at ease. And once Kido told him that the census records had been updated to indicate that his brother was once again alive and unmarried, he began to think of Daisuké's disappearance as a problem for the family to deal with internally.

Kyoichi continued to insist that his brother must have been murdered. What appalled Kido was his suggestion that Daisuké had been "piggybacked" by North Korean agents, a word he had apparently found online. When Kido expressed doubts about the theory, Kyoichi didn't cling to it, but maintained instead that, whatever the specifics, if his brother had been murdered, it must have been precipitated by some nefarious turn of events rather than simple mischief. Something fitting for the sort of person his brother had been—Kyoichi seemed harrowed by the very thought of it.

"We didn't hear anything from him after the earthquake. That's screwy, right? If he was alive, he'd at least give us a ring. Unless his life is so awful he can't even show his face."

Although Kyoichi had shown almost no initiative in searching for his brother, wary of stumbling upon some lurking trouble, his—their—mother, to Kido's surprise, had apparently bawled him out for this. Tearful, she'd urged him to kick up his search efforts, saying that she desperately wanted to see her younger son once more before she died.

By this time, Kido had checked the attachment to Daisuké Taniguchi's family register and found his address prior to moving to Town S. It was for a dirt-cheap, blighted apartment on the Yodo River in Osaka City's Kita district. The building management had an office nearby, and once Kido had explained all this to Rié and Kyoichi, he proposed that the three of them go there together. But before Rié could reply, Kyoichi, claiming to have business in Osaka, stopped by the office himself and met with the president of the company.

According to Kyoichi, the president sympathized with his story about his missing brother and, after studying Daisuké's picture, had said that he felt fairly certain he was the one who had lived there. Just to be sure, Kyoichi showed him a picture of X, but the man shook his head and said that the face didn't ring any bells.

This meant that Daisuké had remained Daisuké up until his time in that Osaka apartment. He'd then had a run-in with X and had everything, from his name to his family register, taken from him. Kyoichi had learned this through the simplest detective work in the world, and he was enraged anew with the police for not even bothering.

Toward the end of the meeting, Kyoichi asked for Daisuké's phone number and forwarding address, assuming they were taken down when he vacated. Immediately, the heretofore cooperative president's expression turned wary, as though he had suddenly wised up to something. He then concluded evasively by saying that he wasn't sure they still had those files but would be sure to take a look.

Kyoichi figured the man was worried about getting mixed up in trouble, which he thought was understandable under the circumstances. He had not heard from him since.

Kido could think of reasons why Kyoichi might have gone to Osaka without them. What he couldn't understand at first was why he'd put Misuzu up to making a Facebook account for his brother. That Misuzu went on posting as Daisuké was simply bizarre and seemed unlikely to achieve anything. But in the process of observing the online exchanges between Kyoichi, Misuzu, and Misuzu masquerading as Daisuké Taniguchi, Kido gradually puzzled out what Kyoichi was really after. And this only reinforced his conviction that their ploy was not something he could get on board with.

Daisuké Taniguchi's account displayed a number of old photos uploaded by Misuzu and Kyoichi, listed his hometown and schools, and liked the pages for Michael Schenker along with two of his former bands, Scorpions and UFO. According to Misuzu, Daisuké had been an especially big UFO fan, so they considered trying to find him through their official page on the off chance that he might be connected, but decided it would be too difficult to sift him out from the two hundred and fifty thousand other followers.

There were several people named Daisuké Taniguchi on the various social media networks—Facebook, Instagram, Twitter—but none appeared to be the one they were looking for. While it was unclear what dealings Daisuké might have had with X, Kido thought it unlikely, assuming he was alive, that he would register using his real name. It was even possible that he had switched names with X.

Kido didn't doubt that Daisuké Taniguchi would be gobsmacked if he saw the imposter account, but wondered if he would just think X was behind it. He wasn't sure if X, in his guise as Daisuké Taniguchi, was supposed to have been aware of the existence of Misuzu. Either way, if Daisuké Taniguchi saw a fake version of himself exchanging intimate comments with his former lover, he would surely be disturbed. But would he take the bait and contact her?

Whatever the answer, Kido could tell from observing the conversation unfolding over the Daisuké account that Kyoichi was attracted to Misuzu. And these feelings had not developed only recently. Rather, there appeared to be history there. Kido's suspicion was that Kyoichi had loved Misuzu, but she had chosen his younger brother. There were also signs that Kyoichi and Misuzu were messaging privately, though Kido never asked them about it directly.

The Daisuké Taniguchi played by Misuzu was vigorous and cheerful, had a competitive streak despite being timid, and displayed his sensitive side when posting about how UFO's "Love to Love" made him cry. He was, in other words, the Daisuké Taniguchi that she wished him to be, the only Daisuké Taniguchi that she could in fact imagine. Playing with her recollection of him, Misuzu was wistfully reliving her past. Embodying those memories, she could feel her love for him just beyond the tips of her fingers.

Kido's perception of Misuzu had changed since the night he'd pretended to be Daisuké Taniguchi in that bar. For once thoroughly intoxicated, Kido was relating everything he knew about the man, when he found himself saying that he had once been in love with her. Now he had a secret wish that he was terrified someone might uncover: namely, he wanted to experience what it was like to be the young man who had loved her and been loved by her, even just for a few hours. So when he thought about meeting her in person, he felt ashamed and flustered, comporting himself exactly like someone trying to hide a crush.

This shift inside Kido only distorted and complicated his feelings about his wife's suspicions. Since her doubts about his fidelity had begun after his trip to Miyazaki, he'd assumed she was having presentiments of him cheating with Rié and had had little patience for it, when in reality she may have been anticipating Misuzu all along. Of course, Kido considered this possibility no less ludicrous.

𝄪

At eleven o'clock on the appointed date, Kido met with Misuzu at Minatomirai Station. She was dressed casually in a loose, slightly-off-the-shoulder blouse and ankle-length jeans that suited her well-proportioned figure. Walking beside her in his necktie, Kido couldn't help feeling like a cornball.

"Sorry to drag you out when you're so busy," said Misuzu with the same laid-back smile he remembered.

At the bar, Kido had been seated on a stool, looking slightly up at her. Now that they were standing face-to-face, he was struck by her big eyes with their thick lower lids and the sleek definition of her nose. Her perfume was conservative, appropriate for the morning.

As it was a weekday before noon, and the exhibit featured the work of only young up-and-comers, the museum was all but empty. They climbed up and down stairwells like miniatures of those in the Musée d'Orsay, hardly speaking as they wandered around and took in the different displays.

Although Kido was no art expert, since he preferred the cultivated simplicity of work like Fontana's *Spatial Concept*, much of what he saw there did nothing for him. The boats made of cardboard. The violent, anime-themed sketches. The portrait of an elementary school student done in countless impressions of three kinds of stamp: "Nice effort!" "Well done!" and "Excellent work!" Now and then he looked to Misuzu, searching for indications of whether these were to her taste; nothing made her stop for long either.

But on the second floor, they soon discovered a work entitled *Three Years Old, A Memory* that was for both of them an exceptional treat. The artist was a Japanese woman in her late twenties based in Berlin. Kido had never heard of her. She had built a large installation resembling the box sets used in theater. Stepping inside, they found a faithful reproduction of the living room of the artist when she was a child, except that the scale of all the furniture and household items was gigantic.

It was supposed to be the artist's very first memory. Her intention was to allow a vicarious bodily experience of the world exactly as she had seen it when she was three years old. The square wood dinner table rose to about Kido's eye level, and the four chairs set around it were too tall to sit on without climbing. Everything from the saltshaker to the grains of sugar on the pancakes was huge, the knives with blades like short swords, everything looming beyond reach. The overall effect was to make the bodies of the spectators small by comparison.

Kido had come up with similar concepts from observing Sota's daily wandering around the living room and kitchen, and sometimes indulged in tender reminiscence over his own early childhood. In the beginning he'd been too small to see the mirror in the bathroom but gradually grew until he could spot the reflection of his hair if he jumped, then his face. Eventually he could brush his teeth unaided before finally being able to see himself up to the waist. What sort of thoughts might have been running through his head at the age when objects at home had been as overwhelming as they were in this installation? Its one flaw was the somewhat shoddy sculpture of a mother standing in the kitchen.

Kido and Misuzu both clambered with some difficulty onto the chairs and faced each other across the table. Unlike when the bar counter had been between them, they were both smiling bashfully. It was as though they'd reverted to the bodies of children and travelled back in time. Having become make-believe childhood friends, they began to hanker for afternoon desserts that they might share, and as they continued to sit there, both sensed that someone bigger might just serve them.

For lunch, they went to a well-known restaurant attached to the station that served Mont-Saint-Michel cuisine. Over souffléed omelets so fluffy the eggs had been whipped into a froth, they shared their impressions of the exhibition and both grinned wryly to admit that it had been mediocre at best overall. When Misuzu apologized for inviting Kido, he shook his head and reassured her that he had enjoyed *Three Years Old, A Memory*, at least.

"It really was great, wasn't it?" she said. "I could practically spend all day just zoning out in there—but that mother in the kitchen! She looked so lonely facing away from us . . . What do you think the artist was trying to express with that?"

"Oh . . . interesting. Given the bad workmanship, I just assumed that the artist lacked the knack for people, but perhaps you're right. There must be a reason she's so poorly realized . . ."

Kido was impressed with Misuzu's insight and eye for detail.

"The artist's note made it sound like she had some issues with her parents," said Misuzu.

"I missed that . . . Come to think of it, while it might be an opportunity to reflect fondly on the past for someone whose early days had been happy, for some people it would be painful—being in that space, I mean."

Misuzu smiled in agreement, and her eyes seemed to ask which category Kido fell into. At the same time, something in her expression told him that she wouldn't judge if he chose not to answer.

"I think that I probably come from a happy home. I was close with both my parents and my younger brother."

"I had a feeling."

"Really?"

"Uh-huh. I had a pretty normal family too. I mean in a good way."

"Yes, we were normal too in a way, but you see, I'm third-generation Zainichi, though I have Japanese citizenship now because I naturalized in high school. So the inside of our home looked a tad bit different from a typical Japanese home in those days. For example, there was Korean calligraphy and commemorative pictures of my grandmother and mother wearing jeogori. Only little things, really . . . That piece we just saw, I imagine when it's shown overseas, the visitors appreciate it because they can translate it to their own memories of being a toddler in whatever country, but inside Japan, I could see it taking flack for the way it portrays the so-called 'normal home.' We have more and more people here with roots in different countries, and the gap between rich and poor is widening—or perhaps I should say it's a work that provokes thought precisely about such issues . . ."

The first time Kido met Misuzu, he had been extremely guarded about his ethnic background, but here he was, putting it out in the open with unhesitating ease. He hadn't even realized he was doing so until after the fact, while still in the middle of speaking. This change in him was probably due to the effect of the art he had just encountered and of becoming familiar with Misuzu's sentiments and way of thinking over the past few months. Although her face showed no signs of surprise, her eyes suggested that she was reviewing her past behavior toward him in her mind.

"Wow, I never thought of any of that. Almost makes me want to take another look."

"Your observation about the mother made me feel the same way."

"So we'll head back to the gallery when we're done?" said Misuzu with a joking smile. Then, looking worried, she added, "That conversation at Sunny must have been uncomfortable for you."

"Not at all," said Kido with a shrug. "Abduction is a real problem, after all—though I suppose your boss did belabor his point."

"Not just that . . ." Misuzu seemed reluctant to go on. "Takagi is prejudiced toward Chinese and Koreans. I guess you could say it runs deep in him."

"Even though he's such a big fan of black music! Hasn't it made him sensitive to discrimination at all?"

"He doesn't see the connection. I don't think he even realizes he's discriminating."

Kido let the unpleasant topic fizzle out with a few polite nods before asking, "Is he your . . ."

Before he'd finished his question, Misuzu cut him short with a pout of dismay. "People jump to that conclusion all the time, but it's nothing like that."

Not wanting to be insensitive, Kido stopped himself from asking if Takagi had unrequited feelings for her. In the awkward silence that ensued, Misuzu reopened their former topic, seeming to feel the need to clarify her position.

"The recent hate speech is the worst. It's just gross."

Her tone of open detestation was so unlike the shallow words of pity Kido was used to. Most people spoke as though it was his problem, not theirs. And he felt the last of the tension he'd been holding on to fall away.

"To be honest, I don't feel hurt or angry when it becomes that extreme, when they're shouting, 'Die!' and 'Cockroach!' . . . though I do find it tiresome." Kido smiled weakly, like a bottle of flat carbonated water being popped.

"How did things get like this? I feel like saying those awful things would have been unthinkable only a few years ago."

"I suppose the dregs of internet language have been stirred up."

"Is there no way to crack down on it legally?"

"There are some movements to do just that, yes, but opinion is split in judicial circles over how to balance it with freedom of expression. Personally I think that hate speech should be restricted once the definition is clarified . . . But—how can I put it?—I'd prefer not to dedicate myself to this problem. Yes, I despise the scum who say such racist things, and my stress levels would be lower if they were gone . . . but only a little. There are plenty of more important things in my life that I should be thinking about. Like the cases I'm working on, and my family, and especially my son . . . not to mention . . ."

Kido stared at Misuzu. He'd almost gotten carried away and told her that the time they were spending together right then was a perfect example of something profoundly important, but held his tongue for fear it would sound like he was hitting on her. Instead, he cut into the hearty, well-fluffed omelet on his plate. Cooked to the ideal golden hue, it was folded in half, and frothy egg overflowed from the seam with such impudence that Kido almost felt thwarted. It made him think of molten lava rushing toward the sea.

". . . Well, various things," he continued. "Just tons of things that are worthier of the fuss and pain of serious consideration. Happy and pleasant things too, of course . . . I grew up like any Japanese person, in a regular town, not in a Korean enclave, so I never experienced bullying. Until recently, I was hardly even aware of the stigma attached to my background."

"It must be tough living with a stigma."

"Yes and no. Having a stigma means that you have some kind of trait that serves as the basis for discrimination, negative feelings, or even attacks. This irrespective of whether the trait is intrinsically bad or not. For example, the circumstances of your birth and rearing, a birthmark on your face, a criminal record. Everything else about you is ignored. All your multifaceted complexity is reduced to that one aspect. So if you're Zainichi, that's all you are and nothing more."

"How unfair."

"Yes, but the implications are not only negative. In all honesty, I don't like when other Zainichi try to claim me, as though we were somehow separate and special. I feel the same way about being from Ishikawa. Our prefecture has traditionally used the self-deprecating nickname 'the Beggar,' and there may be something to it, but it makes me uncomfortable when people refer to it at every available opportunity. Whether it's being a lawyer or being Japanese, the same applies. It's unbearable to have your identity summed up by one thing and one thing only and for other people to have control over what that is."

"That is so true!" said Misuzu excitedly, bending backward and then leaning forward across the table on the rebound off her chair. "I'm always saying exactly the same thing."

"You're putting it into practice, Misuzu, more so than I am. Working freelance by day and mixing cocktails by night."

"My philosophy is Three-Steps-Forward-Four-Steps-Backism."

"Pardon me?"

"Life isn't all unicorns and rainbows, so I'm fine taking three steps forward and four steps back."

"You must mean four steps forward and three back. If you took three forward and four back, you'd be losing more ground than you gained."

Kido thought he'd caught her making a simple slip of the tongue, but Misuzu shook her head.

"Nope. Three forward and four back is the way to go. You might not think so by looking at me, but I'm a megapessimist—true pessimists are full of cheer! That's my personal motto. Our expectations are always low, so when something just a little bit nice happens, we're on cloud nine."

Misuzu laughed proudly. But Kido was somewhat befuddled by her pet theories. Until suddenly it was as though a new visual field were opening up inside him and what she was saying clicked.

"Makes sense . . . ," he said.

"I have terrible luck. Like Daisuké disappearing on me. Honestly, I'd totally settle for two steps forward and four steps back. But I'm setting my sights high with Three-Steps-Forward-Four-Steps-Backism."

"That's a good way to think."

"Right?"

"The way the world is right now, it's as though taking a single step back cancels out the three steps you took forward."

"So you're a pessimist too."

"Yes. I suppose I am."

"Everyone makes this world out to be so much better than it actually is. They just see it the way they want it to be. That's why they blame people for their misfortunes. Meanwhile, they're not even satisfied with their own lives."

"That's very true. Because you never know what might happen . . . And, well, being Zainichi isn't exactly a step back or anything, but it's difficult for me to say how much stress it actually brings—the whole topic is just tiresome. The worst would be if some oddball were to write a novel with me as the protagonist and call it *Tale of a Third-Generation Zainichi*. Not that *Tale of a Lawyer* would be much better."

"You're a funny guy, Kido-san."

"You think so?"

"But I totally understand what you're getting at."

"I don't think that I'm representative of most Zainichi anyway. So, getting back to what we were talking about, I know I have to do something to fight hate speech, but when I see those videos online, it's just . . ."

"Considering joining one of the counter-demonstrations?"

"I'm not interested in those. If I'm going to do anything, I suppose I'll give legal advice to the victims or something of that nature. Though a verdict has just been reached in the civil case over the attack on that Korean primary school in Kyoto . . . I think I've always organized my life to avoid places where I might interact with such people. As I go about my daily business, I simply don't have to worry about someone launching racist remarks at me. Going to a demonstration and hearing their awful train of vituperation would be off-putting to say the least."

"Sure . . . but forget about people you don't know. What about your family? Your parents, your son."

Kido saw Sota's face in his mind's eye and had to take a moment before he could reply. He recalled Kaori saying that she wanted Kido to hide his ancestry. Her point wasn't that his being Zainichi made her feel inferior but that they needed to protect their son from physical harm. Kido had not raised any disagreement.

"Well, yes, fair point . . . But if you're going to say that I should go because I'm Zainichi, then shouldn't Japanese people treat it as a problem with their own country and be obligated to go to the counter-demonstrations themselves? They're the ones who are giving those scoundrels free rein. Since they're not part of the solution, then they must be part of the problem—which I guess forces me to conclude that I should go too, since I'm a Japanese citizen now."

Kido gave Misuzu a playful smile to show he had no intention of arguing. While he was speaking, the sensations he'd experienced on the bullet train the other day had begun to creep up, and he wanted to change the subject.

"Anyway, I suppose deciding who the victims are and who perpetuates their suffering is no easy matter . . . Wherever that line happens to fall, I think a third party should intervene. It is the need for such intervention, after all, that is the basis for the whole legal profession."

Misuzu nodded as though she was convinced, staring at him with kind, narrowed eyes. Though he was surprised by her slight smile, it somehow made him relieved.

"Then I'm going to go in your place, Kido-san," she said.

"Huh?" Caught off guard, Kido didn't know whether to be impressed or bewildered. "That's not what I was trying to suggest . . .

I don't think that's a good idea. It would just make you feel awful. But thank you."

"No need to worry. I want to go for my own reasons," said Misuzu with a laugh.

Siphoning a bit of her mirth, Kido laughed too. Then he thought again what a mysterious woman she was.

He never learned what aspect of the search for Daisuké Taniguchi she had wanted to consult with him about. But one thing soon became clear: their online interactions from that day forward would reach a new level of intimacy.

CHAPTER TEN

Already more than ten months had passed since Kido had taken on Rié's case, and yet he had made no progress with his investigation into the identity of X. The case had remained on his mind even as other work, such as the death-by-overwork lawsuit, kept him extremely busy. But once Rié's family register had been successfully revised and all pressing issues dealt with, he was at a loss for how to proceed. Meanwhile, he wasn't expecting the fake account managed by Misuzu and Kyoichi to yield any breakthroughs.

It was while he was at this standstill that he came across a potential lead thanks to a conversation he had with Nakakita at the firm. For in the process of continuing to provide support to those affected by the earthquake in the Tohoku region, Nakakita had been approached by someone seeking advice about victims of the ensuing tsunami whose existence the government had not kept track of because they lacked a family register.

While some people had ended up without a family register after World War II—when they neglected to report that theirs had been lost after records stored in government offices were destroyed due to American firebombing—improved archiving procedures prevented similar problems from occurring in the recent earthquake. Although the original registers were still stored in local offices, copies were now kept in the applicable Regional Affairs Bureau. Digitization was also in progress. But in spite of such measures, some children still lacked family registers due to the so-called "three-hundred-day problem," and it was about just such a case that Nakakita had been consulted.

As per the Civil Code, a child born within three hundred days of a divorce was legally considered to be the child of the former husband. The law had become controversial of late because women, who, for example, divorced after suffering domestic violence and who had a child soon after with a new partner, sometimes refrained from submitting a notification of birth. This left some children to enter society without a family register. Even though they met all the conditions to obtain Japanese citizenship, the state was not aware that they were alive and consequently could not tally their deaths when they were swallowed up by the tsunami. As far as official records were concerned, the events of both their coming into the world and leaving it had simply not taken place—there was never even anything that temporarily existed for the word "not" to deny, with no unfolding from the beginning, and the circle of nothingness closed.

As Kido was listening to Nakakita's explanation, he began to wonder if X might have been one of these unregistered people, which was precisely what his colleague had been implying all along. Assuming Daisuké Taniguchi was safe and sound, Kido had been imagining him living under X's identity, having swapped family registers with him. But what if X had been unregistered? Did that mean Daisuké had become unregistered in his place? Kyoichi suspected murder. But if Daisuké Taniguchi had taken on the identity of someone entirely absent from public records, the state would be unable to recognize his murder. Even if his body were discovered, it would be disposed of as unidentified. His surviving acquaintances and friends might testify, his DNA might be tested, his photos and personal effects might remain, and on this basis, the fact that he seemed to have existed might be inferred. But supposing he had been taken by the tsunami, all physical evidence might have been completely washed away and the search mired in even more remarkable difficulties.

Kido had been hopeful that Daisuké Taniguchi was still around. Now, even setting aside all speculation about the tsunami, he began to feel a sense of foreboding. For Rié's sake as much as Daisuké Taniguchi's, he didn't want to believe that X had killed him. She seemed to be holding on by a thread and, if it turned out that X was a murderer, he was worried that she might lose her tenuous grip.

X

Nakakita related this story about vanished tsunami victims while he and Kido sat on the office couch drinking coffee. When he was done, they talked for a while about the history of the family register.

Its introduction dated back to the era of the Ritsuryo system, an imperial bureaucracy modelled after China's that began in the late sixth century. Used mainly in the beginning for policing and tax collection, the family register was expanded over a millennium later in the Edo period when it became a tool for cracking down on Christianity. Records of religious affiliation were drawn up to check who was registered with Buddhist temples, and a wider range of information was incorporated for individual identity management, including birth, marriage, adoption, current address, job, and death. From then on, there were always numerous people, such as vagrants, who were not accounted for in the records.

As this system presupposed attachment to land, it was rendered obsolete in the late nineteenth century, not long after the start of the Meiji period, when freedom of movement was recognized, and the first modern family register was introduced. This new family register was employed in the census for the purposes of conscription and tax collection, and the desire to avoid these led many to ditch or falsify their registers.

"Some kids ended up without family registers when they were born out of wedlock and went unreported," said Nakakita as he ate a slice of the Baumkuchen that someone had brought to share. "Others when they were born overseas in wartime and the closure of a diplomatic mission prevented their parents from submitting a birth notification. You might say the system was like Swiss cheese."

"I understand why someone might think that being unregistered would be advantageous before the end of World War II," Kido replied. "The social security system was sorely lacking in those days, and you'd be able to dodge the draft. I suppose that's why the government was so draconian in its promotion of the Imperial Rescript on Education."

"But it was a reinforcing circle," said Nakakita. "Because the basis for imperial citizenship was that all full citizens were connected through the institution of the family to the eternal, unbroken line of the emperor."

"Your point being that people were excluded from the spiritual body of the nation and became second-class citizens if they weren't included in the family register."

"Just look at the Korean Peninsula. That's exactly how Japan's assimilation policies worked there." Nakakita's tone suggested that these policies were naturally deserving of criticism, in respectful acknowledgment of Kido's heritage. When Kido merely nodded in agreement, Nakakita went on.

"In any case, the government mostly conducts identity management with residence certificates these days. Once they tie together taxes and social security with the My Number system, the family register will finally become redundant."

"True. Though that may only make it easier to trade identities."

"Until they're managed together with biometrics. Then the system will be pretty much inescapable."

"Good point. Anyhow, it's because of the family register system that someone like Daisuké Taniguchi would want to make a clean break from his family."

"And what about X? If he wasn't unregistered to begin with, then I'd wager he was hiding a criminal record. And for a very serious crime. Nothing worse than having society and the state eyeing you suspiciously all the time."

"Hmm . . . I see what you mean."

"Daisuké Taniguchi's record is clean?"

"Sparkling."

"Well, then . . ."

With arms crossed, Kido began to consider this. Nakakita shrugged, not bothering to belabor his point.

After his conversation with Nakakita, Kido tried researching criminal cases related to social security, and soon hit upon a peculiar ruling from six years earlier.

It involved a then fifty-five-year-old man in Tokyo's Adachi ward. Pretending to be another man aged sixty-seven, he'd illegitimately received his pension. But he hadn't merely gone fraudulently by this other man's name. He had traded family registers with him upon their mutual agreement. The other man had made the swap in order to convince his fiancée, a woman in her thirties, that he had never been married before and that he was a decade younger. In court, the verdict was that the fifty-five-year-old man was guilty of false entry in an original notarized electronic document and of sharing this false document. He was sentenced to one year in prison with a three-year suspension of sentence.

What caught Kido's attention was that the case involved a third person who served as the broker for the exchange. Although this middleman was given only a suspended sentence as an accomplice, he was later arrested, this time for an investment scam involving fundraising for a nonexistent business, and sentenced to three years in prison. It seemed that he had arranged numerous other register exchanges, charging a handling fee each time.

The case dated to 2007, the exact year that Daisuké Taniguchi moved out of his apartment in Osaka and X appeared in Town S, and as Kido was reading the record, he began to wonder if they might not have met through this man. Further research revealed that he was currently serving his sentence at Yokohama Prison. As it was only thirty minutes by train from his condo, Kido decided to arrange a visit.

X

Kido told the man by letter that he wanted to ask him about an incident from six years ago, and the man wrote back to say that it would be "his pleasure," an odd response given that Kido was nothing to him but some lawyer he had never met.

The sky was overcast and the air was chilly on the morning Kido went to Yokohama Prison. The man had said that he preferred to meet early in the day, so Kido arrived at ten o'clock and told the guard at the entrance that he was there to see one of the inmates.

It was his first visit to Yokohama Prison in ten years, as he had only overseen civil cases of late. If not for the surrounding wall, the building might have been mistaken for a school, and Kido was reminded of Michel Foucault's *Discipline and Punish: The Birth of the Prison*, which he had read in university. Incarcerated there were two types of convict: those in the B class, with "advanced criminal tendencies including repeat offenders" and those in the F class, defined as "foreigners requiring different treatment from Japanese." At the reception, Kido filled out a visit request form and checked in his bag. The man had the unusual family name of Omiura.

Presently, Omiura appeared in the visiting room escorted by a corrections officer. He was a bald, chubby man said to be fifty-nine years old. His right eye was bigger than his left, and the deep lines of his forehead were accentuated by short, sparse eyebrows. The moment he saw Kido, Omiura smiled delightedly with a mouth like a carp's.

"To what do I owe the honor of a visit from such a handsome lawyer?" Omiura exclaimed as he took a seat on the other side of the clear acrylic partition, looking Kido over with his head tilted obliquely as though sizing him up. "You see, I've got an inferiority complex about my looks. It's on account of overcompensating that I ended up here."

Omiura spoke with a faint slur and, although he was affable enough, had a strained air about him that seemed to quietly threaten murder if you belittled him. The bit about Kido being handsome reeked of insincerity, and yet the admission of his lack of confidence—intended to better convey the initial flattery—came off as genuine. To Kido, his pinched left eye and wide-open right seemed in a peculiar way to symbolize this contrary impulse in his words, as they strove to instill belief in one thing while simultaneously concealing another.

Not taking up Omiura's strange greeting, Kido was about to launch into the topic he had come to discuss when Omiura said, "You must be Zainichi, eh, sensei?"

Kido scowled, but could not immediately find the words to reply, as though his throat were being strangled. When he let out a soft sigh, he realized that his breathing had in fact stopped for several seconds. The corrections officer remained in his seat beside Omiura, showing no signs of interest.

"So?" said the convict.

"Am I supposed to respond to that?" said Kido.

"Your face says it all. Especially the shape of your nose and eyes. I can see through you in a second."

Across Kido's mind's eye flitted his own face in the mirror each morning.

"I'm third generation," he said. "But I'm a naturalized Japanese citizen."

Kido pushed down his anger, not wanting to waste any of the visitation time. As though this exchange had allowed Omiura to balance out his feeling of inferiority with a kind of superiority, he smiled, his lip peeling back to reveal only his upper teeth.

Kido gave a simple self-introduction and explained the reason for his visit. Omiura distractedly nodded along to what he was saying before soon interrupting.

"Sensei, there really are people out there who live to be three hundred years old, aren't there?"

". . . Huh?"

"Isn't that what they always say? People. Out there. Three hundred years old."

"I've never heard that."

"Just as I thought. They can't be found in the world your kind lives in—between you and me, there used to be one in this prison, but they let him go."

I meet a lot of people in my line of work, thought Kido, *but I've rarely come across anyone so shady*. He checked his watch and tried to get the conversation back on track. But Omiura prattled on heedlessly in a low voice about his impression of the Three-Hundred-Year-Olds, now and then drawing his face close to the partition. The whole thing was sheer nonsense. When there were about fifteen minutes left in the visit, Kido lost patience and cut him off.

"This is truly fascinating," he said, "but today I'd like to ask you about an incident from six years ago. Are you familiar with a man by the name of Daisuké Taniguchi?"

After taking one glance at the photo Kido held up, Omiura let himself fall back against his seat rest in a display of obvious annoyance, and then stared up at the ceiling, looking bored. Kido's gaze turned vacantly to the corrections officer for a moment before he continued.

"A man who went by his name has passed away. But he wasn't Daisuké Taniguchi, and the real Taniguchi is missing. It's just a hunch, but I thought you might know something about their family register exchange."

Omiura gave a flick of his chin and said, "You're talking about the second son from Ikaho Onsen?"

"Exactly!" said Kido, his eyes going wide. "Do you know him?"

"Maybe I do, maybe I don't . . . Should we cut our losses and call it quits for the day?"

"I'm trying to find out who he exchanged family registers with. Would you be so kind as to tell me?"

"It was no exchange. It's called identity laundering. Think how many people want to clean up their past, just like with dirty money. They've been trying to climb the social ladder by messing with their family trees since forever. I bet you're one of them, aren't you, sensei? I can see right through you."

Kido didn't grace that with a reply.

"Hey, sensei. Next time you stop by, could you bring me some little gifts?"

". . . Pardon me?"

"I'd like that tabloid, *Asahi Geino*. Also, a book on the Heart Sutra. Preferably something not too complicated."

The corrections officer told them that their time was up. Kido nodded in acknowledgment, but Omiura looked disappointed that Kido would be leaving.

"You're not a very Zainichi Zainichi," he said, rising to his feet and looking down at Kido. "Which is one way of saying that you're as Zainichi as it gets. Just like I'm not a very con-man con man."

Omiura peeled back his lip to display his front teeth in another smile. Kido was on the verge of exploding with rage. But he found that his knees had gone weak and could do nothing but sit there and watch as Omiura left the visiting room.

❭❬

As time went by, Kido felt an emotion that approached hatred for Omiura swelling inside him. He told himself that Omiura was just a scam artist he'd met once by necessity for work. That the stuff about him being "not a very Zainichi Zainichi" was probably a meaningless psychological game. But every time Kido stood in front of the mirror after his visit to Yokohama Prison, he felt as though he was facing the man through the clear partition. It was deeply unsettling, and he wished that Omiura's existence would be wiped away from both the world and his memory.

Learning that Omiura knew Daisuké Taniguchi had been a surprise. In all likelihood, he knew something about X's identity too. But thinking about going back to meet him invariably put Kido in an awful mood. He never wanted to speak with that man again. And as much as he would have liked to prove that X hadn't been a criminal for poor Rié's sake, the case had taken an ominous turn, and he now worried that something might have happened to Daisuké Taniguchi after all.

Kido wrote another letter to Omiura. His hope was to disengage from the case as soon as possible. While he couldn't simply drop it, he wanted to wrap things up quickly.

Ten days later, he visited Omiura again, this time with a copy of *Asahi Geino* in hand. Omiura thanked him for the gift and provided a lengthy appraisal of the nude spread of a female pop idol inside.

"When you get to be around my age, nude pics of young girls just don't do the trick anymore. Ladies around fifty are where it's at. Say you're taking turns using the same bathwater with your family at home. You know how the water is kind of stiff if you're the first one to get in? It's exactly the same thing when you're screwing. Young girls have tight bodies that are just stiff as hell, even to look at in a photo. But the feeling on your skin of a woman getting on into middle age is like bathwater that's gone a bit soupy after two, three people have had their soak. You're still young, sensei, so I know you feel me on this."

After that, Omiura told a story about the time in university when senior players on the rugby team had pressured him to appear in a "homo video," forcing him to skinny-dip in the sea at Kujukuri Beach in the still-cold early spring before gang-raping him later at a hotel. He related this as though it were an amusing anecdote about an unfortunate bit of bad luck, and the visit ended, once again, with him merely hinting that he knew something about X.

On Kido's third visit, two days later, Omiura told a braggadocios tale of the big earnings he'd made privately importing Viagra. He tried to recruit Kido for the scheme once he got out of jail, assuring him it was both legal and lucrative. When Kido delicately declined and asked again about the connection between Daisuké Taniguchi and X, Omiura finally turned away from him and began to whistle as though performing some kind of comedy skit, cutting the visit short. After that, he ignored Kido's letters.

Omiura was an eccentric, mercurial man. Truth and fiction were so intricately glommed together in his stories that any attempt to strip away the lies seemed to risk tearing the facts to indecipherability. To Kido, this seemed more pathological than merely a matter of personality, and he decided to hold off on contacting him for a while to see how he might react.

Eventually, Kido received eight postcards in the mail, one after the next. They were copies of the nude picture from that issue of *Asahi Geino*, done with a ballpoint pen. As Kido was studying these sloppily drawn reproductions, he became somewhat sad. He began to suspect that, out of everything Omiura had talked about, it was his experience of being raped in the porno that he had most wanted to convey. Kido had dismissed the story as farfetched, but now wondered if Omiura might have been hoping for some kind of lawyerly advice or maybe just human compassion.

Omiura seemed to grow tired of reproducing nudes, because he then began to send drawings of the bodhisattva Kannon sitting on a rock by the waterside looking at a reflection of the moon. At this point, Kido sent him a letter of thanks and applied for another meeting. Omiura's response came immediately. The letter was addressed, "Dear Korean!" and Kido couldn't tell whether this was meant to be friendly or mocking. The main body simply read, "Are your eyes just empty holes, Handsome Lawyer Sensei? C-H-U-M-P!" The lines of the characters had been traced over numerous times for emphasis.

After this, his drawings reverted to raunchy nudes. The subject of his copying had switched from the tabloid photo to what appeared to be an image from a manga in which a middle-aged woman with fulsomely exaggerated breasts held them up in an iron grip. But when Kido looked more carefully, he discovered that encircling the right nipple were small characters that read, "Daisuké Taniguchi" and encircling the left nipple, "Yoshihiko Sonézaki."

When Nakakita passed by his desk, Kido showed him the postcard without a word. Nakakita frowned, looked at the front, and broke into exasperated laughter with his neck crooked in disbelief.

"This Yoshihiko Sonézaki,'" he said, turning to Kido. "I guess Omiura's trying to say he's X?"

"That's how it appears . . . though it's the first time I've ever come across that name . . ."

Kido wrote a letter seeking confirmation but received no reply, and Omiura would no longer accept his requests to visit.

CHAPTER ELEVEN

On the last Sunday of October, Rié, her mother, Yuto, and Hana drove to Burial Mound Park on the outskirts of town to view the cosmos blossoms, which were set to reach full bloom slightly earlier than in most years.

Hana often referred to the park as "my park" and was delighted to join them for a visit, but Yuto, who had been spending an increasing amount of time indoors of late, was reluctant at first, saying that he wanted to read a book. As Rié had not started reading books for pleasure until well into her adult years and had never been a big reader, she was astounded by Yuto's voracity. Even more so because the books he brought home from the library were all literary classics, including works by Soseki Natsume, Naoya Shiga, and Saneatsu Mushanokoji. Yuto seemed to especially like Ryunosuke Akutagawa and would buy the bunko editions, flipping through them at every spare moment. Whenever she asked him if he enjoyed what he was reading, he would reply simply that he did, without elaborating any further. Just last autumn, she had been warning him about playing too many video games; now, only a year later, he never even touched them.

After lunch, Yuto had gone upstairs and refused to come down. It was only after his grandmother asked that he obediently agreed to tag along. Without Rié making any serious effort to instill this quality in him, Yuto had always revered his grandparents. Not once had she seen him take a rebellious attitude toward them, and he would listen to his grandmother about something when Rié only made him grumble. Of course, his grandmother, for her part, felt profoundly sorry for him after the series of misfortunes he had undergone and lavished him with attention, not to mention an excess of sweets and toys.

Although this does not directly concern their trip to Burial Mound Park that day, it is worth mentioning at this point a certain incident. Not long after Rié's second marriage and the second anniversary of the death of her father, Yuto and his grandmother went to the local pet shop to buy goldfish and installed an old aquarium in the entrance to their home. Neither Rié nor her now late husband had been informed and were startled when they stepped in the door after work.

"What's this?" she had asked. "I didn't know you wanted a pet goldfish."

"It's just because Grandma looks so lonely ever since Grandpa died," Yuto explained.

Rié recognized the aquarium, having used it herself as a child until all her goldfish died. It had then ended up in the shed, where it had been collecting dust for more than thirty years.

"So when you went out with your grandmother to buy them, that was for her?"

"Yeah . . . I thought it might take her mind off things."

"Why goldfish?"

"Because I saw Grandma looking at the aquarium in the shed. Just fish are OK, right, Mom? I'll look after them."

Rié was deeply moved by Yuto's kindness.

"Yuto is growing up to be a good boy," her late husband had said, his eyes narrowed with tenderness. "A very thoughtful boy."

That night, after the kids were in bed, Rié asked her mother what had led them to visit the pet shop.

"It's just because little Yuto looks so lonely ever since Grandpa died."

Rié couldn't help laughing. "So you didn't want goldfish?"

"They're for Yuto," her mother replied, looking at Rié distrustfully, not seeing what was so funny.

"Yuto said exactly the same thing," Rié explained.

"What?"

When Rié related what Yuto had told her, her mother looked dumbfounded, but was soon laughing along with Rié and eventually grew teary-eyed. Apparently, the two of them had discovered the aquarium while Yuto was helping his grandmother look for something in the shed. Yuto had then cleaned it with the garden hose; searched online for the gravel, air pumps, and other items they would need; gone with her to buy them; and even installed the aquarium himself.

Rié was glad that her mother and her son had been forming a connection unbeknownst to her. Two people that she loved also loved each other without the need for her to mediate their affection. And sharing in their sadness and isolation, they were trying to soothe each other's pain and assuage each other's loneliness. For Rié, it was a mysterious joy, and the mere thought of what they might be talking about when she wasn't around brought a ticklish warmth to her breast.

Although Yuto was easily bored and tended to lose interest the moment he'd found something he was passionate about, taking care of the goldfish was the one thing he never neglected or burdened his family with. He kept it up even after his second dad died.

ᚷ

The tumulus mounds at Burial Mound Park stretched in an ellipse with a diameter half the width of a soccer field, like a bellybutton surrounded by fields of cosmos that covered the park as far as the eye could see. Said to number some three million, these red, pink, and purple blossoms ensconcing yellow stamen and pistils shimmered atop their green stems. Counting the smaller mounds, there were a total of 319 tumuli scattered throughout the vast park. Originally they had formed a barren landscape that seemed connected to nothing but the past, until a city initiative began to add color. Now each season revealed different flowers: cherry and mustard in the spring, sunflowers in the summer. Going to see them had been a family tradition since Rié was a child. Her late husband had loved the scenery so much that he named their daughter Hana, or "flower," which was why the little girl thought of it as her park.

When they arrived at Burial Mound Park that day, the usually empty parking lot was full of cars with license plates from various regions, both inside and outside Miyazaki Prefecture. The neatly arrayed walking paths that cut through the fields of flowers bustled with families, and in every direction, amateur photographers could be seen cradling tripods topped by hefty cameras. The weather was pleasant and clear, with a mild wind—the sort of bright, vibrant day that one wished would continue all year round.

"Hana, go stand beside those cosmos," said Rié's mother. "Are you just about there?"

Hana stood in front of the field of flowers and begged Rié to take a picture. It always thrilled her to check her height against the cosmos and to compare the pictures from each year side by side. She was still small enough to disappear amidst the flowers if Rié wasn't careful and had kept Rié busy the previous year chasing her down every time she scampered off. Now, as Rié steadied her phone to take the shot, she thought that within a year or two Hana might outgrow the flowers. Behind her daughter, the rearing blossoms began to sway from left to right under a slight breeze, as though stretching to get a look at Rié and her family through the tight crowd.

Yuto had been silent on the ride over and had remained so since they stepped out of the car. Now, he gazed vacantly at the flowers as he kept a watchful eye on Hana, his hands stuffed into the pocket of his gray hoodie, stretching it down as though his belly were carrying an anchor.

Rié studied him from behind, considering his profile whenever it angled into view, and wondered again how he must have felt to lose his brother, his grandfather, and the man he had thought of as his dad. In spite of his growth spurt this past year, he was still just a boy, as his gangly build attested. Even as an adult, Rié felt empty, as though the most precious parts inside her had been shorn away, leaving her so off balance and dizzy she could barely stay on her feet. She should have realized earlier that, like her, he was enduring the pain without expressing it. No doubt as he tended the goldfish, looked out for his little sister, read books, he was struggling just to hold himself together.

Her poor son. He hadn't fully grasped the meaning of death when Ryo passed away, but he was bound to come to his own thoughts and feelings about it in the coming years. Even Rié had contemplated death as a teenager, albeit vaguely, despite having yet to experience the loss of a loved one herself. Yuto had been deeply attached to his second dad, more so than X's actual child, Hana, because of how old they were when he was alive. And whenever Rié racked her brain for things she might do for Yuto as a mother, she wished, paradoxically, that her late husband were there to give him advice.

With each passing day, her grief seemed to grow indistinct as it gradually, soundlessly crumbled, spilling into the flow of time and slowly unburdening her heart. This brought her relief—she was leaving the crisis behind—even if, in place of the anguish immediately following his death, a new kind of loneliness sometimes seeped through the depths of her body. There were some who suggested she remarry, but she would only shake her head with a smile and tell them she'd had enough.

Now Rié was more aware of her age than ever. She compared herself to her father, who had died at only sixty-seven, and sensed her own approach to the end gaining ineluctable momentum. Death terrified her, and yet imagining Ryo and her father waiting for her always took the edge off her dread. Even Ryo, a wee toddler, had accepted his death, a death that she had not been able to undergo in his place . . . The thought that he might be waiting anxiously to see her almost made her want to die as fast as she could. More than anything, she wanted to finally apologize for subjecting him to that pointless treatment.

Rié wasn't sure when she had begun to conceive of Ryo's death not as something that made him vanish in the past but as something that allowed him to wait for her in the future, his existence not receding but approaching. Unfortunately, she wasn't the sort of person who could fully convince herself of this. Taking the belief seriously entailed that she might keep Ryo waiting in heaven for another forty-odd years, and that was something she could not bear to do to him, even with his grandfather there as guardian. Nevertheless, as admittedly unreasonable as it was, the idea that her most cherished loved ones had gone to the great beyond for her sake soothed her fear of following them and gave her something to lean on in the solitary here and now.

It was impossible for her to picture her father aging in the afterlife. But what about Ryo? If he was alive, he would be eleven. Moving had spared her the pain of having to watch his day care playmates grow up. Those diapered, toddling infants would in two years be donning uniforms for middle school. Next year would be ten years since he passed. *Time flies*, she thought to herself. *Time flies.*

Rié received word from Kido that, although he still hadn't figured out X's identity, he had made some progress with the case. As apprehensive as she was to learn the truth, worried it would be an unsettling tale, she still wanted desperately to know who her husband had been. For upon this knowledge hinged not only the possibility of clearing the haze around his existence but around her own past as well. And unable to rush Kido, especially considering the modest sum for which he was investigating, she had no choice but to be patient.

Yuto continued to keep his back turned toward her, and Rié could tell that this was his way of criticizing her for not explaining why she had neglected to deal with the death of his second dad. Afraid she might hurt his feelings further, she had been unable to broach the topic openly since that time in his bedroom.

"Yuto, what book were you reading before we left?" Rié asked. They had just reached the rows of cherry trees, already bare of their leaves.

". . . Nothing really," he replied.

"I've never heard of a book called 'nothing really,'" said Rié, poking him lightly in the shoulder with a smile.

"It was one of Ryunosuke Akutagawa's," said Yuto.

"You really like him, eh, Yuto? I read some of his short stories years ago. Like 'Yam Gruel' and 'Flatcar.'"

Yuto let that pass without comment, his face downcast, wearing a look of indifference.

"What's the story about?" asked Rié.

"It's not a story. It's kind of a poem." Yuto told her the title, but Rié couldn't catch it.

"Sorry, what's that?"

"'Asakusa Park.'"

"I've never heard of it . . . That's by Akutagawa?"

"Yes."

"What's it about?"

Yuto shrugged.

"Don't be like that to your mother. Tell me."

". . . When the main character passes in front of an artificial flower shop, a tiger lily goes, 'Look how beautiful I am,' and he replies, 'But aren't you an artificial flower?'"

"I don't get it. That's weird." Rié gave a wry smile. "You find that interesting, Yuto?"

". . . Yeah. But it's difficult."

"You're learning how to think thoughts that are beyond even your mother. When you're done, let me read it."

"Not happening."

"Why?"

"For one thing, I underlined parts of it."

Rié studied her son's profile with tender concern, smiling. "I see," she said. "Then I guess I'll just have to go buy a copy."

"I doubt you'd . . . find it interesting."

"Hey! What are you trying to imply?"

At last a hint of a smile crept onto Yuto's face.

"Even if it's not interesting for me, I want to know what sort of things you're into."

"Don't worry about it, Mom. It's got nothing to do with you."

"Nope. I'm just going to have to read it myself, whether you like it or not."

"Quit it about my books already."

Scratching his head, Yuto waved his other hand as if to shake off his mother's nosiness. He then glanced back to check on Hana and Grandma and, finding them looking at something along the edge of the path, turned to face Rié again.

"Mom," he said, "do you remember Dad's tree?"

"Of course. That one, right? The third tree over, with branches like this . . ."

After Rié remarried, they had all come to this spot in Burial Mound Park, and she had proposed that they each pick out their favorite cherry tree. Rié's tree was a bit farther ahead, Yuto's was two removed from his dad's, and Hana's had been chosen for her by Yuto since she was still in utero. The strange thing was that, the next time they came, the trees they had claimed for themselves had become different from all the others somehow, the object of their special affection.

Every year after that, they would visit in spring and compare the blossoms on their trees to decide whose had the most impressive bloom. While Yuto's tree had lost out to Rié's husband's in the year of his death, it took the prize the year after. Ever since, Yuto had wanted to stand before his dad's grave and tell him, but was still waiting for the opportunity. Now another spring had passed. And this year Rié had not brought them to see the flowers here.

Rié stopped in front of her dead husband's denuded tree and looked up at it. She doubted he had seen all two thousand trees said to have been planted in this park. But of those he had considered, this one had called out to him for whatever reason, and with each turn of the seasons, he had stood right here in this spot and stared at it as though it were his doppelganger. She still didn't know anything about his past. But she knew that, whoever he was, he had been the sort of person who, with so many trees to choose from, preferred this one.

"Mother. The anniversary of Dad's death has come and gone again," said Yuto. "But you still haven't made a grave for him."

He spoke in a controlled voice that Rié wouldn't have thought possible for a child. She didn't think she had it in her to explain right then. But she could tell that he wasn't going to let her get away with a vague reply this time.

"There's something I've been keeping from you," she said.

"What?"

"Dad . . . His name wasn't really Daisuké Taniguchi."

". . . Huh?"

"I know . . . it's strange . . . But when he died, I found out it wasn't his real name. Daisuké Taniguchi's brother came to visit, and he told me Dad wasn't his brother."

"I don't get it . . ."

"He was going by someone else's name."

Yuto's pupils quivered, his lips parted. "Then . . . who was he?"

"That's what I've been trying to figure out this whole time. I went to the police. I hired a lawyer."

"And who was he?"

"I still don't know. That's why I can't make him a grave."

"Then . . . My name, Yuto Taniguchi. What is that?"

"Taniguchi is just a name Dad used for a while. The name of someone we don't know."

"Is that why you went back to your maiden name?"

After Rié nodded, Yuto just stared at her in bewilderment. It was as though he wasn't even sure what to feel.

"Then . . . what about the story Dad told me? About his home in Ikaho Onsen, and having a fight with his family, and coming here after he ran away."

Rié hesitated for a moment but decided there was no use being evasive, and looking Yuto straight in the eye, said, "That isn't his past. It's Daisuké Taniguchi's."

"He was lying?" Yuto tensed his paling cheeks.

Saying nothing, Rié gave two slight nods.

"What the hell . . . he tricked us. All of us? Huh . . . why? Dad . . . Why did he lie? What did he do?"

"I don't know any more than you do. There was no way for me to explain. I wanted to wait until everything became a bit clearer before I told you . . . I just don't know."

They stood together in silence for a time. Presently Hana skipped over, holding hands with Grandma.

"Mama, look, it's Papa's tree!"

"It sure is."

"This I think. Um, Papa thought maybe we'll be coming today, so he went inside his tree to hide and wait."

Rié was reluctant to turn her attention away from Yuto, but she looked down at Hana with a smile and said, "Could be."

"Hey. Mama. Take a picture."

"OK. Want me to take one of you with Papa's tree?"

"Yeah! Then I want one with my tree too."

Hana was the first to take her place in front of the tree, followed by Grandma. Yuto remained where he was at first, but upon his grandmother's urging slunk over beside them.

"OK. Smiiile," Rié said in singsong. But through the display of her smartphone, she saw Yuto giving her a deadpan stare. And with a click of the shutter, she captured his expression.

"Rié, you go stand over there too," said her mother. "I'll take this one."

As instructed, Rié took Hana's hand and lined up beside Yuto, but found herself no better able than him to put on a bright face.

CHAPTER TWELVE

In the capacious lobby of the Yokohama District Court, Kido stood, talking with his two clients about the fifth oral argument hearing that had just concluded. These were the parents of the man who had committed suicide after working unconscionably long hours. Kido had been serving as their lawyer in the suit for almost two years. Now, with public outcry growing ever more heated, the accused izakaya chain was finally showing signs that it might be moving toward a settlement.

As Kido and his clients would report on the hearing later that day at a debriefing session attended by the labor unions, they reconfirmed their strategy going forward. Then the father looked Kido straight in the eye and said, "Sensei, it's not about whether we win or lose. We want to know what actually happened, why our boy died."

"Yes, of course," said Kido with a nod, conveying his understanding of what drove them on this long fight.

While the father's forehead was broad, he had a full head of mostly white hair, which he kept close-cropped and tidy. With long eyebrows slanting out over eyes shaped like set squares that always glittered moistly, his face universally aroused pity whenever it appeared in the media, contributing to the already growing sympathy for the case.

"Let's keep marching on. We're headed in the right direction."

Kido used these phrases regularly, and his clients never seemed particularly heartened by them, but over the past two years they had grown fond of his tone when he said it, and this time it appeared to stir their emotions.

"You've been a great help to us, sensei, I mean it. In the beginning we were completely at a loss. It's thanks to you we've managed to keep our heads on straight. Even if the case can never bring our boy back to us . . ."

"Let's keep marching on," Kido repeated, acknowledging what the father had said with restraint and decorum. In his heart he was moved, knowing that the man's words were sincere.

※

Kido had been in a state of constant irritation all day after shouting at his son for being sulky and uncooperative about getting dressed that morning.

He had been holding down the fort with Sota since the previous day when his wife left for a business trip to Osaka, and the two of them had had an uneventful evening together, eating a quick dinner at a family restaurant before bath and then bedtime as usual. The problem had begun that morning when Kido awoke to find Sota watching a Doraemon movie on DVD on the TV in the living room. From that moment on, whatever Kido tried to get him to do, whether it was have breakfast or wash his face, Sota invariably dragged his feet. At first Kido was worried that he might have caught a cold, but Sota had no fever and shook his head when asked if he was feeling sick. After Sota nonetheless persistently refused to come to the breakfast table, Kido's tone grew increasingly harsh. And with an appointment at 9:30, he watched the clock with growing impatience.

Sota hadn't been his usual stable self since Kaori gave him a fierce scolding for not doing his Kumon math homework two weeks earlier. As Kido had never been one to approve of forcing huge amounts of study on young children, he had tried to defend his son, claiming that there was no need to teach him arithmetic so thoroughly at this stage because he was bound to learn it soon enough anyway. This had set Kaori off, and the conversation quickly flared into an argument. From his divorce mediation work, Kido knew just how common it was for disagreements around childrearing to cause deep-rooted discord between couples. But his and Kaori's inability to have a calm discussion about such a trifling issue was unusual. And telling Kaori, out of consideration for her, that she seemed tired out from escorting the boy back and forth to his many lessons only succeeded in fanning the flames. The end result was that Sota received a savage earful from his mother.

When Kido saw how Kaori treated their child, it was the first time he seriously considered divorce. That their life together stressed her out was obvious, and since he wished her the best whatever might happen between them, he wondered if she might do better to start over with a new partner. Then perhaps she would regain her former composure. Perhaps Kido would too.

He had trouble finding any sign that she loved him, and if someone were to ask him whether he loved her, he would have been at a loss for words. Even so, he could never have outright denied his love for her.

After ten years living in wedlock, their relationship was slowly coming apart, without any particular inciting incident he could point to, and Kido kept trying to think of some way that they might set it right. Over the past few months, they hadn't touched once, maintaining a wary distance between their bodies like strangers, as if to ensure that they didn't brush against each other even by accident. In all fairness to Kaori, she too was making efforts to restrain herself and prevent their fights from escalating. She took great care not to become emotional with Kido, though in compensation, her berating of Sota would sometimes rise to a furious pitch. Never before had Kido seen her behave the way she did with him at such times, not in the whole decade they had lived together.

Sota had his own role to play in the friction between his parents. Recently, he had been rebelling ferociously against his mother's imperious commands, as an entirely normal part of the development of his sense of self, and their relationship could only be described as a vicious cycle. Kido's attempt to bring this problem to Kaori's attention had been utterly inadequate, no more than a timid suggestion, fearful that the slightest interference might destroy their marriage forever. To make up for this failure, he consoled Sota in his room and in the bath, hugging him and letting him talk, all the while hating himself for this disingenuous evasion of his responsibility. How far he had strayed from the sort of father he wished to be.

Kido was aware that he was the cause of his wife's growing discontent. At the same time, he could tell that something more fundamental underlay the irritation that engendered her preposterous suspicion of his infidelity, and he invariably shrunk back whenever he reached the threshold of understanding it. Instead he would seek a momentary escape from reality in his go-to diversion, the ongoing search for X.

If their falling-out had only concerned husband and wife, Kido might have accepted it. What tore him apart was the impact it was having on their son. Not that he had some grand theory of childrearing he was trying to live up to. His only hope was that Sota might one day look back and feel certain that he had been raised with love. This was a goal that even Kaori should have thought worth pursuing.

As Sota had never been disobedient to his father, Kido had deluded himself into believing that they had a special relationship of mutual trust, even as he despised his own mendacious kindness. But as soon as Kaori had left town, Sota's frustration at the position they placed him in found a new outlet, the only one at hand. And although Kido should have seen it coming, he flew into an unseemly rage at Sota's willfulness that morning, pelting him with the socks he refused to put on, placing his hand on his head, and bellowing, "Behave!"

Perhaps "placed" isn't right. More likely, that gesture of rebuke was a slap. And realizing this instantly, Kido left his hand where it was, gripping his son's head in anger, in a half-unconscious attempt to conceal what he had done. Frightened, Sota stopped crying, and Kido stared at his hand. Everything about violence that he rejected could be found in the force of that grip.

Kido felt as though something vile had burst inside his chest. When he stepped away for a moment, Sota put on his socks, sobbing, his face beet red. Kido hugged him until his tears ceased. Then, without a word, he took him to day care, and the moment he watched his son disappear inside, was stricken with sorrow and regret.

Every time Kido encountered tragic cases of child abuse in his divorce suits, his heart went out to the children. At the same time, he tried to have some understanding for the parents who could not help their behavior due to their innate disposition and environment. He was able to maintain this outlook because he had seen himself as belonging to an entirely different category of person. Now, for the first time, he took seriously the possibility that if the conditions of his life were different, he might have become a child beater. Picturing this hypothetical scenario amounted to a profound loss of faith in himself. Even his comforting Sota at the end was just like the honeymoon phase in a textbook cycle of domestic violence and reconciliation.

Just after six o'clock, Kido went to pick up Sota from his day care in the Motomachi-Chukagai Station building. When Kido arrived, Sota hurriedly put away the blocks he and his friends had been playing with and scampered over to Kido, wearing a broad smile. The teacher reported that Sota had made it through the day without any problems. Sota cavorted with his friends as though reluctant to leave, and the kids all gathered to say their usual parting words, "Together, farewell!" before Kido and Sota left.

The ocean wind was strong that night. A Christmas light display sparkled on the silhouettes of trees lining the streets.

With the vibrant glow of Motomachi in the corner of his eye, Kido was waiting with Sota for the light when he spotted a strange man repeatedly kicking a utility pole for no apparent reason. Instinctively, he squeezed Sota's hand and retreated a few paces. As the man remained where he was after the light turned green, they immediately left him behind. Sota was silent, but Kido thought he sensed him speeding up.

Every time they reached an intersection, a chill wind blasted them from the canyon of buildings. As Kido buttoned up the front of his coat, he grew concerned about Sota's fingertips sticking out from his sheltering hand.

"Are you cold? Everything OK?"

"Yeah . . . Hey, Daddy?"

"What is it, son?"

"How come Ultraman can shout '*shuwatch*' and stuff when his mouth doesn't move?"

"Oh." Kido pictured Ultraman's immobile, metallic face. "I wonder." He shrugged with a smile.

Eyes wide and fervent, Sota explained how little sense it made.

"True . . . ," Kido acknowledged. "But, well, Ultraman can fly and shoot his Specium Ray and do all kinds of incredible things, so I bet talking without moving his mouth is a piece of cake."

Kido was quite pleased with himself for this answer, but his reasoning did not seem to satisfy Sota in the least.

Upon returning home, they had a dinner of spaghetti with meat sauce and frozen hamburger patties. Then, before Sota could turn on the television, Kido went over to the couch, sat Sota on his lap, and said, "I'm sorry for shouting at you this morning."

"That's OK," said Sota with a nod, more interested in turning on the television ASAP than in what his father was saying.

"I was in a rush because I thought I was going to be late for work. You wouldn't have wanted to be late for day care either, would you? See, that's why I got mad."

"OK."

"Tomorrow morning—look at me—let's make sure to get ready fast enough so we can be on time."

"OK."

"Good. That's all. You can go ahead and watch TV now." Kido patted his son on the head and embraced his tiny body once more.

After bath time, they went to Sota's room and lay in bed with the lights out.

"Daddy."

"What is it, son?" said Kido, stretched out in the darkness beside him.

"If you saw me and my double, would you know which one was the real me?"

"Um, what do you mean?"

Sota told him about the Anpanman picture book the day care teachers had read them in which the villain, Baikinman, went around posing as Anpanman.

"Ah, now I get it . . . Of course I'd know. You're my son."

"How could you tell?"

"Just by looking at you. And by your voice."

"But what if he looked and sounded just like me?"

"Then . . . I guess I'd ask him about things only you would remember. Where did we go for vacation last summer?"

"Hawaii!"

"Exactly. Even if your double looked like you on the outside, he still wouldn't have your memories, now would he?"

"Oh yeah. You're amazing, Daddy! So if your double shows up, should I ask him about his memories too?"

"Definitely."

"Then . . . When we went to Hawaii, did you eat a steak as big as a straw sandal or not?"

"I sure did—but better not ask my double like that or you'll give away the answer."

As they continued to talk in this way, the gaps in their conversation gradually widened until eventually Kido could hear soft, peaceful breathing beside him. He waited in the dark while it rapidly deepened before fixing Sota's blanket and slipping quietly out of his room.

Kido had been putting off decorating their Christmas tree and decided to get it done before bed. So, throwing on a CD of Masabumi Kikuchi and Masahiko Togashi duets, he took out the cardboard box with the decorations. Inside, he found the lights and silver and gold ornaments exactly as he had packed them a year earlier. Somehow, at the sight of the components of their fake tree, he remembered that Rié had contacted him seeking advice about X at around the same time. The speed at which the year had gone by astonished him. It was a feeling that came upon him on an almost monthly basis.

While assembling the tree, Kido recalled the night he had sat in this room, drinking vodka by himself after putting Sota to bed, and pondered the meaning of that intense feeling of joy he had experienced. Once the tree was ready, he placed it by the glass door leading to the veranda, wrapped it with LEDs, and hung the stars and baubles from the branches for the finishing touch. After all that procrastination, it had been a mere fifteen-minute operation. Turning on the Christmas lights and dimming the ones in the room, he inspected his work from a few paces away. Reflected in the glass behind the tree was the room with him standing there all alone.

Kido was thinking of having a few drinks like the last time, when a song he worshipped came on—Masabumi Kikuchi's solo piano rendition of "All the Things You Are"—and suddenly he lost all desire to be anywhere else. The tempo seemed to slowly dismantle time, each note a clear droplet that fell and spread overlapping ripples through the silent interior. It wasn't amidst the music itself but in the melding of his anticipation of its sounds and their lingering resonance that Kido stilled his breath, gazing at the lights as they cycled through their repeating pattern.

He was interrupted finally from his reverie when his cell phone beeped with an incoming Line message. He reached for his phone atop the table. It was Kaori.

> How are you two holding up?
> Is Sota being a good boy?

It was unusual for her to contact him during a business trip, and Kido thought this might be her way of expressing her concern about their recent conflict. Although the message was a mere two lines long, he was happy to see it, hopeful that she might come back refreshed by the change of scenery. She had said she would be travelling with her new boss, but Kido wasn't worried about her because he was supposed to be a capable man, so much so that Kaori had recently stopped complaining about her job.

> Yeah, we're fine.
> He's being good.
> Good luck with your trip!

To his reply, Kido added emojis for the first time in he couldn't remember how long.

Kaori sent back a sticker with the English phrase "Thank you!!" attached to a character he didn't recognize. It was smiling more cheerfully than Kido had seen Kaori smile for ages.

After fiddling with his phone at the dining table for a while, Kido recalled Misuzu's Three-Steps-Forward-Four-Steps-Backism. He now clearly recognized his attraction to her. Still, he was not prepared to carry their relationship to the next stage. He never had been. The very idea of them getting together was so unrealistic that he didn't even treat it as a serious possibility. Nevertheless, there was something about her that irresistibly stirred up visions of what life might be like with her as his partner. He felt more comfortable with himself in their online communications than in any other context. And whenever he saw her picture on Facebook, with her happy-go-lucky vibe and joyful, spontaneous smile, he imagined the days passing with her by his side, wondering how everything might have turned out if he had married her and she had been Sota's mother instead. Of course this was nothing more than a fantasy of an alternate life that, while possible perhaps in another world, could never have been a reality in this one.

Kido doubted that he would have approached this conundrum with such hesitation and putative good sense if he had been younger, whether married or otherwise. And yet the impulse that, back then, might have prodded him into action and forcefully yanked him along—namely, his libido—had marked a shy retreat and would now only be there for him in the pursuit if he insisted. To think, this was the very same libido that so tormented him over his sexless marriage! The idea of, conversely, having to give his libido a prod and yank it along was simply too daunting to consider. Though, in his twenties, Kido would have flatly dismissed such pretense to enervated maturity as a bunch of bald-faced lies . . .

In any case, giving himself over to a sudden destructive urge for some giddy middle-aged pipe dream, throwing away the life he had painstakingly built and starting a new one with Misuzu, had to be the exact opposite of the grounded, compromising way of according with existence exemplified by the philosophy of Three-Steps-Forward-Four-Steps-Backism that had so greatly impressed him.

For the first time, Kido wondered if X might have been a perfectly normal guy who simply got bored with his life and decided that he wanted a new one. As the conversation with Sota suggested, memories make people who they are. Thus, if you possessed the memories of another, wouldn't it be possible to become them?

Perhaps X was sitting alone late one night, overburdened with the weariness of life, just like me right now, when he discovered Omiura on the internet. Just a frivolous man who yearned for a touch more stimulation, and murder had nothing to do with it.

Kido had tried searching online for Yoshihiko Sonézaki, one of the names from Omiura's nude manga copy, but had failed to turn up a criminal record, or, for that matter, any sign that the man existed. Given that X seemed to have been involved with a shady character like Omiura, Kido leaned toward the supposition that X had been mixed up in some kind of crime, and felt less inclined to sympathize with him. At the same time, something told him that X's life had to have been innocuous enough that Daisuké Taniguchi would deem it worth trading for simply to escape his poor relationship with his family. Or could he have been after money?

Whatever the truth might turn out to be, Kido knew that Rié would want to know it. There was no other way for her to heal the rifts in her family, and Kido reminded himself how urgent it was to sort out his own home situation once this empty game of make-believe detective had drawn to a conclusion.

That night, Kido's interest in that game was fading fast, and he might have soon convinced himself to call it quits. But thanks to an unexpected turn of events two weeks later, he stumbled upon the true identity of X and found himself fully absorbed once again.

CHAPTER THIRTEEN

It was three days before Christmas when Kido, after finishing up some work at the Tokyo District Court, headed to Shibuya for an exhibition of art curated from the submissions of convicts on death row. He had heard about it from one of the event organizers, a lawyer friend named Sugino who was an ardent supporter of the movement to abolish capital punishment in Japan.

Although Kido was opposed to capital punishment, he had never been directly involved in the movement, nor did he have experience defending clients in criminal cases where the prosecution sought the death penalty. Rather, what drew him to the exhibition was a newly discovered interest in the art of convicts, kindled by his encounter with Omiura and the peculiar postcards he'd sent from prison. What if this tragicomic puzzle of a con man had been awaiting that fatal retribution? His drawings would no doubt have had a completely different character. He would be living between a murder he had committed in the past and an execution at the hands of the state that awaited him in the future. Kido was curious to see what sort of art people actually in such a predicament might create in the present.

Snow was falling as he walked from Shibuya Station to the small gallery beside the Tokyu Department Store where the exhibition was being held. With the weather report warning of accumulation that night, even in the center of Tokyo, the front of his jacket was covered in white in spite of his umbrella. He walked swiftly, bringing a glow of warmth to the inside of his numbed cheeks.

The gallery was on the sixth floor of a building stacked with bars and restaurants. As Kido was dusting himself off at the entrance, Sugino thanked him for making the trek in such atrocious weather, and Kido commiserated with him about the cold. Sugino was scheduled to serve as the moderator for a talk later on.

Inside, the white hardwood floor was wet with tracked-in snow and Kido watched a woman in front of him almost slip and fall. Chairs had already been set up for the audience, and he was surprised to see that the large event space was packed. Worried about his train home being delayed or cancelled, he slung his coat over a chair at the back, planning to slip out early.

✕

The exhibition showcased several dozen artists. Their work ranged in size from large pieces that reached toward the ceiling to those pieces no bigger than a postcard. Cobbled-together papers and ad hoc additions of color betrayed the great pains the convicts had taken to make the most of their limited materials. Listed beside each piece was its title, the name of the creator, and the unofficial name of the case for which they had been convicted. As no other details were provided, some attendees searched on their phones while making their way around the room.

Near the entrance was a large piece made up of two paintings. Each was composed of conjoined B4 paper sheets, hung one on top of the other to form a single continuous scene. One depicted a naked woman on her knees at the bottom of an enormous dry well, trying to climb up the brick wall. The painting above revealed a narrow view of the blue sky far, far above and green flowering plants in the tranquil sunlight. Kido interpreted this light as the artist's accumulated memory of the glimmers seen daily through the prison window. The thirsting after freedom suggested by the perspective gestured toward hopelessness, while the contrast between the dazzling light and the increasingly thick gradations of darkness down the well elicited a sense of anguish.

The case was of a married couple who owned a pet shop and who had killed four customers in succession before destroying the bodies. The artist was the wife. She had claimed innocence ever since her arrest. As the incident was well known, the piece had been featured prominently in the flyer for the exhibition.

Another piece of hers beside it depicted the ground in what had to be early fall. Through a scattering of young pine cones and fallen green leaves marched a line of ants. Oddly, the scene incorporated countless grenades and the white foot of a woman trying to walk through without shoes. Kido noted that the bare feet of the woman in the well had likewise been emphasized. Both works seemed to imply the artist's innocence, while a third work made a more direct declaration in words. It was more like a poster than a painting, and Kido was immediately taken by the excellence of the image.

Beside these was work by another woman. She also claimed innocence, in this case for the crime of mass poisoning, and was in the middle of petitioning the Supreme Court for a retrial. Displayed were about ten of her pieces, each the size of a square of origami paper. Kido followed a couple ahead of him in the crowd and stopped in front of one: against a black background, a thick red line ran horizontally through the center, drooping in the middle, and a droplet like a tear of blood hung down. According to the explanation Kido had read on the exhibition website, the line represented the neck laceration left by the rope in a hanging and the droplet the tears of the family.

In a second neighboring work, a square the size of a bean enclosing a red circle had been drawn against a blue background. The website had said that this represented the entrapment and loneliness of being cut off from blue skies in prison. The works of this artist appeared to be abstract diagrams of her fear of death and belief in her innocence set within squarish frames. While they suffered from a shortage of drawing implements and a lack of finesse, Kido thought that all possessed a certain power that seemed to compress the being of the spectator. He stopped in front of them one by one, each time holding his breath at first and then eventually letting it out in a long sigh.

Her work seemed to him closer to graphic design than anything else. This reminded him of the familiar concept of the artistic quality of promotional representation, but he decided that there should be more discussion of its contrary, the promotional quality of artistic representation. The purpose of graphic design was to make people aware of the existence of something, whether an event or a commercial product or anything else. Otherwise it would be ignored as though it had truly never existed. Posters, for example, borrowed the power of the sublime to inform people of their subject's existence, and in the process, that representation was occasionally elevated into the domain of art.

But irrespective of capitalism and mass consumer society, didn't art in fact originally function as publicity? For example, a blazingly vibrant sunflower in a flowerpot. A horse galloping across a prairie. A life of loneliness. The tragedy of war. Hatred borne inside. Loving someone. Being loved by no one . . . Couldn't all artistic representation be thought of in the final analysis as an advertisement for these?

※

With his eye on the time, Kido began to pick up his pace.

The work he saw showed a surprising diversity of form. From illustrations, manga-style doodles, and tattoo-book-style renderings of waterfalls and carp, to reproductions of famous paintings, surrealistic watercolors, and a meticulously compiled chart of the toppings for the miso soup served in jail at breakfast, lunch, and dinner—no two were alike. While the skill level of the artists varied, some demonstrated obvious talent. This, Kido supposed, was because the most creatively inclined death row convicts had responded to the call for submissions.

Some of the pictures were almost alien to the space of the gallery. Others were so beautiful and heartwarming, it was hard to believe they had been conceived in prison. Among the work of convicts who acknowledged their guilt, a few decried the brutality of capital punishment as an institution, but many were depictions of birds, flowers, cats, or any other subject the artist happened to have felt like taking up.

Although Kido had some reservations about fixating on the first idea that came to him, he went on contemplating what the artists might be trying to "advertise." In spite of their claims of innocence, a surprisingly small number directly denied committing the crime. Rather than say what they had not done, they screamed with grave urgency that they were not the sort of person that could have done it, defending not their actions but their existence. The state was, after all, proceeding toward obliterating them.

Some of the convicts had drawn cute pictures that seemed incongruous with the crimes they'd committed. In this, they sought to moor traces of their existence to something external, something other than their soon-to-be ruined bodies. In particular, to a side of themselves that no one would have suspected they possessed, one scheduled for extermination along with the rest of them when the appointed time came. If the human personality could be carved up into parts, then perhaps they were desperately advertising, out of the pit of fear for their own death, the presence of these blameless others that would be dragged off with them to doom.

As it was nearly time for the talk to begin, Kido made his way through the crowd along the display wall to view the last remaining pieces.

In the center of a frame crammed with rallying cries that might have come from a political leaflet—"DOWN WITH THE SECURITY TREATY!" "BANZAI TO THE DICTATORSHIP OF THE PROLETARIAT!" and "NO SALES TAX INCREASE!"—was a series of nude female illustrations in the style of a bordello flyer. At the sight of these, Kido's eyes boggled. The composition, the breast-accentuating poses, everything about them was just like Omiura's postcards—or rather, the other way around: Omiura's drawings were obvious imitations of these. The display even included a hand-copied version of the Heart Sutra, a text Omiura had asked Kido to procure for him.

Could he have seen this exhibition somehow? Kido wondered. *Or an article about it in a magazine . . . ?* He recalled Omiura's writing that he was a "C-H-U-M-P." Had that been an expression of his exasperation with Kido for failing to notice that he had copied pictures by an inmate on death row?

"So . . . Ahem. Can we have your attention please? As the talk will begin shortly, we ask everyone to please take your seats. There will still be time to view the displays afterward."

As Kido began to follow the flow of the crowd toward his seat, he took a glance at one last picture and stopped. Unlike the fraught imagery of the other convicts' pieces, this one depicted a serene landscape of hills and fields with a stream running through. While poorly realized, it succeeded in emanating a sense of modest simplicity. Beside it was a picture by the same convict of small birds and cherry trees in full bloom, and another of a street corner in an old town with a mailbox, utility poles, a road enclosed by plank barriers.

Kido was overcome by the peculiar feeling that he had seen these pictures somewhere before. But he didn't see how he could have; they looked like something a middle school student might make in art class. Omiura, perhaps? No. Not him . . . So who then? The artist was described as the perpetrator of murder and arson in Yokkaichi in 1985. As Kido had been ten years old, his vague memories of the incident began to come back. After racking his brain for an explanation for his reaction, he began to suspect it was merely déjà vu and allowed the staff to usher him to his seat.

The talk consisted of an art critic involved in curating the exhibition explaining the significance of each piece. As he made a forced attempt to treat them exclusively as "works of art" in his analysis, Kido soon grew bored. In his role as master of ceremonies, Sugino seemed to appreciate this approach, and Kido resolved to set him straight later on.

All throughout, the landscapes continued to nag at Kido's attention. He found his gaze wandering to them past the heads of the crowd but was still thinking about ducking out early rather than taking another look. Only about fifteen minutes remained in the hour-long talk.

". . . Now then, as we are running out of time, let's take a quick look over here, shall we?" said the critic. "See those racy pictures of nude women? Those are the work of one of the perpetrators of the Insurance Fraud Switcheroo Murder in Kitakyushu. This was a very convoluted case. To describe it as simply as possible, it begins when A, the manager of a karaoke bar in Kitakyushu, and B, one of his staff, who are both hard-up for cash, cook up an insurance fraud scheme. First, the two of them are adopted by a certain financial backer in order to legally become brothers. Then, they have B take out an expensive life insurance plan, make A the recipient, and kill a homeless man in B's place by force-feeding him alcohol. Now they're ready for the switcheroo, and they try to fraudulently collect life insurance. But here's the slipup. The man they killed is not even close to B in either age or height, and the police are onto them in no time. As it turns out, B has already committed arson and a murder-robbery, so they slap him with the death penalty. And here are his pictures . . ."

Kido had been listening without really taking it in, but when the significance of the unofficial case name, Insurance Fraud Switcheroo Murder, finally sunk in, his eyes snapped to the speaker.

To kill the homeless man in B's place, they must have switched their identities . . . At this thought, Kido broke out in ticklish goose bumps around his biceps. When he made the connection to X impersonating Daisuké Taniguchi, his jaw fell open, his lips shaped into an unvoiced "Oh." He remained frozen like that for several seconds, staring not at B's nude illustrations but at the landscapes beside them, until suddenly it hit him where he had seen them before.

They're just like X's pictures, he realized. And pulling out his cell phone, Kido searched for the photos of X's personal effects that he had taken at Rié's place. Quickly he found several sketches. X's work depicted landscapes geographically distant from the ones here. And yet the style was identical.

Kido's heart pounded with urgency against the wall of his chest, trying to tell him something. He took a deep breath and tried to think more carefully how it might all fit together. The critic had just shifted to the landscape pictures. He explained that the artist was a man named Kenkichi Kobayashi who had been executed twenty years earlier. But X's name was supposed to be Yoshihiko Sonézaki.

How can I be so sure? thought Kido, knitting his brow and tilting his head in perplexity. His sole justification was the names written on the woman in Omiura's enigmatic postcard. But just because the right breast read "Daisuké Taniguchi" and the left "Yoshihiko Sonézaki," did that warrant the conclusion that those two men had switched family registers?

He pictured the text written in a circle around the nipples. *Are your eyes just empty holes, handsome lawyer sensei? C-H-U-M-P!*

Why did he call me a chump in that letter? Kido wondered. Had Omiura just been trying to rile him, or had he actually been hinting at something substantial as Kido had assumed? Perhaps there was some significance to his imitating the pictures of the man executed for the insurance scam murder. If he had seen this exhibition, perhaps he was familiar with the pictures by this Kenkichi Kobayashi that so resembled

X's. Is that what he was trying to get at? But wasn't Kobayashi long dead? What was Omiura's point?

Kido's excitement faded as quickly as it had arisen, leaving him grasping only an empty trace. The sound of applause alerted him that the talk was over. Without any break, the Q&A began.

Most of the audience seemed sympathetic to the capital punishment abolition movement. Many stated their opinions rather than asking anything, and one woman got so worked up that her eyes grew moist. Of the few with actual questions, most stuck to uncontroversial topics: the challenges of organizing such an event, the speakers' outlook for the future. Everyone chose their words with excessive care.

"Yes, the gentleman at the front," said Sugino, finally picking out a man who'd had his hand up from the beginning. "We're going to make this the last question."

"Thank you for the valuable talk," said the man. "I'm also grateful for the opportunity to speak. My name is Shuichi Kawamura. I'm a nonfiction author writing a book about the families of victims of crime."

Wearing a white shirt and navy-blue sweater, Kawamura looked to be in his early twenties. While he came off as serious and spoke politely enough, his voice sounded as though it was always on the verge of bursting with emotion, which set the audience on edge. Kido had never heard of him.

"Um . . . so this is going to sound a bit brash, but I think this exhibition is intentionally misleading. In fact, to be perfectly honest, I'm actually kind of ticked off. Before you held this event, how come you didn't exhibit the pictures of the victims? Why did you make no effort to understand and relate to their feelings first? Before you went, 'Wow, look how talented these death row convicts are, look at their amazing pictures,' did you bother to consider how much talent, what dreams, how beautiful were the minds of those who were murdered? Were they given the time to draw pictures before their lives were taken? You say that the death penalty is barbaric, but don't we all reap what we sow? Why are these people privileged with the freedom to make art? However much they want to express themselves, let's not forget that they themselves deprived others of the freedom to do the same. These murderers! Without considering any of this, you look at the pictures here and think to yourselves, 'Oh, those poor convicts.' Kind of one-sided, maybe? Shouldn't you put up a sign that properly describes how horrible their crimes actually were? Even in cases of murder, it's only, like, 0.2 percent that are sentenced to death, you know. It is beyond clemency, what these people have done! Can you spare a thought for the pain and suffering of not just those who died but their surviving family and friends and loved ones? All exhibitions like this achieve is to pour salt in their wounds! That's all I have to say."

Kawamura said all of this in a rush, trembling. When he was finished, he plonked himself hard into his seat and held out the mic for the staff. Piercing feedback ripped apart the silence of the gallery. One person in back applauded vigorously, and several others looked over their shoulders to see who it was. Then Kawamura jumped back up as though suddenly remembering something he'd left out.

"Oh, and by the way, I think the execution of innocent people is a serious problem and I'm opposed to it. That's all I wanted to add."

Saying this, he returned to his seat.

Prior to Kawamura's tirade, it had been bothering Kido that no one had even mentioned the victims. He thought the issue deserved a question from the audience and was planning to tell Sugino later. In fact, this lacuna in the abolition movement was part of the reason he wasn't comfortable becoming actively involved.

It seemed that Sugino was acquainted with Kawamura, because without batting an eyelash, he nodded and gave his response.

"I think we need to draw a distinction between legally guaranteed rights and our emotions. Legally speaking, Japan's approach to punishment is not absolute retributivism but proportional retributivism. The idea of lex talionis embodied in the common expression 'an eye for an eye' is in fact a precept for constraining retaliation, which tends be overly emotional, from extending beyond the degree of the initial harm. In penology since the advent of the modern era, corporal punishment that takes the form of 'an eye for an eye' has been replaced with removal of freedom. If a victim is blinded, the perpetrator does not have their eyes poked out. Even though the victim is deprived of all the visual beauty of the world, the person who inflicted this damage has no limitations placed on their sight. Instead of such retribution, a punishment is assigned that restricts the criminal's freedom in accordance with the severity of the crime. This is punishment meted out not through the body but through freedom. The institution of the death penalty falls completely outside this principle. Emotionally speaking, I can understand what you're trying to say, but since the dead victim has been deprived of all of their freedom, it follows from your reasoning that death row convicts should never be allowed to think or feel anything."

"Which exactly sums up my opinion," said Kawamura, not using the mic. "They should be executed immediately. Each and every second that goes by until then is an extravagant luxury relative to those who've been murdered."

"The death penalty is a form of corporal punishment, and I'm opposed to recognizing it as an exception. Moreover, artistic creation is one of the most basic activities of human life, and I support the right of the condemned to engage in it. That being said, I believe this is an issue for us to resolve as a society and would be profoundly interested in an exhibit of artwork created by the surviving family of the victims. Only I think the onus is on advocates of the victims to hold it. Citizens should of course view both and make up their minds for themselves."

Kawamura repeatedly shook his head in adamant disagreement while Sugino was speaking but argued with him no further, his back visibly tense with unexpressed anger.

Sugino was rare in that he had turned away from a judge-track career path, despite high hopes for him since his legal intern days and numerous invitations, to instead become a lawyer. While his response was orthodox from a legal history standpoint, Kido nonetheless felt he could understand Kawamura's frustration with his sheer impassiveness.

𝕏

Once the talk was over, Sugino began to schmooze with the guest art critics, so Kido decided to extricate himself from the crowd rushing out the door and wait in front of the landscape paintings. According to the explanation earlier, Kenkichi Kobayashi had murdered the married owners of a local construction company, along with the sixth grader who was their only son. But Kido, while fully acknowledging his own naivety, struggled to believe that these landscapes could have been the work of such a person.

The gallery gradually began to empty out. Just as Kido started to look up "Kenkichi Kobayashi" on his phone, Sugino appeared from the back.

"Sorry to keep you waiting," he said. "Thanks for listening to the end."

"Thanks for putting it on. I learned a lot tonight."

As Kido went to put his phone in his pocket, his eye caught a photograph of a face on the screen and all words abandoned him. It was X. As Sugino seemed to think that Kido was checking his messages, he stood there, waiting for Kido to finish with his phone. Kido skimmed the text attached to the photo.

"See this . . . ," he said, showing his iPhone to Sugino.

"Ah," said Sugino, bringing his face closer to the display. "That's the man who painted these, Kenkichi Kobayashi."

Kido looked back and forth between the photo on his screen and the landscapes on display, puzzling over what this could possibly mean. He realized the photo wasn't X, only someone who looked incredibly similar. How? Why? Suddenly he was ready to make a guess, but gobsmacked and excited, he lacked the presence of mind to grasp any of the implications.

CHAPTER FOURTEEN

According to Sugino, Kenkichi Kobayashi had a son named Makoto. As the boy had taken his mother's maiden name, Hara, when she and Kenkichi got divorced, he now went by the name Makoto Hara.

It was in 1985, in a city called Yokkaichi in Mie Prefecture, that Kenkichi Kobayashi committed the crimes for which he was later executed. A typical gambling addict, when Kobayashi inevitably slipped deep into debt, he went begging at the house of an acquaintance who operated a construction company, demanding money and going berserk when he was refused. After a few hours back at home, he returned in the middle of the night to rob the house, at which time he stabbed the acquaintance, his wife, and his child to death with a kitchen knife before setting a fire to destroy the evidence.

Kido could just barely remember this gruesome incident, but it gained new immediacy when Sugino mentioned that Kobayashi's son, Makoto, had been born in 1975—the same year as Kido. Kido recalled vague glimmerings of the faces of his classmates and of himself playing with them. To think there had been another kid in grade four who'd had to cope with the fallout of his father's murders.

The story had been all over the news, bringing reporters in droves, and Makoto's mother had immediately moved out of town with him. Makoto was later recorded as living in an orphanage in Maebashi. Little was known about his activities after he left.

Then, in 2006, an unexpected turn of events brought Makoto Hara back to public attention. Starting around this time, he was repeatedly reported to the police for shoplifting. In 2008, he was finally charged and given one year in prison with a three-year suspension of sentence. During the probation period, he was then apprehended for shoplifting again, slapped with one and a half years of actual jail time, and found guilty of the same offense for a third time soon after his release. Now, after finally serving out his term at the beginning of the year, he was living on the outside again.

When Makoto Hara was sent to prison the first time around, one of the weeklies published a feature exposé entitled "After the Crime" that used him as an example of how a convict's offspring could turn out. Kido had been able to glean details of the exposé from extracts posted on a die-hard crime-enthusiast website that he had found in the course of looking up Kenkichi Kobayashi. Although the article made a show of protecting Hara's identity with a pseudonym, the fact that he went by his mother's name had already been outed by the site, every page of which was a jumble of sordid hearsay. What surprised Kido most about the article was that Makoto Hara, after leaving the orphanage, had reportedly belonged for a period of time to a boxing club in Kita-Senju, had later debuted as a professional boxer, and in 1997 had taken the bantamweight championship title in the East Japan Rookie King Tournament. As Kido had some familiarity with combat sports, he knew that this was no small feat.

But, as the feature went on to explain, Makoto had been grappling with psychological problems and, before the All Japan Rookie King Championship Match, suddenly withdrew from the bill and disappeared. He then spent nearly a decade making ends meet as a day laborer, never staying anywhere long as rumors that he was the child of a murderer inevitably surfaced in his workplace wherever he went. The exposé noted that, after his first conviction for shoplifting in 2006, the crime quickly became habitual. It sympathized with Makoto Hara's plight even while concluding with cruel speculation about how criminal proclivities might be genetic.

As Sugino explained, the exposé was discovered soon after it was published by a lawyer named Kadosaki, who was also involved in the abolition movement. Dismayed at its treatment of the son of an infamous convict, she'd taken Makoto Hara on as a client and represented him the second time he was given an actual prison term. In court, she drew attention to his early childhood trauma and history of psychiatric treatment in an attempt to establish that his continuous shoplifting was the result of mental illness, but none of this was taken into account in the sentencing. According to Kadosaki, she had introduced him to a psychiatrist upon his release, fearing his kleptomania would drive him to yet another repeat offense, and now sometimes checked up on him.

✕

After Sugino put him in touch with Kadosaki, Kido arranged to talk with her on the phone. As he had been unable to find photographs of Makoto Hara despite his best online search efforts, one of his first questions was about Hara's appearance, and Kadosaki told Kido that he bore no resemblance to his father. When, in the natural course of their conversation, he later asked where Hara had been serving his sentence, Kido was flabbergasted at her response.

"Yokohama Prison," she replied.

"What? Yokohama?"

"Yes. I guess that's your neck of the woods?"

"It's very close by. It's just . . ."

Makoto Hara had been locked up with Omiura. There was nothing peculiar about this in itself, given that Yokohama Prison was one of the few jails in the Tokyo Correctional Precinct with accommodation blocks for B-class convicts. Except it meant that Omiura and Hara had almost certainly known each other as fellow inmates, which astonished him because it added plausibility to a conjecture that he had been entertaining but still found too unbelievable to be true. Namely, that X was the son of Kenkichi Kobayashi. In other words, X was the real Makoto Hara, while the man formerly incarcerated for compulsive shoplifting had merely switched family registers with him via Omiura.

"What?" said Kadosaki when Kido pitched this to her on the phone. She remained speechless for some time.

"If X is indeed the son of Kenkichi Kobayashi," Kido continued, "then I have an explanation for why he would feel it necessary to take on a new past. It must have been tough for him . . . being descended from the man who committed that awful crime."

"Wait . . . What? Are you being serious about this?"

"A hundred percent."

"I think you're taking a logical leap here."

"Oh, OK . . . Well, I should mention that X is his spitting image—he looks just like Kenkichi Kobayashi, I mean."

"Is that all you've got?"

"Their art is also remarkably similar. That's what drew the connection for me. The idea that something like that might be hereditary."

"Still a bit flimsy."

"Does the Makoto Hara you had as a client ever talk about his father?"

"No. Never."

"How about his days as a boxer?"

"It came up once or twice. I remember he laughed and said that all the punches he took made him stupid."

"How tall is he?"

"How tall . . . Um, I guess a little bit over 170 centimeters."

"That's pretty big . . . Is boxing an interest of yours, Kadosaki?"

"No. Not in the slightest."

"The bantamweight category Makoto Hara competed in was for boxers around fifty-two or fifty-three kilograms."

"Wow . . . That's even lighter than me . . ."

"X was around 163 centimeters tall. That's another example. His height matches up with the weight range."

Kadosaki went silent again as she mulled this over.

"But Hara-san's psychiatrist agreed that his kleptomania could stem from boxing," she said eventually. "Of course, I imagine his father was a big part of it too."

"The police never checked his identity? What about the photo on his ID cards, his driver's license?"

"I don't think he has a license. He's homeless."

"Is that right . . ."

"He has a mild cognitive deficit. He blames boxing, says the brain damage took away his ability to do math, but the psychiatrist thought he was always like that."

Both lawyers were silent for a moment.

"Fine," she finally said. "Let's assume this X was the real Makoto Hara, and my client is someone else . . . Don't you think that's just terrible? No matter how much you hate your past, there's no excuse for tricking a mentally handicapped drifter into swapping registers."

"I don't see how it could have been a trick. Your client is aware that Makoto Hara is the child of Kenkichi Kobayashi, is he not?"

"He'll say yeah, but it's hard to tell if he really understands. He replies yeah to everything. Swindling someone like that just isn't right."

". . . Could he have agreed for money?"

"Maybe, but I guarantee it wouldn't have been a very large amount."

"That could very well be."

✗

Kadosaki made a good point. While it was understandable that X might have yearned for emancipation from the fact that he was the son of Kenkichi Kobayashi, assuming that was indeed who he was, foisting that fact on someone else was a dubious move at best. And if that someone happened to have a slender capacity for decision-making, it was simply atrocious.

The possibility that X might have done such a thing disrupted Kido's perception of him while simultaneously making it harder for Kido to comprehend himself. Throughout his investigation, Kido had wanted X to turn out to have been a decent person, whatever hardships might have driven him to lie. Kido had, after all, taken on the investigation out of sympathy for Rié and hated to think, after the tragedies she had endured, that her late husband might have been a monster.

At the same time, Kido suspected that he envied and admired X for being able to discard his past and start anew. Otherwise, there was no satisfactory way to explain his interest in the man. Kido told himself that this desire, the wish to experience the life of another, was not exclusive to those who had lost all hope in the present. It was perfectly normal, an inevitable response to the human predicament, to our entrapment within a single, finite existence. If anything was unusual, it was following through with this ubiquitous aspiration, which required a certain recklessness that few possessed. For most, such a fresh beginning could only ever be a dream. And while Kido's Zainichi background allowed him to imagine and relate to the many circumstances that might force people to hide their identity, what ultimately sustained this dream for him was his conviction that X had been someone worthy of the love of a woman like Rié.

Initially, Kido had dismissed Kyoichi's insistence that X had been a dangerous criminal as delusional and only began to take it seriously after he met Omiura, who'd forced him to accept that X and he might be not as similar as he'd imagined. He was then able to put himself in X's shoes again when he began to believe that X was the son of Kenkichi Kobayashi. For in this version of events, X was blameless, having suffered at the hands of fate. Strange as it was, directing his compassion toward X's ordeals had brought Kido some modicum of relief from his own anxiety. Now, with Kadosaki's description of the drifter's mental handicap, his faith in X had been shaken once again, filling him with a vague sense of gloom. And in his moments of clarity, Kido worried for his own sanity that he would react this way.

X

Setting such problems aside, Kido's inference was as follows.

The real name of the mentally handicapped man was, making use of Omiura's hint, Yoshihiko Sonézaki. This was the first man that Makoto Hara exchanged family registers with. After living as "Yoshihiko Sonézaki" for a while, Hara then crossed paths with Daisuké, with whom he performed another swap—or perhaps Hara had taken Daisuké's register without his consent. Either way, Hara became "Daisuké Taniguchi" and eventually met Rié in Town S, while the real Daisuké Taniguchi, assuming he was still alive, went by the name "Yoshihiko Sonézaki."

To check if he was right, Kido wanted to speak with the shoplifter who called himself Makoto Hara and asked Kadosaki to arrange a meeting. As the man was fond of Kadosaki, he quickly agreed.

When Kido and Kadosaki stepped into the appointed café beside Higashi-Nakano Station, the man was already waiting at one of the tables. The first thing Kido noticed was his age. While Makoto Hara's family register put him at the same age as Kido, this man looked to be in his fifties or late forties at the youngest. Skinny, he kept his gray-speckled hair buzzed, revealing the contours of a flat cranium that looked as though it were being compressed by some kind of weight. With thin eyelids that drooped heavily, the leftward bend of his features came together—if they could be said to come together—in the tip of his small, off-kilter chin. Kido took note of the sharp, narrow rise of his unbroken nose. The man's face did not in any way resemble that of a former boxer who had been clocked so many times it had diminished his intelligence, as the man himself had supposedly claimed.

"Hey, sensei!"

The man's exuberance at the sight of Kadosaki was palpable. When he approached, seeking a handshake, Kadosaki—a lawyer in her early thirties and the very picture of normcore, from her haircut to her attire—affectionately asked how he was doing. When she introduced him to Kido, the man bowed respectfully and smiled with glee much like that he had shown Kadosaki. Kido briefly explained who he was and, when the waitress came with water, ordered a coffee. Although it was a weekday afternoon, the café was crowded with middle-aged and elderly women. When they had settled in at their table, Kido cut to the chase.

"Sonézaki-san . . . ," he tried, testing the man's reaction.

Remnants of the man's smile lingered, but he looked confused.

"Do you know Yoshihiko Sonézaki?" Kido asked, trying a different tack.

"Yeah."

"How do you know him?"

"Yeah. I don't know him."

"Oh . . . So you're not acquainted?"

"Yeah."

"I don't mean to be rude but . . . is your real name Yoshihiko Sonézaki?"

"I'm Makoto Hara. That's *definitely* true."

Beside Kido, Kadosaki seemed startled by the word "definitely."

"Sorry, Hara-san," she said in a nurturing tone. "I know it's a weird question to spring on you so suddenly. You must be very surprised."

The man appeared upset and looked to her to rescue him, showing an obvious dislike of Kido.

"This is about the husband of a woman that Kido-sensei is representing," Kadosaki began and briefly summarized the situation for him. ". . . Then Kido-sensei thought, *What if the man who died was Makoto Hara?*"

"Apologies for being so blunt with you," said Kido. "The wife of this man is beside herself with anguish over the mystery of his identity. My aim is to assist her in whatever way I can—I heard from someone that your real name might in fact be Yoshihiko Sonézaki. So, while I knew it would be very impolite of me to ask you, I felt that I simply had to."

The man poured large quantities of milk and sugar into his coffee, pinched the handle of his cup, and circled his eyes from left to right, his mouth agape, saying nothing.

He's not Makoto Hara after all, thought Kido. He was beginning to feel certain of this, when it occurred to him that Omiura might be intimidating the man into holding his tongue.

"OK. Let me ask you something else," said Kido. "Are you acquainted with Norio Omiura?"

"Yeah."

"So you know him?" Kido asked.

"Yeah," the man repeated, this time more resolutely.

"Did Omiura set up the exchange of your family register?"

The man looked to Kadosaki, silently asking her whether to swallow down the words stuck in his throat or pull them out.

"You can tell us," she said. "It will make it easier for me to help you. Is your name actually Makoto Hara?"

"Yeah."

"Alright, so what's the name you were given at birth?"

"Um . . . Will I have to go to jail again?"

"I promise that I will never repeat what you tell me here," said Kido, looking him straight in the eye.

The man hesitated before blurting, "My name is really Shozo Tashiro."

Kido frowned and could sense Kadosaki's breath catching beside him.

"That's your real name?" he asked.

"Yeah."

"And you traded it with Makoto Hara?"

"Yeah. You got it. My family register, everything."

"Why would you do that? For money?"

"Yeah. Also, finding jobs and borrowing money and that is hard when you're homeless."

"Is that what they told you?"

"Yeah."

"And then you traded your family register with Makoto Hara."

"Yeah."

"Did you know what kind of person Makoto Hara was?"

"Yeah."

"Did Makoto Hara tell you?"

"Yeah. The middleman did."

"You never met Makoto Hara himself?"

"Yeah. I met him."

"So you're telling us your name is Tashiro? Not Sonézaki?"

"Yeah. I don't know who that is," said the man who had reclaimed Tashiro as his name with a decisive shake of his head.

Kido had the sense he wasn't lying. He took out a photo of X.

"Is this the Makoto Hara you swapped family registers with?" he asked.

"Yeah. It's not him," Tashiro declared, leaving no room for equivocation, as though his self-respect depended on it. "I don't know this guy!"

X

After this, the three of them had cake while Kido asked Tashiro what his life had been like. Tashiro told them that, after graduating from high school, he had moved from job to job. He never lasted long because people would always call him terrible names like "moron" and "waste of space," and for the past ten years he had been homeless. The sum he'd received for the family register swap after Omiura took his cut had been barely enough to cover food for a month. Tashiro said he didn't know how much Makoto Hara had paid.

When Kido asked whether he had ever worried that becoming the child of Kenkichi Kobayashi might make his life more difficult, despite what Omiura had told him, Tashiro replied, "Yeah. But I never tell people about it and they don't link Hara to Kenkichi. We have different family names."

In total, the meeting lasted about an hour and a half. When they left and it was just Kido and Kadosaki, she was still struggling to find words.

"All the things I did to support him . . . what was that? His name's not Hara—it's Tashiro? He never wanted to talk about what happened when he was a child. But I just thought that was natural. It didn't seem right to press him about it."

"That's perfectly understandable."

"I always thought his kleptomania was from the strains of boxing and the incident with his father and . . . The way he presented himself, he fit the part perfectly. Every time I looked at those little creases on the side of his eyes, I would think of all the trials and tribulations he had been through as the child of a murderer and my heart would go out to him."

"Yes . . . Well, I doubt his past was exactly uneventful. One can see the isolation and sadness in his face."

As Kido tried to console Kadosaki, he thought of X's impassioned telling of Daisuké Taniguchi's tale as though the pain were his own.

Although Kido felt certain that Omiura would continue to ignore him, he tried requesting another visit. If he was going to elicit a response this time, he decided that his letter would need a hook.

"After our last meeting, I did a lot of research of my own," Kido wrote. "Now I finally understand what you were trying to convey with those postcards."

A reply came from Omiura immediately. It was a letter unaccompanied by any illustration. He would be glad to have Kido visit whenever he liked.

Kido would have been unfazed by such a change of heart from any other inmate, as most were eager for contact with the outside world. But because it was Omiura, the reply struck him as peculiar.

On December 29, Kido went to meet him in Yokohama Prison. It was a snowless but wintry day, the sky overcast with a chill wind blowing, and Kido found himself walking faster than usual, his dress shoes clapping dry and hard on the asphalt walkway. The firm had gone on break the previous day, and the crowds on the trains were waning. As Kido had never visited prison during the Shogatsu holidays, his heart filled with a sort of tender sentimentality, the end-of-year calm piling on the weight of the year with unfaltering melancholy.

The moment Omiura stepped into the visiting room, he pointed his chin at Kido, one eye stretched wide, and said, "Hey, Korean lawyer. Long time no see!"

At this, the tension dropped from Kido's cheeks.

"It's been a while," he replied with a nod.

Despite the fact that Omiura's attitude had stirred such fierce hatred in Kido before, for some reason, this time, it brought only the slightest annoyance. Kido felt no fondness toward the man, and Omiura showed no more deference than before. Nevertheless, something in that moment made Kido smile.

"You're looking good," said Kido.

"Don't mess with me," said Omiura. "I'm holding on for dear life."

"I met with Makoto Hara."

At these words, Omiura momentarily pursed his lips and homed in on Kido with a single eye. "Is that right?" he said. "He was in here till recently."

"Were you his middleman too?"

"For what?"

Kido waited silently for him to say more.

"OK. I don't know what he told you, but I've got nothing to do with it."

"He's actually a different person, isn't he?"

"Who is?"

Kido ignored this obvious attempt to play dumb. "The real Makoto Hara had no compunctions about dumping his past on him?"

Hearing this, Omiura sucked his cheeks in with surprise and gave Kido a sly smile. "You still don't understand a thing, do you, sensei?"

"Why would you say that?"

Omiura cast his gaze down with a smirk as though the situation was too funny for him. Kido had been worried about the corrections officer recording their conversation in the log but now realized there was no need. The man's professional and utterly imperturbable boredom made him aloof and distant from all manner of hassle. Although their exchange ought to have triggered his suspicion, his hand was barely moving.

"OK. Fine. Maybe you're right," said Kido. "I learned the real name of the man who used to be in here, but in the process, I've become confused about who Yoshihiko Sonézaki is. You wrote in the letter . . ."

Indifferent to Kido's frank admission, Omiura seemed to find their conversation so tedious that he was about to get up and walk away.

"Sensei, you've really put your stupidity on parade here," he said. "Don't you feel ashamed to exist?"

All Kido could manage was a bitter smile. Even this reaction seemed to annoy Omiura, and he spent the next while viciously mocking the content of all Kido's letters as if to thoroughly pulverize his self-respect. The corrections officer finally took interest and observed the abuse in fascination, looking not at Omiura but Kido. Omiura's invective raised Kido's ire and hurt his feelings, but something told him it was an attempt to psychologically prime him for manipulation, and he tried not to let it get to him.

"You look down on me even though you're Korean, don't you? You never believed a word I said from day one because in your eyes I'm nothing but a con artist. How can you think I'm a bigot when it's you who's discriminating?"

Kido came close to saying that he wasn't discriminating because Omiura was an actual con artist doing actual time for it, but took his point about how he'd looked down on him and couldn't bring himself to make the retort. Then he became aware of how Omiura's mishmash of justified claims and specious distractions was affecting him and took note of the authority the man seized as he came into his element, cunningly deploying words to gain a foothold on the threshold of his listener's mind and make whatever inroads he could. If they had been having this conversation somewhere else, like a restaurant or a café, Kido might have swallowed every word. He couldn't help shuddering at the thought.

"You want me to tell you the biggest reason you're a dumbass?"

"What's that?"

"I bet you think I turned out like this because they made me appear in that gay porno."

"I wouldn't go that far. But I did take that anecdote to be something I was supposed to view quite seriously because of how strongly you emphasized it, even though we'd only just met."

"You look down on me for being a pathetic con man, and you still think that story I fed you was true?"

Kido said nothing.

"Now you know why I call you a chump." Omiura slowly brought his face up to the partition, bearing in on Kido as though he were now beneath dignity.

"How do you even know my name is Norio Omiura? Is it because I look like a 'Norio Omiura'?"

Speechless, Kido could only return his gaze.

"It's the same with tattoo artists. They don't just tattoo other people. First, they tattoo themselves. With all the family registers being flipped, why would you think I was an exception? Moron."

". . . Are you actually someone else too?"

Omiura laughed sneeringly. When the corrections officer told them their time was up, he left Kido with these words:

"Listen, Korean lawyer. I feel sorry for you, so I'm going to let you in on one thing. The man you're trying so hard to figure out is just a boring schmuck. You seem to have some weird expectations about him, but the children of killers are nothing much. You've got your own family, don't you? As the saying goes, beware the snake in tall grass. If I were you, I'd leave it alone."

CHAPTER FIFTEEN

At night on New Year's Day, Kido lay in the dark on a futon, thinking back on the past two days.

They were at his family home in Kanazawa. He, Kaori, and Sota had arrived there that morning after spending New Year's Eve at the home of his in-laws in Yokohama—a pattern they repeated annually. On the surface, it had been a perfectly ordinary Shogatsu holiday. Kaori had relaxed with her brother and parents at her family home and engaged genially with Kido's parents at his. Around both dinner tables, Kido had smiled and conversed naturally with her, and after retreating to their rooms, they had spread their futons on the floor and discussed practical matters such as their plans for the following day.

But unlike the years before, Kido found himself unable to sleep, both the previous night in Yokohama and now here in Kanazawa. It was too stimulating to have Sota and Kaori stretched out on each side of him on their futons, as he had grown accustomed to the routine of one of them putting the boy to sleep and then being alone until morning.

He dreaded the thought of explaining the situation to their parents if he and Kaori decided to divorce. A custody battle would no doubt ensue, and while, on the one hand, he never intended to simply give up his son, on the other, he knew he would feel bad to take Sota from her. At the firm, they had often discussed the ramifications of introducing joint custody to Japan, but that was a long way off, if it ever even happened. As Sota's grandparents all loved him deeply, Kido could anticipate his guilt toward whichever side lost. And he was all too aware that if the question were put to Sota, he would surely choose his mother, however much he seemed to favor Kido under the present circumstances.

The whole scenario reeked of savagery, and as Kido stared at the ceiling in the dark, painfully aware of his wife doing the same beside him, he told himself that their relationship was not so far gone as to force such an extreme decision just yet.

Ever since Kido had learned of the boxing club Makoto Hara had belonged to, his curiosity had been piqued. So in the new year, once the busy period at work had settled, he took the train to Kita-Senju in the northeastern corner of Tokyo for a visit.

Kido had been watching live televised broadcasts of world championship boxing since he was a child, and after the combat sports boom kicked off in the late nineties, he had become more interested in the technical side, turning for a while into an avid viewer of big fights streamed online. Nevertheless, this represented his first time going to an actual club. And, as he stepped out of the station beneath the winter sky and began to walk along a stretch of local shops known as Showakai, he recalled not actual boxing, but the boxing manga that he used to love as a boy, like *Champion Joe* and *Genki, the Boy Champ*.

Presently he reached a narrow residential street. There were so few passersby that the streetlights made him think of people hunched over their cell phones as they waited for a friend running late. It did not strike him as the sort of place likely to have a boxing club, and he had to check his map repeatedly to convince himself he was going the right way. But soon enough, he spotted what appeared to be the right sign and building.

The moment Kido slid open the glass door, three young people, one warming up in the ring and two on the floor, glanced at him and called out "President!" in the direction of the office at the back. The man that stepped out looked to be about fifty and wore a black training suit. It was the club president, Kosuge, with whom Kido had been communicating by email.

When Kido had initially requested a meeting to talk about Makoto Hara, Kosuge had replied swiftly and been all too eager to comply, saying that he "remembered him well" and that he was shocked to hear he had died. After Kido explained that Hara's widow wanted to know what sort of person he had been, Kosuge agreed to reach out to his old practice buddies. Now, at Kido's greeting, he gave him a ruddy-faced smile.

Kido knew that the building that housed the club had originally been a meat-packing plant. Fluorescent lights hung haphazardly from the high ceiling. There did not seem to be enough of them to cover the floor area, as the room was somewhat dim even though it was uncomfortably bright to look up.

Kido passed between a number of dangling black-and-red punching bags as he followed Kosuge to the back. Techno music pounded, punctuated every three minutes by the sound of a buzzer. Posters of classic fights such as Mike Tyson versus Evander Holyfield and showcase matches organized by the club plastered the walls in every direction. The exception was one section adorned with the championship belts of those who had trained there, alongside the memorial photo of the club's founder, his motivational advice, daily training protocol. To Kido, it was all strange and fascinating.

Waiting in the office was an ex-professional boxer who was said to be a few years older than Makoto Hara and to have trained with him in the past. He introduced himself as Yanagisawa and handed Kido a business card for a fishing gear shop in the Kinshicho area, which occupied his time now that he was retired from the sport.

Kido briefly rehashed the series of events that had led up to their meeting, which he had already described by email, and showed them a picture of X.

"Is this man Makoto Hara?" he asked.

Both Kosuge and Yanagisawa took one glance at it and nodded.

"That's Makoto alright," said Kosuge.

"Are you certain?"

"Without a doubt. We dug up some old pictures for you—that's him, right?"

Kosuge showed Kido a photo of Makoto Hara, wearing red boxing gloves and taking a fighting pose. Although he had been much leaner back then, there was no mistaking that it was X.

I've finally done it, thought Kido as he studied the image, speechless for some time. A shiver began around his shoulders and ran repeatedly down his back, spreading also to his arms and legs, as though it could find nowhere else to go. His intuition at the convict art exhibition that X was the son of Kenkichi Kobayashi seemed to have presaged this moment. If that hunch had turned out to be off the mark, he would have had little recourse but to sigh at his failure. Now he savored the uncanny discovery that it had been correct, slipping into a daze.

"How did Makoto die?" Kosuge asked when Kido's silence had stretched out to an awkward length. This brought Kido back to his senses, and he looked up at Kosuge.

"He worked in forestry and was involved in an accident at a logging site," Kido replied, and explained what had happened, leaving out any sensitive details.

Kosuge listened with his arms crossed and his mouth half open. Yanagisawa nodded along attentively, wrinkling his chin like the pit of a pickled plum. From their reactions, Kido could tell that they knew about Makoto Hara's troubled youth.

"When did he start coming to this club, approximately?"

"The spring of '95," said Kosuge. "I remember it well because it was after the Kobe earthquake and the Aum terrorist attack."

"Oh . . ." Kido recalled his horror when, only a few short months after the disaster in Kobe, he had seen the news of the Aum Shinrikyo cult releasing sarin gas in the Tokyo subways. "In that awful year."

"When Makoto first showed up, weren't some people saying he was an Aum runaway?" said Yanagisawa with a laugh.

"Only because Makoto never said a word about himself to anyone," Kosuge hurried to explain when he saw Kido looking perplexed. "You gotta understand, he had this look in his eyes, and there was something about him that told you he'd been through some stuff, you know. Plus, he was a sensitive kid that mostly kept to himself but with this power and determination at his core."

"As far as I can tell from his photos, his eyes look gentle to me."

"From the one you just showed us, I get the feeling he mellowed out after he was here. Do you think he was happy with that woman?"

"Yes. That seems to have been the case," said Kido, meaning it sincerely.

"Remember, this was in his boxing days," said Kosuge, gesturing toward the old photo of Makoto Hara.

Kido took another look. If he focused only on his eyes, Hara did indeed seem like a different person.

"Anyhow, he was a real nice kid. And I'm not saying his eyes were ferocious or anything like that. More like, how can I put it . . ."

"They picked up on all sorts of things," Kido supplied.

"You got it. The man was perceptive. You see, boxing is the kind of sport where you've got an opponent, so it's all about your attitude when you're face-to-face with someone just like we are right now. That's how you can tell if someone's got the knack."

"Huh. Is that right?" said Kido. Then after a pause, "Why do you think he took up boxing? Was he aiming to become a pro from the beginning?"

"It was just a whim for him at first. I was standing right there at the entrance to this office, observing the training, when he stepped into the club out of the blue. I remember it well, that moment."

Kido recalled Rié's story of when Makoto Hara first appeared at the stationery shop in a similarly sudden way, and in his mind's eye, the two scenes melded into one. Perhaps that had been Hara's furtive way of interacting with different fragments of the world.

"And over time, I guess he started to show promise?"

"You got it. You got it. Kid didn't know a thing about boxing, but his reflexes were solid and he was a fast learner. Plus, he threw himself into the training like it was the only thing he had. That's what it comes down to in the end."

Kosuge stuck out his thumb and tapped it several times against his chest. In doing so, he had made a loose fist and Kido sensed the power in its sinewy contours, so unlike that of a nonboxer.

"Makoto came to the idea himself and I told him to go for it—I mean take the test to be certified as a pro. Yanagisawa here was working hard toward the same goal."

"Is it uncommon to aim for the professional level?"

"It sure is these days. Take this club here. Pretty much all our eighty or so members are amateurs. I'm including, for example, women's box-ercise. It's tough to pay the bills as a pro. That's for sure. Plus, nowadays people who are serious about boxing can just look up clubs online and take their pick. Where do you suppose that leaves a little club in a working-class neighborhood like this one?"

"I see . . . How much money is in it? Sorry, I'm just curious."

"The sign-up fee here is ¥10,000. Association rules fix the monthly fee at no more than ¥12,000. Then on top of that, you've got to get mouthpieces made, buy gloves, and other little expenses like that. It's not as bad as other sports though because you compete without clothes."

"I think he was asking how much money boxers make," Yanagisawa interjected, looking at Kido with an apologetic smile.

When Kosuge just stared back in confusion, Yanagisawa answered on his behalf.

"Pros fight about three times a year, give or take. The fight money you take home for a four-round match is about ¥60,000, and then ¥100,000 for a six-rounder. Good luck putting food on the table that way. And for someone like Makoto with no one to depend on, it's just impossible 'cause they don't pay you in cash, just tickets to the matches that you have to sell yourself."

"So everyone is moonlighting on the side?"

"You got it," replied Kosuge. "Usually at bars and restaurants. Makoto worked at a Chinese joint."

Kido had decided it wasn't necessary to record their conversation, but he took notes on what he had heard thus far.

"Do you need to show some form of identification when you take the professional certification test?"

"Not when you take the test, but when they issue the license, you need either a family register or a residence certificate."

As Kosuge was speaking, he looked over his shoulder to check on a trainee who was shadowboxing in the ring. Kido followed his gaze to a young man of around twenty with hair parted down the middle. All alone in the squarish space, he launched punch after punch at the person meant to be there. As if to dodge this person's incoming jabs, the man moved his feet constantly, his upper body swaying left to right. The fruit of his efforts would be revealed in the flesh of an as-yet-unseen opponent; the young man was isolated from that future by the cage of the present. Suddenly, Kido imagined Makoto Hara in this run-down gym doing the same lonely exercise day after day.

"Oh, sorry," said Kosuge when he looked back, and Kido took advantage of this disruption to broach the topic he most wanted to ask about.

"Are you aware who Hara-san's father was?"

Kosuge exchanged a glance with Yanagisawa. "Yeah," he said. "We heard."

"When did he tell you?"

"So, when Makoto was about to debut in a pro-level fight, he came to me for advice. Told me he was thinking of giving himself a ring name. I said go for it. Boxing is pretty dull entertainment compared to, say, kickboxing or MMA. You've got to become the kind of fighter that draws crowds. So I suggested he come up with a crazy ring name, one that would really stand out. But Makoto disagreed. Said he wanted something run-of-the-mill so he could blend in."

"Did he explain why?"

"He wouldn't say at the time. I heard the reason from him later. After he became the rookie king of east Japan."

"I see."

"Boy oh boy . . . I was as shocked as anybody. But I tried to encourage him. Said, look, you can't confuse a parent with their kid. They're not the same. It's your life to lead, so just give it your all and let's go for the gold."

"Is this when he told you about his past?"

"You got it . . . Makoto said that, after the incident, him and his mom stayed with his aunt and uncle for a while. They were kind to them at first, till his uncle got fed up with the situation. His aunt was his mom's younger sister, and she got caught between Makoto's mom and her husband, slipped into a kind of depression. Then they had to leave."

"How awful . . ."

"After that, Makoto's mother ditched him and he ended up in an orphanage till he graduated middle school. Sounds like school was tough as hell too, getting bullied and all the rest of it."

"But hadn't he already changed his name from Kobayashi to Hara?"

"He told me that the first school he transferred to was pretty close by, so they figured out who he was lickety-split. You gotta remember that Makoto's old man killed a boy not much older than Makoto himself. It was the boy's friends who really hated him. Blamed him for what his old man did. No one knew who he was at the middle school after the orphanage, but he'd already turned into an introvert, and got bullied basically just for that."

"He never went to high school?"

"He told me he enrolled in night school but dropped out almost immediately. Then he left the orphanage and, during the two, three years before he came here, lived as sort of a vagrant. He never got into the details. I bet it was tough as a minor. No residence certificate, thrown out there all by yourself, the poor kid."

"Kenkichi Kobayashi was executed in 1993, when Hara-san was eighteen. Is that the period when he was homeless?"

"Makoto had a grudge against his old man like you wouldn't believe. He was a quiet kid, but when he got going about his father, asking why he had to be born to such a monster, he'd start shaking and this eerie look would come over him like he was possessed. Eyes turned so sharp they bored right into you . . . He told me he was friends with the boy that got killed. That was one thing he could never get over."

"Did he ever visit his father in jail?"

"Nope. Never went to meet him that I'm aware. He'd get letters, though. Makoto said they were full of all this stuff about how guilty his old man felt and how much he regretted everything, but that when you got right down to it, it was really just about his own suffering, and his apologies to the victims rang hollow. Apparently, he begged Makoto not to forget the happy memories they had together."

Kido sighed as he recalled the serene landscapes Kobayashi had painted in jail. "Had he been a good father to Hara-san? Before, I mean."

"Beats me. Going through something like that is bound to change the way you look back on things . . . But one thing's for sure—Makoto never said that he wished his old man could have lived. I couldn't tell you how he felt on the inside."

"No . . . I suppose there isn't any way to know."

"It was about two years after his father was executed that he showed up here. Said he saw normal kids his age going to university and starting careers and felt like he should find some purpose of his own . . ."

Kido nodded to indicate that he could relate.

Kosuge turned to the ring again and said, "Excuse me a sec. That alright? I won't be long. In the meantime, ask Yanagisawa whatever you like. Also, if you're interested, feel free to take a look around."

Kido was in no position to insist that Kosuge stay, and stood up to give him a bow as he abruptly left the office. The air-conditioning had been going on and off fitfully, and when Kido returned to his seat he felt chill air around his feet. He realized now that more than an hour had already passed.

Yanagisawa remained in the office with Kido. After briefly watching Kosuge take shots to punch mitts in the ring, he narrowed his eyes slightly and said, "Kosuge gave Makoto a sermon once. Yup."

Kido turned to face Yanagisawa. "A sermon?" he said, in a casual tone of the sort he might have used with someone close to his age.

"Makoto was a talented guy. I couldn't tell you if he had what it takes to be champ, but he was way better than me. Good thing he was in a different weight class or we might never have been so tight."

"I suppose not."

"Makoto passed the pro test on his first try. Everything up to then was smooth sailing. Then he won the East Japan Rookie King Tournament, and suddenly he was the center of attention. Even more than usual 'cause he KO'd the guy in his title fight. This was before the internet, so it was only some people that knew about him, of course. But that didn't change anything for Makoto, and when he was set to fight for the All Japan Rookie King Championship, he told Kosuge he wanted to pull out. Yup. Asked for my advice too."

"I see. What ring name did he choose in the end?"

"Katsutoshi Ogata. You write 'Katsutoshi' with the kanji for 'win,' like this, see . . ." Yanagisawa used the tip of his finger to air-write two ideograms that together meant "win" and could be pronounced "katsutoshi." "Me and him closed our eyes, flipped the phonebook to a random page, and there it was."

"That's how he picked his ring name?" asked Kido with a bemused smile.

"You better believe it. He thought a name that meant 'win' was good luck. Regretted it later, though."

"Why was that?"

"You know how when a boxer wins they write 'win' beside your name in the newspaper and everything? Well, that meant for him it was 'win win.' Everyone that saw it thought it was hilarious."

Although the investigation into Makoto Hara had absorbed Kido's thoughts for more than a year now, this was the first time that he imagined him smiling before he met Rié. And suddenly, what had until then been an empty shell of records and anecdotes seemed to pulse with vitality.

"Did Hara-san smile often?"

"Nope, not really. He wasn't a downer or anything like that, just not much of a talker. That's why he looks like a different person in that picture with his wife. He's aged a bit, but it's the gentle expression on his face that does it. It's good to see him like that."

"I know what you mean."

"And . . . What was I talking about again? Oh yeah, right, right. So the prez—you know I mean Kosuge, right?—the prez, he asked Makoto why he wanted to pull out of the rookie king title fight. And that was the first time Makoto talked about his father."

"Had someone in the boxing world recognized him?"

"Nope . . . He wasn't worried so much about being outed. It was more about whether he deserved the glory."

"Oh . . ."

"The poor guy. He took up boxing 'cause he was sick of being an outsider, but when his moment to shine finally came . . . I think he was scared of taking flack for who he was. No doubt. But it was more than that. There was his friend that got killed too. He felt like he owed him something."

". . . I understand."

"Makoto was, let's say . . . Well, you ever heard of gender identity disorder? You know where your body and mind just don't match up? For Makoto it was something like that. Yup. Like someone's stuffed you into this disgusting mascot suit and you're stuck in there for your whole life."

"By that you're referring to Hara-san being seen by others as the child of a death row convict?"

"Well, that's part of it. But, you know, he used to talk about his body. Yup. They're basically mirror images of each other, him and his father, I mean."

"Oh, yes . . . That's right."

"He said it grossed him out so bad to think that his father's blood ran in his veins that he wanted to scratch himself open and scrape his own body off. You could never make love to someone if you saw your body like that, now could you? That's how come he was still a virgin, back when he was here."

Not knowing what to say, Kido lowered his head and nodded several times. This brought his arms and legs into view, and he began to study them. He tried to imagine the agony of perceiving what was supposed to be each person's last refuge, the body, as hell, and to believe that you were therefore unqualified to love and be loved.

"You know how people are always saying, 'Oh, you look more like your father' or 'You look more like your mother.' Makoto couldn't have that conversation. 'Cause saying he resembled his father was the same as saying he didn't deserve to exist . . . His body and mind just didn't mesh. He was terrified that his body might go berserk and slip out of his control. That's what his bullies used to tell him would happen. A normal person would never make a move to actually kill someone, no matter how angry they were. But Makoto was terrified that he might. Hurting his body was his way of coping. Unless he took punches and punished himself through training, he was just miserable. He told me that boxing was supposed to teach him how to master his violent impulses."

"That was his motivation?"

"According to him anyway. I tried to help him get over it, asked him who'd ever heard of a murderer that had a parent who was a murderer too. But I guess all the bullying really did a number on him. I get that—I was bullied too. When someone's beating you up every day, the only way to accept that reality is to think of yourself as the one who's doing the beating, or, like, tell yourself that getting beaten is inevitable, that you're powerless to do anything about it."

"Huh . . . I can think of situations where people use pain and self-harm to cope with self-negating emotions. It happens with teenagers, for example."

"For sure. But I don't think the prez, Kosuge—I don't think he understood where Makoto was coming from. He thought that Makoto was putting himself through the wringer to make up for his father's sins and told him straight up how crazy that was. As if any amount of suffering was going to bring the victims back to life. And how was showing off his pain to everyone any different than the shit-eating nonsense in his father's letters? But Makoto never meant it that way. At least I don't think so. To be fair to the prez, he was really worried about Makoto, and it ticked him off that he would think of backing down at the last minute after they'd come so far, so I don't think there was any other way he could have reacted. In the end, he gave him some advice. Said, look, your life is your own to lead, so if you're really so torn up about it, why don't you go and speak with the surviving family. Yup. Then it won't matter what anyone else says. So long as the family approves of what you've decided to do with your life, you can keep on going and hold your head high."

Kido looked toward Kosuge in the ring, keeping his gaze unfocused. He recalled that the murdered president of the construction company had had surviving parents and a younger brother.

"Oh Makoto, the poor guy," said Yanagisawa, looking troubled and wistful.

"Back then, me and him used to go running together in the morning, around this area," he said after a time. "One day, when it was getting to the point where he had to make a decision about the fight, I invited him to come out for a run, do some roadwork. So we're ripping along as usual till we get to the local park, when suddenly he starts slipping behind. I look back, like what the heck, and I see he's just stopped . . . Then he falls to his knees like all the strength has gone out of him and, when I go over and ask if he's alright, he drops flat onto his belly and starts to cry. Right in the middle of this big park. Rubbing his face into the dirt and just wailing. On that chilly morning. Cold enough for frost."

"Oh my . . ." Kido felt his chest tighten as he imagined the scene. He was fairly certain he'd passed that very park on his way over from the station.

"That's when I told him he didn't have to do it. Whatever the prez said, he had no obligation to speak with the victims' family . . . He'd just make them uncomfortable anyway."

Saying nothing, Kido gave him a frown of concern. Then after a pause, he asked, "Did he end up going?"

"Nope, never did—or, well . . . it was right after that he got himself into an accident."

"An accident?"

"He fell off a balcony. From the sixth floor of his apartment building. Got badly injured. Broke a bunch of different bones. Only thing that saved him was landing on the roof of the bicycle parking lot."

"Was it . . ." Kido left the sentence unfinished.

"Makoto claimed it was unintentional," said Yanagisawa, guessing his meaning. "But said he couldn't remember what happened. Yup . . . Obviously, a full-grown man doesn't just fall off a balcony by mistake. I mean, there was a railing . . . But personally, I don't think he wanted to die. He was just at his wit's end and needed some way to escape from it all. The injury forced him to forfeit the rookie king fight. To me, he looked kind of relieved."

"What was Kosuge's reaction?"

"He was as shocked as the rest of us. It had been ages since the club churned out a pro. Makoto apologized, but once he got out of the hospital, he just vanished. The prez really beat himself up over it. He's back to his old self now, but for a long time he was in the pits. You saw the way he rushed off just now? I think it's painful for him to remember."

Kido looked at Kosuge again and felt sorry for him.

"The prez would have done anything to make Makoto champ. He wanted to help him turn his life around and move past all the suffering he'd been through. Then he'd have confidence, you know?"

"Yes."

"But Makoto didn't want to be champ. He just wanted to be a normal person . . . He just wanted to live a normal, quiet life. A boring life that no one would take notice of. That was his deepest, truest desire. Same time, he was torn 'cause he knew how hard the prez was trying to help him become champ."

After Kido wrote the words "normal person" in his notebook, he stared quietly at them for a while. He accepted the intense longing Hara had imbued this phrase with, dismissing the clichéd counterarguments that hounded the very idea of normal. These did not apply to someone who had lived such a troubled life. When at last he had stared so long at the word "normal" that it lost all meaning for him, Kido put another question to Yanagisawa.

"And that's the last time you saw Hara-san?"

"That's right."

"When would that have been?"

"Nineteen—um—ninety-eight, I guess."

"And you've heard no news of him since?"

"Nothing."

Kido gave a nod to shake his thoughts into order and began filling in his patchy notes. Only nine years of Makoto's life remained unaccounted for, between his disappearance from the club and his reappearance in Town S as Daisuké Taniguchi.

"Um, can I ask you a question?" said Yanagisawa when Kido at last raised his head.

"Certainly."

"Was it suicide?"

Kido's eyes went wide for a moment. Then he gave several small shakes of his head. "As far as I can determine, no."

"Yeah? Phew . . . See, when I heard a lawyer was coming all the way out here, I had a bad feeling about it."

Kido was tempted momentarily to let him in on a few more of the details but decided to change the subject.

Yanagisawa seemed to pick up on Kido's evasiveness, but left off on questioning him about the issue and sounded as though he were ready to tie up their conversation when he said, "Did Makoto do any more boxing after that?"

"It seems not."

"Oh yeah? OK . . ." Yanagisawa reached for the photo of Makoto Hara and Rié on the table to take another look. "It's a shame he died so young . . . but I'm glad he was happy in the end."

Kido wasn't sure if Yanagisawa was speaking to him or to the photo but replied anyway. "Yes," he agreed. "I really do believe he was happy."

"I'm also really glad to hear that he made it to the finish line without hurting anyone like he always feared. I wish I could tell him I told you so. Yup . . . There are so many things I wish I could say to him now . . . the prez too, I bet."

Although Kido was still concerned for the safety of Daisuké Taniguchi, he felt in the moment that what Yanagisawa had said was true and merely replied, "Indeed."

CHAPTER SIXTEEN

When Kido returned home from the boxing club, he wrote out the story of Makoto Hara told by Kosuge and Yanagisawa as best he could remember it with the aid of his hurriedly scribbled notes. At the same time, he reorganized the information he had gathered in his yearlong investigation, bringing cohesion to his scattered memories. His intention was to finally report his findings to Rié. And in the process, he noticed something so simple, he was amazed it had until then eluded him.

Omiura had originally come to Kido's attention when he'd read about the 2007 case of a family register swap between a sixty-seven-year-old man and a fifty-five-year-old man from Adachi ward. According to the blog of someone writing under the pseudonym "Courtroom Fiend," who had listened in on the trial in person, Omiura's career in "past laundering" had begun the previous year. Oddly, what seemed to have inspired him to get into the racket was a news report concerning the murder of James Bulger in 1993.

In this infamous case, a pair of ten-year-old boys abducted a two-year-old named James Bulger from a shopping center in Liverpool, UK, proceeding to torture and then murder him. Shock at the incident reached global proportions, spreading outrage and a kind of cynical frustration. When the two murderers completed their eight-year prison terms at the age of eighteen, they were given new identities so that they could start over as "different people" before being released, despite a vociferously opposed protest movement. Then, in June 2006, a tabloid revealed that one of them was working an office job and had gotten married without anyone realizing who he was.

At news of this development, the blog claimed, Omiura had a "eureka moment" and came up with the idea of selling and swapping family registers. Purportedly, he had laundered many more registers than the police ever detected, and Kido now supposed that the reason he had continually called him "Korean" was that his clientele had included many Koreans and foreigners or else that he'd had expectations of such demand. The blog went on to explain that many of Omiura's customers engaged in multiple register trades if they were dissatisfied, and it was this fact that finally jogged Kido's mind into a realization.

The suggestion that X, aka Makoto Hara, had foisted his family register on Shozo Tashiro, making a mentally handicapped vagrant adopt the identity of an infamous murderer's son, had nagged at Kido, making his drawn-out game of detective seem futile. As naive as it was, he simply could not reconcile that deed with the kind husband that lived in Rié's memory. But if Tashiro's tenuous testimony could be believed, it had not been Hara who traded with him after all. Or at the very least, Tashiro had never met the real Hara, merely someone using Hara's name.

This forced Kido to modify his initial conjecture. For if Hara's first register swap hadn't been with Tashiro, then it had to have been with a different man. In all likelihood, it had been this man who'd dumped Hara's undesirable identity on Tashiro. And it was Kido's supposition that this man had originally been "Yoshihiko Sonézaki," the name written on Omiura's postcard.

So from Hara's perspective, the series of events would have been as follows: First, Hara had learned about Omiura online or through some other source and become Sonézaki. Then, probably dissatisfied with the

Sonézaki identity for some reason, he had swapped his new register with Daisuké Taniguchi and gone to Town S, where he met Rié.

If this was correct, the upshot was that the real Daisuké now went by "Yoshihiko Sonézaki." Assuming of course that he hadn't swapped his register again. And assuming that he was still alive.

※

Kido watched as Makoto Hara, a long-neglected and for some time nebulous person, remerged through the text on his computer screen and took on a definitive existence once again. He was used to putting events and people into words—this was the essence of his work as a lawyer—but unlike the documents he drafted for court, he was under no requirement to pare down his writing for any specific purpose, and did his utmost to include as much detail, even trivia, as possible. He performed this task with the devotion of family members at a crematorium, trying to gather up as much of the ashes of their kin as they could.

In the days when Hara still existed in the flesh, the past Kido now revealed had been left to slide into oblivion. Or perhaps Hara had sought to erase it, to slough off what could only ever be a burden and a fetter so long as he was a corporeal being that wished to be alive. But now that his physical matter was gone and the woman who loved him was willing to open her heart and understanding to all that he once was, there was no longer any obstacle to restoring him in his entirety, past and all.

Whether the individual fashioned in the process still ought to be called "Makoto Hara" Kido wasn't sure. But no longer beguiled by mere fragments of information, he found his anxiety begin to fall away and perceived himself coalescing, kneaded into unity, in sync with this new person taking form.

✕

Kido was keenly aware that his game of detective had stretched on far too long. Nevertheless, his anticipation of its approaching end and the emptiness that would surely follow called forth unspeakable loneliness.

Yes, loneliness. He did not shy from this word to express the dark emotion that had been seething in his chest of late. It was a bottomless, middle-aged kind of loneliness that he never could have even conceived of when he was younger, a loneliness that saturated him with bone-chilling sentimentality the moment he let down his guard.

At such times, Kido often pictured Makoto Hara wailing facedown in that park in Kita-Senju. The spectacle appeared to him cut loose from time and place, like a scene from myth. No doubt collapsing in tears on the spot was a superhuman deed. And yet somehow, Kido felt the pain of the man's cheek scraping against the pebbled, sandy ground as though it had been his own.

✕

According to an article about Kenkichi Kobayashi, he was born in Yokkaichi in 1951. When he was a young child, his parents were too poor to provide him with enough food, and he was forced to endure his father's frenzied violence. In his teenage years, he turned delinquent, dropped out of high school, and idled around until he eventually found work at a local factory, cut off his parents, and began to live alone.

At the age of twenty-one, he married a woman two years his junior and, three years later, she gave birth to his only child, Makoto. Kobayashi physically abused both Makoto and his wife on a daily basis, but just as in his formative years, it was not an era in which such things were treated as a serious problem. Until Makoto turned five, anyone on the outside would have seen them as a typical family.

Then, as Kobayashi was approaching thirty, he reunited with a shady friend from his middle school days, who triggered his obsession with gambling and thereby precipitated his plunge into debt. By the time Kobayashi committed his murders in the summer of 1985, collectors had reportedly been hounding him for some time.

Kobayashi became acquainted with the construction company president who would refuse his pleas for cash through the local kids' club that Makoto belonged to. During the slaughter of this man along with his wife and child, Kobayashi stole ¥136,000, enough for two months' rent, and set fire to the house before going straight home. He was apprehended a week later. The article described his crimes as "inhuman" for their rashness, ruthlessness, and inclusion of a child. Given that Kobayashi had murdered three people, it was seen as a foregone conclusion that he would receive the death penalty. He didn't even bother disputing the charges against him nor did he seek to appeal the lower court verdict.

Kido considered the possibility that he might run into someone like Kobayashi and that for a similarly absurd reason he, his wife, and his son might be killed. The very idea put him in an awful mood, and when he imagined the murder weapon—a long-bladed chef's knife—piercing Sota's smooth, youthful, fragile skin, he could barely hold himself together.

And yet, his dread and indignation at the irrationality of it all did not automatically translate to hatred for Kobayashi. His feelings would certainly have been different if he had been affected directly. But partly due to his professional experience, Kido knew that such tragic situations were all too common and perceived them as something destined and accidental.

Unfortunately—yes, this was literally unfortunate—people like Kobayashi actually existed. None of the innumerable

factors—whether inherited or acquired, contingent or necessary—
that had been involved in propelling him to commit his crimes were
in any way exceptional or unprecedented in human history. If anything, the whole matrix of conditions had been so banal as to elicit
a sigh.

Kido did not think that this in any way absolved Kobayashi of
responsibility for what he had done. At the same time, while Kido
could not take the extreme position of completely denying individual
free will, it was an established fact that Kobayashi's early childhood
environment had been deplorable, and Kido took it as self-evident
that this had contributed significantly to his degeneration.

In allowing this, the state had neglected to remedy the misfortune of one of its citizens. It had nonetheless exterminated him via
capital punishment for violating the legal order it upheld, looking
on with implacable righteousness, as though reality thereby accorded
with justice. Kido believed this was wrong. For the judiciary to cancel
out such a failure of the legislative and executive branches by nul-
lifying the existence of the resulting lawbreaker was simply disingenuous. If such a system went unchallenged, a vicious cycle would
emerge in which the blighted citizenry needed to be executed in ever
greater numbers as the state slipped further and further into decline.

Despite his firm convictions, Kido had never actively tried to discuss
them with anyone. He wasn't sure if other people would understand—
least of all his wife, who, he knew from one conversation they'd had,
found his reasoning incomprehensible. This was back when Sota had
just turned one. While the two of them were watching the news, they
began to discuss what ought to happen if someone murdered Sota.

"The murderer should be executed," she said. "Don't you think?"

"Under Japan's present laws, murdering a single person does not garner the death penalty, I'm afraid. It simply wouldn't be on the table, legally speaking."

"Fine. Then what if it was the two of us, Sota and I? You must agree that the murderer should be executed then?"

Kido could tell that Kaori wasn't going to let him dodge the question and braced himself before giving his reply. "If we are ever going to wipe away the evil of murder, then as a fundamental baseline condition, we need to reject the idea that it is acceptable to kill in extreme cases. It may not be easy, but I believe that that is what we should be aiming for. Offenders will surely never be forgiven, but the state should bear the blame for the social conditions underlying their crimes and take responsibility by providing substantial support to the victims, instead of feigning innocence and pandering to punitive sentiments. Whatever policy is chosen, my view is that the state must never descend to the same ethical lows as the evil of murder."

Kaori's eyes trembled, red with anger and disappointment. She stared at him as though doubting that human blood flowed through his veins. But perceiving that continuing the conversation would beckon an irreversible and devastating shift in their relationship, they quickly broke it off. What point was there in fighting over a tragedy that hadn't even occurred?

X

Another reason that Kido found it difficult to bear ill will toward Kenkichi Kobayashi was that, after everything he had learned, he had developed a strong affinity for his son, Makoto Hara, relating viscerally to his many ordeals.

He imagined how Hara must have felt the morning he learned about the murder of his friend and his friend's parents. Although the boy his father killed was a few years older than Hara, they were in the same kids' club and practiced softball together. Hara had often been over to play at their house—what would later become the crime scene—as the boy's parents had let them keep bats, bases, and other equipment there.

Kido pictured the uproar on the block as ambulance and police sirens blared, the crowds of parents thronging the elementary school auditorium where crying voices rang out. The morning the police arrived, the cameramen roaring as they pushed and jostled for a shot, Hara's father apprehended and taken in. Then the reporters who singled him out for questioning on his way to school, asking about his dead friend and the condition of his father. And finally, Hara himself looking confused as he studied the look of disbelief that his mother had worn since it all began . . .

Kido felt troubled and disturbed on Hara's behalf. Saw him as an adult walking up ahead. Couldn't think what to call out to him.

From the underground platform of Motomachi-Chukagai Station, Kido rode escalator after escalator up through the building. His destination was America Yama Park on the roof, where the kids from Sota's day care often played around this time of day. Although he was already set to pick up Sota earlier than usual, he was anxious as always to see him as soon as he could and, on his long ascent, time seemed to move inexorably slow.

The park consisted of lawns and flower beds divided by gently inclining cobblestone paths that stretched toward the Yokohama Foreign General Cemetery. It had been completed by the city of Yokohama in 2009 to commemorate 150 years since the opening of the port.

When Kido arrived, it was twilight. In spite of the brisk early February air, the twenty-odd children had the zippers of their down jackets undone to their chests as they gamboled about ecstatically in their yellowish-green hats. Sota was some ways off, laughing uproariously as he toddled after his friend at full tilt.

Kido greeted the young teacher. After reporting that his son had had a safe, uneventful day, she called out loudly to Sota. Several kids had already noticed Kido and were pointing at him, shouting, "Look. Sota's dad!"

Sota's eyes sparkled bashfully when he spotted his father. The nuance of his smile shifted, his expression suggesting both embarrassment at being watched by his dad and expectations of him that his friends could never fulfill.

"Sota's dad!"

Before Sota could reach Kido, several little ones charged in and pounced. The kids at the day care seemed to have pegged him as an ultraplayful dad ever since he had casually hugged them when they rollicked around him on parent observation day. As usual, a pack of them surrounded him in a flash and made Sota jealous.

"He's my dad!" he cried as he arrived on the scene and began to yank the kids off Kido.

"Hey! You'll hurt them if you pull like that," said Kido as he gently drew Sota against him.

"Today, when Ryo and Kohei were fighting, Sota told them it was wrong and made them stop!" one of the kids reported to Kido.

"It's true!" said another. "Right, Sota?"

"Oh wow, did he really?" said Kido. "Good job, son."

It suddenly occurred to him that the day might come when one of these innocent children killed someone. Even if none of the kids present ever did, there was another five-year-old child out there, frolicking with his friends in just the same way, who undoubtedly would. Either backed into a corner or through ignorance of what is right. Whose responsibility would that be? Kido maintained his broad smile as he considered the question.

When Kenkichi Kobayashi was five years old, perhaps he'd been just another innocent child like these. But no, more likely his pain and trauma had been plain to see. As far as Kido could tell from the reports of the James Bulger case, the conditions in which his ten-year-old murderers had grown up were just as abysmal—the fierce pressure from British public opinion to make them answer for their crimes notwithstanding. According to Japanese criminal law, anyone under nineteen fell under the Juvenile Act, and only perpetrators older than that were culpable. But it wasn't as though cumulative negative influence suddenly vanished the moment a person reached adulthood, like a debt being reset to zero.

Individual effort was surely worthy of praise, but did it amount to anything more than having the good fortune to encounter the right people and events to orient you toward it? Nakakita, for example, was convinced of the perspective taken by recent biology that a person's character was determined by the synergy between genetic and environmental factors and believed that the exclusionary dichotomy between nature and nurture was specious. It went without saying that he dismissed the assertion that everything is the responsibility of the individual as the pinnacle of folly. Kido was of exactly the same opinion.

X

After Kido returned home, such thoughts continued to pester him. And eventually he recalled a recent conversation with Kyoichi that had some bearing on them.

Several days earlier, Kido had called Kyoichi to fill him in on what he had uncovered about Makoto Hara thus far. It was the first time they had been in touch in many months, and part of the reason Kido had decided to reach out was that Rié had requested he keep Kyoichi informed. At the same time, he wanted to solve the one remaining mystery: Hara's doings over the nine years between his leaving the club and meeting Rié. Most important of all was confirming whether Hara had harmed Daisuké during that period, and to that end, enlisting the Taniguchis to help find Daisuké seemed like the key.

"What? Are you fucking serious? What?" Kyoichi had said repeatedly on the phone, bringing the conversation to a temporary stall. "So it's just like I told you. That guy bumped off my brother." His tone was far graver than at their previous meeting. "I mean, he's the kid of a crazed murderer."

"We can't go jumping to any conclusions," said Kido, feeling uncharacteristically worked up. "His goal, remember, was to free himself from that background and be accepted by society. Killing someone would have undermined everything he'd worked toward."

Kyoichi snorted as though rankled both by what Kido had said and how he'd said it. "Not if he made sure no one found out. You make him sound *way* too logical for a guy with a father like that. If he lost it, there's no telling what he might do."

"By the time Hara-san met your brother, he was most likely going by the name Sonézaki. In other words, he was no longer the child of a convict. That is the reason, I expect, that your brother was willing to trade family registers with him. With a middleman arranging everything, there would have been nothing to gain by killing the other party for his register."

"I'm sorry, but you're just guessing, right? How is that any better than wild speculation? Got any evidence to back it up? I can think of a million reasons why that guy might have killed Daisuké. Like, what if he wanted to silence him after Daisuké learned the secret of who he was?"

"Extremely unlikely."

"How so?"

"I just don't believe he was that sort of person."

"Huh? Sensei, are you off your rocker? Based on what?"

"I spoke with people who knew him well."

"He's a damn human being. Everyone has something they're not showing, you know."

"Be that as it may, in order to ascertain the truth either way, I'm asking you to help me find your brother. Please."

Kyoichi should have had no reason to refuse, whatever his history with his brother, but he was just as angry as Kido and refused to give him a clear answer.

After Kido hung up, he continued to stew over Kyoichi's infuriating remarks about how the child of a murderer would take after their parent. But as he was rehearsing rebuttals in his head, he found his confidence in his own arguments beginning to wane.

※

Kido had tried to understand Kobayashi's murderousness as resulting from the influence of his father's violence. But if he were going to take such a line of reasoning, then he had to admit that Kyoichi's belief that Hara was prone to criminality had some merit to it, as Hara's home environment had been just as wretched. A case could also be made for their genetic similarities, including—to Hara's endless dismay—their looks. Was it too cruel to the memory of Hara to point out the irony of his artwork, like reflections of his pure heart, being nearly identical to the paintings his father had produced on death row?

Kyoichi wasn't alone in seeing Hara as a threat to society. Countless others had done the same. In fact, no one had fretted more over the risk that Hara might have posed than Hara himself. Even though the child is their own person and no one is obliged to rectify the deeds of their parents, he took it upon himself to balance out the asymmetry between the family of the victims who went on grieving and the family of the perpetrators who did not. That is, he lived in constant danger of being crushed between the past and the future, between his need to suffer for his father's sins and his terror of recapitulating them.

But something about this train of thought struck Kido as beside the point. Ultimately, none of it overturned his belief in what he had said to Kyoichi. *I just don't believe he was that sort of person.* For if everyone who met Hara had declared this from the start, Hara would never have felt the need to trade his family register. And he might have been able to go on being Makoto Hara even to this day.

CHAPTER SEVENTEEN

After a dinner of sukiyaki, Sota said that he wanted his mother to put him to bed that night, so Kido left him in Kaori's hands after bath time and did the washing up in the kitchen. Then he lay on the couch listening to Meshell Ndegeocello, as his mind rambled through memories of playing bass in his university days. *If only I'd been as good a player as Nakakita, I might still be in a band and have a great way to get some downtime.* Vague thoughts came one after the next. At some point, he drifted off, exhausted.

It was after eleven o'clock when he awoke. The tips of his bare toes were cold, so he turned up the heat. On impulse, he then flicked on the television, though he rarely watched it. After channel surfing for a while, footage of a menacing crowd caught his eye. Holding aloft Rising Sun flags and screaming such obscenities as "Send the Koreans to the gas chambers!" they paraded along a street in broad daylight. It was part of a news feature on hate speech and, cursing his luck, Kido went to turn it off.

But when the caption shifted to "Counterprotesters on the Scene" and a woman holding a placard that read, "Can't we just get along? *Chinhage jinaeyo!*" appeared, Kido leapt to his feet in astonishment. Though she was only on screen for a split second, he felt certain it was Misuzu.

What was she doing there? he wondered and at that moment heard a voice behind him.

"Daddy."

Turning around, he found Sota standing there rubbing his sleep-filled eyes.

"Oh. Is something wrong?"

"I woke up . . . ," said Sota, ambling over to the couch. "What are you watching?"

With the sound of two crowds of demonstrators shouting at each other over a line of police in his ears, Kido couldn't even begin to think how to explain. And before he had the chance to try, the screen suddenly went black.

"Come along, Sota," said Kaori. "You've got to sleep."

She seemed to have come in search of Sota and now placed the remote noisily on the table. It annoyed Kido to have the TV turned off on him without warning. And Kaori said not a word before she returned to the bedroom with Sota in tow.

Kido made a move to turn the TV back on with another remote within arm's reach but immediately realized that he was no longer in the mood and was forced to yield by default to his wife's intervention.

He tried to recall whether it had indeed been Misuzu a moment ago. Already the memory was hazy. He remembered how she had brought up the counter-demonstrations over lunch near the Yokohama Museum of Art. "Then I'm going to go in your place, Kido-san," she had said. But Kido hadn't taken her seriously. In fact, he had almost forgotten all about it. They hadn't been in touch of late, and it surprised him to learn that she had secretly fulfilled that promise. He smiled, thinking how quintessentially Misuzu it was, but realized that his feelings about what she had done were complicated, somewhere between joy and dismay. Kido was glad that he occupied a significant place in her world. What she had done could not have been easy. Yet he could not welcome her participation in the counter-demonstration with categorical approval and had to sigh at his own nitpicking.

His reservations were connected with the way he perceived Zainichi, which he had often thought was more or less the same as the way Levin in *Anna Karenina* perceived peasants:

> If he had been asked whether he liked or didn't like the peasants, Konstantin Levin would have been absolutely at a loss what to reply. He liked and did not like the peasants, just as he liked and did not like men in general. Of course, being a good-hearted man, he liked men rather than he disliked them, and so too with the peasants. But like or dislike "the people" as something apart he could not, not only because he lived with "the people," and all his interests were bound up with theirs, but also because he regarded himself as a part of "the people," did not see any special qualities or failings distinguishing himself and "the people," and could not contrast himself with them.

Moreover, Kido's sense of discomfort when those with whom he felt an ideological affinity attempted to involve themselves in Zainichi issues was expressed well by Levin's frequent criticism of his elder brother, Ivanovitch:

> Just as he liked and praised a country life in comparison with the life he did not like, so too he liked the peasantry in contradistinction to the class of men he did not like.

Basically, Kido hated the very idea of collecting human beings into categories. That was the sole reason he found his Zainichi background bothersome. It should have gone without saying that some Zainichi would be good people and some bad, and there would be things about the good Zainichi that he disliked as well as things about the bad Zainichi that were good even if he didn't know it.

Another of Levin's criticisms of Ivanovitch illustrated his qualms perfectly:

> Sergey Ivanovitch, and many other people who worked for the public welfare, were not led by an impulse of the heart to care for the public good, but reasoned from intellectual considerations that it was a right thing to take interest in public affairs, and consequently took interest in them.

But hold on: Wasn't this also the exact reason that Kaori was mistrustful of Kido's own "care for the public good"? Not for the first time, Kido hit upon this contradiction within himself and hugged his knee as he lost himself in thought.

The problem of whether Kido was personally embroiled in Zainichi issues was clearly no simple matter. Since he had grown up almost entirely as a "Japanese person" even before he naturalized, he was profoundly uneasy with the idea that he was either a direct victim or perpetuator of the troubles that beset Korean enclaves. And while Levin had discovered sincere love for "merry common labor" on that ineffably beautiful night after he had exhausted himself toiling with peasants for a day, Kido found it inconceivable that the same sort of fellow feeling with other Zainichi might one day sprout in his own heart.

Kido grew tired of thinking and turned the TV back on absent-mindedly. The news feature had now returned to the studio, where commentators were discussing xenophobia. They denounced it explicitly, a rare sight on TV of late, while making mention of the massacre of Koreans.

The Great Kanto Earthquake that preceded this atrocity had occurred in 1923, making the previous year its ninetieth anniversary. Ninety was a number of marginal import, but Kido somehow felt disconcerted to think that it was only ten more years to the centenary. A future earthquake in the Nankai Trough and another epicentered in the

Tokyo region were seen as near certainties. While some proclaimed that this would be the end of Japan, no one knew when such disasters might strike. In Kido's neighborhood, there were concerns about buildings collapsing and damage from a potential tsunami. The latter he might ride out if he was lucky enough to be at home on the ninth floor, but if he happened to be, for example, playing with Sota on the waterfront at Yamashita Park, they might not have time to run from harm's way.

The devastation in the city would surely be catastrophic. One hundred years since the Great Kanto Earthquake—in another decade, would terrified fools who took the cry "Death to Koreans!" seriously come for Kido and his family, whether in a grand display of mischief or release of pent-up resentment? If so, the fact that he was a lawyer, a father, a music lover, a "good person," and all of the above would be utterly irrelevant. Or relevant only insofar as his being endowed with such characteristics stoked their hatred further.

You're overthinking everything. Exasperated with himself, Kido tried to push these worries from his mind. But his tense cheeks trembled, and in spite of his efforts he could not put on a cheerful face. Having consulted several records of the Great Kanto Earthquake, he knew that there were fifty-three cases involving Koreans being murdered just counting documented prosecutions, and that, according to the Ministry of Justice at the time, the resulting death count was 233. In actuality—though there were many differing theories—the tally was estimated to be several times larger, with the lives of some Chinese taken as well. And the methods of killing chosen were so ghastly as to make one want to throw up in disbelief.

Kido pictured the great number of brutally defiled corpses and felt a chill as though the cold of those robbed of their existence were touching his skin. He suddenly felt as though they were his compatriots. He recalled his bone-deep anxiety on the bullet train after his friend's wake in Osaka: the pressure that threatened to implode the region of selfhood he had spatially monopolized via the contours of his body since birth without ever needing anyone's authorization. Now, Kido could feel himself identifying with Zainichi sentiments of victimhood. While at the same time, he was forced to take on the historical responsibility of the persecutor insofar as he was a Japanese citizen.

When a commercial came on, Kido turned off the TV, chewed over his thoughts of the past while, and began to feel that he had been mistaken about something earlier. While it was true that there were all sorts of different Zainichi, Misuzu hadn't joined the counter-demonstrations because she had an idealized conception of them. Rather, she had become involved because their existence was currently under threat. Japan was in a bad way.

"Shouldn't Japanese people treat it as a problem with their own country and be obligated to go to the counter-demonstrations themselves? They're the ones who are giving those scoundrels free rein," Kido had told her, even though, as a Japanese person, he should have been rushing to the scene to show his support from day one . . .

As he was ruminating in this way, Kido felt the sickness coming over him again and lay facedown, trying his best to clear his mind of thoughts. And in an effort to distract himself, he called up the memory of the day he visited the art museum with Misuzu, wishing he could see her.

※

Presently Kaori returned to the living room.

"What were you thinking, showing him something like that?"

Since her trip to Osaka in December, a string of events, including Christmas and the Shogatsu holidays, had forced them to converse amiably in order to keep up appearances for the sake of Sota and their respective parents, and this had brought a slight improvement to their relationship. Now, confronted with her stern gaze, Kido could only dread the conversation that was about to unfold.

"He woke up and came out here while I was watching it," said Kido, as nonchalantly as he could manage.

"You should have turned it off immediately."

Kido nodded in agreement, aware that his annoyance showed on his face. Kaori stood there looking at him for a while, until she could no longer resist giving him another piece of her mind.

"You know that I'm understanding about your ethnicity," she said. "You know I married you with full knowledge of who you are. It wasn't as if my family all thought it was a good idea, I'm sorry to say. I had to persuade them—but the reality is that there are people out there like the ones on TV just now, and we have to protect Sota from them. Didn't we agree that you'd tell him about your background when he's a bit older?"

Kido changed his position on the couch and stared over the backrest at his wife still standing there. He tried to find words, feeling the urgent need for them to talk and a readiness to accept whatever course the conversation might take, unsure where to even begin.

Strangely, it struck him with keen intensity how beautiful she was, as though he were admiring a stranger. When Kido's wife came up at the firm, she was invariably described as a "beauty." The teachers at Sota's day care seemed to concur, and Sota was proud of this. Meanwhile, Kido knew that he had taken Kaori's looks into account when he married her. That he would suddenly become aware of something so well established could only be a sign that they were on the verge of discussing divorce, and Kido just could not bring himself to initiate it.

Kaori's eyes tensed apprehensively, watching as her husband's speechlessness dragged on. She seemed to sense that he was about to overstep the line that they had both made it to this point without crossing. Fearing that she might preempt him by making up her mind first, Kido felt he had to say something, anything.

"It's agonizing for me, this situation . . . ," he blurted. "We need to talk about how to improve it because I don't want our marriage to end."

An almost imperceptibly faint smile flickered across Kaori's face.

"Where is this coming from?" she said, tilting her face obliquely in puzzlement.

Her reaction was not what Kido had been expecting. Though several months earlier, she seemed to be about to broach the topic herself, she did not now appear to have any intention of seeking divorce—on the contrary, she seemed concerned that he would feel the need to divulge such worries.

"First," Kido said quietly, letting his face relax, "let me say, as I've said many times before, that I'm not being unfaithful to you."

"Oh, I'm done with that. Have I brought it up lately? Even a word?"

"The silence has been disturbing in its own way."

"You're just projecting your fears."

"You've got nerve saying that when you're the one who doubted me," said Kido, twisting his cheeks to form a bitter grin. Then after a pause, "I wasn't being unfaithful, but it may have appeared that way because there is a certain individual that I've been absorbed in investigating for the past year. Not a woman. A man. The investigation relates to my job, so I never brought it up."

"Who is he?"

"The only son of a death row convict."

Kido began to tell her the story of Makoto Hara. He began with Kobayashi's upbringing and the murders he committed, before going on to describe the bullying Hara was subjected to, his ending up in an orphanage when his mother abandoned him, his time at the boxing club, and finally the collapse of his dream due to the "accident" after his professional debut.

At first, Kaori looked on skeptically, as though confused why he was telling her all this. Since he related the story with great enthusiasm, she appeared to be more intent on studying him than on listening to what he was saying. But when he reached the part about Hara trading his family register, she humored him by asking, "Does that sort of thing really happen?" Although Kido fudged the precise details surrounding Rié, he explained that Hara had married an unfortunate woman who had lost a child, started a family with her, enjoyed a brief period of happiness, and then died in a logging accident. Kaori listened to the end, by which point she seemed perplexed.

"That sure is a tragic and incredible tale . . . but what does it have to do with you?" she asked, cutting to the chase as usual.

"Good question," he said in a self-deprecating tone. "At first, nothing. It was just a job I took on because I felt sorry for the client. Then I grew fascinated with the idea of leading the life of another, started to picture the life he had wanted to throw away and . . . an escape from reality maybe? I guess it's kind of like reading an interesting novel for me."

"What a sick hobby."

"You think so?"

"What are you trying to escape?"

Kido looked at her, struggling to come up with an answer.

"All kinds of things," he said after a pause. "After everything that's happened . . . I think part of it is that I'm still reeling from the earthquake. Because it wasn't merely a natural disaster. It triggered other disasters, like those people they were just showing on TV."

Kido thought of the decline in their relationship that stemmed from such developments but did not include it in his list out loud.

"You're not the only one."

"True . . . I should have been more sensitive to the way it was affecting you too."

"Why don't you go to therapy or something?"

"Pardon me?"

"Instead of making a mountain out of a molehill, I bet just having someone listen to you would put you in a better space. Isn't that what your job is all about?"

"I'm not a therapist."

"I know, but you offer consultation to people who can't resolve issues among themselves. Talking to me isn't going to help you."

"I could say the same about you. To put it bluntly, there is something about our relationship that just isn't working anymore. I'd been thinking that what we needed was to talk, but perhaps you're right. If we're going to have a discussion, it might be more productive after counselling. And not just me. I want you to go too."

"I'm fine."

"What makes you say that?"

"I consult with people when I need to."

"But they're not specialists, are they? I doubt you're talking about what really matters."

"For example?"

". . . Well, for starters I want you to be nicer to Sota. You scold him too much."

"How so?"

"That's where your counselling can begin. You can tell the counsellor what I just told you."

Kaori shook her head in disgust. Kido stared at her and relaxed the muscles in his face. Released from the suffocating imperative to resolve something right then and there, he felt relieved, and words began to gush out of him.

"My issue is that I have all these problems that I want to find practical solutions to. But whenever I start to think about them, I become nauseous. I get this excruciating sense that my existence is radically insecure. And . . . for whatever reason, investigating the person I just told you about takes my mind off it. I don't really understand it myself. But the result is that I'm able to get in touch with my life indirectly through someone else's. And I'm able to think about the things that I need to think about. There's no way for me to do this directly. My body rejects it every time I try. That's why I said it's sort of like reading a novel. No one can deal with their suffering on their own. We all seek someone else to be the conduit for our emotions. And . . . I probably seem gloomy all the time, so I can understand why you'd think I'm no fun to be around."

Kaori took a seat in a chair with her arms crossed, shaking her head softly, her look of concern somehow changed.

"But you and that man are from completely different walks of life," she said.

"That must be why it works for me," said Kido. "The gap between us must put me at ease."

"I don't get it."

"OK, so what I'm trying to say is that I want us to get along, I really do. It wasn't easy for me to say that, but I had to. I just can't have you give up on me. It would tear me apart. I thought long and hard about it, but I'm certain of that now. I know I can't force you to do anything you don't want to, so I've been racking my brain for some way to make you love me. It's a conundrum I've been fretting over with far more urgency in our twelfth year of marriage than even when we were first dating."

At the end, Kido put on a tone of farcical melodrama. He laughed at himself, and Kaori couldn't help joining in. Kido could hardly remember the last time they had engaged in such a joking, ostensibly sincere exchange, and it made him happy to see a long-absent tinge of joy on her face.

"You're taking everything way too negatively," said Kaori, staring Kido in the eye.

Kido nodded in agreement.

"Are you OK?" she asked.

"In what way? I'm fine . . ."

"Are you sure? You're not getting any crazy ideas, are you? I couldn't bear it if you did something selfish like that."

Kido truly had no idea what she was talking about. When he eventually gleaned the meaning from her grave expression, he was shocked. This new suspicion was even more fatuous than his alleged cheating.

"Of course not," he said indignantly. "Crazy ideas. How could you even suggest such a thing? With Sota around, I couldn't possibly."

Recalling the "accident" that had ended Makoto Hara's boxing career, Kido could not hide his surprise that she was worried he might do something similar. Kaori's face had gone pale, and she kept her eyes on him, as though trying to divine the true meaning of his words.

"Then I guess there's no problem," she said.

Has the thought of such a crisis crossed her mind before? Kido wondered, suddenly stricken with worry. They both remained silent for a time. Then Kido slapped his knees with finality and said, "I'm glad we could have this talk. So I guess we'll be going separately to therapy, then."

"You're too stuck on that idea. I don't really understand it, but if it helps you cope, why don't you keep investigating that man for a while? Just make sure to be cheerful around the house."

"The investigation is almost over—if there's anything you'd like to get off your chest, I'd like you to speak with a therapist, or with me, if you like."

"I'm fine . . . Thanks for talking . . . OK, I'm off to take a bath."

Kido watched his wife's back as she left the living room. Then, after gazing out on to the veranda for a while, he lay prone on the couch and slowly shook his head. His breath had been caught in his chest, and now he let it all out.

CHAPTER EIGHTEEN

In the death-by-overwork civil suit that Kido was overseeing, a settlement was reached on February 15. The accused izakaya chain and its directors were required to pay a combined total of ¥82,000,000 and agree to put in place eight different preventative measures. It was, for all intents and purposes, a total victory for the plaintiffs.

After giving a press conference with the family, who carried a photo of their deceased son, Kido joined them for dinner at an Italian restaurant, where they chatted for close to three hours. Mostly it was small talk with barely a mention of the trial, but when it came time to say their goodbyes, the two parents shook Kido's hand firmly with both hands and expressed their gratitude. While this was exceedingly gratifying for Kido, he could not feel straightforwardly happy for them when he imagined them in their old age. And he noted how he had maintained good form as a lawyer while bringing this job to completion, not allowing himself to get caught up despite the profoundly tragic nature of the case.

After his talk with Kaori, Kido felt a renewed need to bring his investigation into Makoto Hara's life to some kind of resolution. To achieve this, he had to somehow locate Daisuké Taniguchi, confirm that he was unharmed and, if possible, ask him about his meeting with Hara. Unfortunately, the search for Daisuké was still at an impasse.

Kido had by this time given up on the idea that Kyoichi might help out. For Kyoichi had looked up Kobayashi online and, reacting with visceral revulsion to his crimes, seemed to want nothing to do with the whole affair. He denounced Daisuké with more vitriol than ever, saying that he deserved whatever he got for seeking out the places where such monsters operated despite being born into privilege. To willingly step into this "other world," as Kyoichi repeatedly described it, was the decision of an idiot beyond all hope of salvation. Kyoichi wasn't going to be so stupid as to get involved and risk being drawn into the same chain of crimes as his brother.

Thankfully, Kido soon discovered that he didn't need Kyoichi after all, when an email he happened to send Misuzu about seeing her on TV yielded a sudden breakthrough in the case. It was his first time contacting her in months. In her reply, Misuzu expressed surprise to hear about her appearance in the TV feature, and told him excitedly that she had participated in two separate counter-demonstrations. What followed was not a drawn-out description of her experience, as Kido would have expected, but a piece of news.

"By the way, I quit Sunny at the end of last year," she wrote. "I have my reasons, but I'd better tell you in person next time we meet."

Learning that he would never again sit across from her at that bar left Kido disappointed and forlorn. As recently as the end of January, after his visit to the boxing club, he had toyed with the idea of popping in to see if she was there. He now realized that she would have already been gone.

Misuzu went on to describe another surprising development: someone had reported the Daisuké Facebook account as fake, and it had been temporarily blocked. Although Misuzu's access had quickly been restored, she had stopped posting to the account, having had reservations about impersonating Daisuké from the start. Moreover, her relationship with Kyoichi had become, in her words, "unmanageable." She then happened to discover a separate Message Requests folder in her personal account and, realizing she had several years' worth of unchecked messages, had gone back to the fake Daisuké account and located the same hidden folder. There, she found a warning message from a "Yoichi Furusawa," the name written in Roman letters rather than Japanese script. The account had no photos and hardly any posts. The message read:

This is a warning from the legal representative. Erase this fake, imposter account immediately. If you do not comply, appropriate legal measures will be taken.

No mention had been made of who he (assuming from the name "Yoichi" that it was a "he") supposedly represented. The account did not appear to have been updated since, and there were no signs that any "legal measures" had been taken against the still-noncompliant Daisuké account. It was only natural to suppose that the account freeze had been this user's doing. Misuzu's intuition was that Yoichi was Daisuké himself.

"Like, he's doing his best to sound scary, but the way he can't really pull it off convincingly is just pure Daisuké."

Kido's own suspicion was that the message was part of an "aftercare" package provided by Omiura's associates for the family register swappers. But whatever or whoever was behind it, he decided that the best approach was to contact the user.

Misuzu's email concluded with the line, "How is everything going with you?" It was a typical question, but one that left Kido with a tingle of excitement.

✕

When Kido spoke to Nakakita, the only person at the firm with whom he consulted about the case, and explained how Misuzu was assisting in the search for Daisuké, Nakakita stared at him in disbelief.

"I think you're being a bit reckless here. She's his ex, right? What are you going to do if it turns out she's a stalker? Maybe this Daisuké guy skipped town to hide from her. The story we've gotten so far is that he ditched his register because he didn't get along with his family . . . but I wonder. What if she's feeding you elaborate nonsense so she can track him down?"

This unexpected criticism rendered Kido speechless. While it was hard for him to believe that this might be true of Misuzu, he could think of nothing to say that would justify his behavior. After all, there was no way to know the "true past" of another. Unless they were right in front of you, there wasn't even any way to know what someone was doing or where they were in the present. In fact, it might very well be hubris to believe that you could understand a person's true thoughts and feelings even when looking straight at them. Nakakita's words spread a dark shadow over the impression of Misuzu that had captured Kido's heart for the past year. He found it almost unbearable.

"Are you OK, Kido-san?" asked Nakakita just as Kido started back toward his desk.

Kido's eyes widened. Nakakita's question was exactly the same as Kaori's.

"Why do you ask?" said Kido, forcing a smile to show him he was fine.

)(

Kido considered what the best approach would be for contacting the "legal representative," Yoichi Furusawa. If he was Daisuké Taniguchi, it would be prudent not to bring up Kyoichi, since he would be averse to interacting with him. Kido also took Nakakita's point and decided to exercise caution about mentioning Misuzu as well. Writing a message that would inspire trust in an unidentified recipient was a challenging task. Whoever the user turned out to be, withholding some of the details seemed like a good way to arouse their interest. Kido settled on using the initials Y. S., rather than the full name, Yoshihiko Sonézaki, that Daisuké presumably went by. What he eventually came up with was the following:

Please excuse my impropriety in contacting you so unexpectedly. This is regarding a message sent to the account of a Mr. Daisuké Taniguchi on October 8 of last year.

My name is Akira Kido. I am currently serving as the attorney of Mr. Taniguchi's wife upon her request. I am registered as a lawyer with the Kanagawa Bar Association and am a partner at the legal firm listed below. Please visit our home page via the link if you are interested in learning more about us.

Allow me to inform you that Mr. Taniguchi passed away due to an accident that occurred in September three years ago. I cannot provide the precise details here. The reason I am contacting you is that, in the process of conducting research in the hopes of reaching a Mr. Y. S., who is said to have been acquainted with the late Mr. Taniguchi, I discovered an account under Mr. Taniguchi's name. Upon contacting the administrator, I was made privy to a message from you requesting the deletion of said account.

My apologies for the impertinent question, but are you not perhaps the legal representative of Mr. Y. S.? If I am correct in this, I would very much appreciate if you could reply, as there is a matter I dearly wish to communicate to him.

Conversely, if this is all a mistake on my part, then
I ask that you forgive my lack of discretion. Please, by
all means, discard this message after reading.

Kido was not very optimistic about receiving a response. Even he
found the message fishy. But if it was indeed Daisuké Taniguchi who
received it, Kido guessed that his curiosity would be piqued when he
learned that his former self had died, his abandonment of the family
register that linked them notwithstanding. Something told Kido that
part of him longed for the life he had thrown away. And if Daisuké
had indeed traded registers with Hara when Hara was Sonézaki, then
Daisuké, assuming he still went by Sonézaki, might be worried about
this exchange coming to light through Hara's widow.

※

"Yoichi Furusawa" replied that night just after 2:00 a.m., while Kido
was asleep.

"Oh boy," Kido muttered when he saw the message the next morning. The "legal representative" displayed as much wariness as was to be
expected, putting on a show of sangfroid but ultimately failing to hide
his distress. It was at this point that Kido came around to Misuzu's
hunch that he was in fact Sonézaki, that is, Daisuké. With this shift
in perspective, the ineptitude of Daisuké's efforts to disguise himself
became readily apparent, and Kido began to feel sorry for him.

"Yoichi Furusawa" began by saying that he doubted Kido was in
fact a lawyer. While there was, as claimed, a lawyer named Akira Kido
listed on the firm's website, Kido had provided no proof that he and this
man were one and the same. The "legal representative" then launched
into a long stream of questions, asking who Kido thought the initials
Y. S. referred to, who had created the Daisuké account, what Kido's
relationship to them was, etc.

In his reply, Kido proposed that they talk on Skype. That way, the "legal representative" could check that Kido was who he claimed to be through the video feed. If he preferred to turn off video on his end and only transmit audio, that was perfectly fine. And while Kido would prefer to speak directly with Y. S. if possible, he had no objections to speaking with "Yoichi Furusawa" to prove his own identity beforehand.

Kido's message was marked as read immediately, but a reply didn't arrive until evening (the interval suggesting to Kido that Daisuké worked during the day). While "Yoichi Furusawa" could not say who he represented, his client still sought the deletion of the Daisuké account and wished to know more about Daisuké's death. Therefore, he would Skype Kido at 11:00 p.m. that night.

Kido wavered about what clothes to wear but eventually chose his usual work outfit: a dress shirt and jacket. It felt strange to put his arms through well-ironed sleeves after giving Sota his bath and putting him to bed. The call from "Yoichi Furusawa" came at five past eleven.

"Good evening. This is Kido . . . Are you there?"

Kido waited for a response.

"Is this Furusawa-san? Can you see me OK?"

Kido put on a mild expression that stopped short of smiling, as he did when meeting a client for the first time. There was no reaction. For a moment, Kido began to worry that he had lost the connection forever.

"Kido here. Can you see me? Furu—"

"Yes . . . I can see you."

"Oh . . ." Kido shuddered at the sound of the man's trembling voice coming from beyond the blacked-out display window. *Could this be the real Daisuké Taniguchi?* he wondered. *Is this the man I've been seeking for more than a year now?* Kido was holding his breath and realized that he had to respond.

"And you can hear me?" he asked, using a genial tone so as not to startle him.

"Yes," said the man.

"Great. Thank you for agreeing to talk."

"You're welcome."

The way the man's words reverberated in the silence conjured a cramped studio apartment. Although his voice had the muffled timbre common in middle age, there was an awkwardness to it that suggested he was altering it on purpose. By audio chat, he seemed incapable of dissembling his fear and doubt, in contrast to the attempted magisterial tone of his messages. This struck Kido as both comical and sad. Out of the blue, he recalled Nakakita's claim that any fan of Michael Schenker had to be a "good dude."

"So was I correct in supposing that you're the legal representative of Yoshihiko Sonézaki?" Kido asked, not beating around the bush.

"Yes," the man immediately replied.

As his tone was uncertain, Kido suddenly felt discouraged, doubting again that it was Daisuké Taniguchi and suspecting it might be one of his friends or another stand-in.

"As I explained by message, Daisuké Taniguchi passed away three years ago. His widow is seeking information about certain aspects of his life."

"Taniguchi-san . . . was . . . married?"

"Yes. Married with two children."

"What does his wife do for a living?"

"She runs a stationery shop."

"Does she? What does she want to know?"

"I cannot discuss those details with anyone other than Sonézaki-san himself."

". . . Like . . . I'm his attorney."

"I have no way to confirm that," said Kido with a bland smile.

"How much do you know already?"

"Most of it, I expect. I'd like to meet with Sonézaki-san first. Then, if he so desires, I can fill him in on everything that's been happening."

An awkward pause followed.

"Listen," said Kido, "the deal that was made between Taniguchi-san and Sonézaki-san is none of my concern. But as a legal expert, I want him to be aware of certain problems that could arise when he dies and am willing to offer my advice pro bono. This is a rare opportunity. I believe I can be of service to him."

Kido said this in the hopes of enticing the man, feeling almost certain again that he was Daisuké Taniguchi. The silence beyond the black window stretched out again. Kido heard a sound like the click of a tongue as the man moved his mouth, apparently in thought.

"Have you met with Misuzu Goto?" the man asked with new authority, as though he had just absorbed the authentic manner of a legal representative from Kido.

"Y-yes," said Kido, surprised that he would bring her up so abruptly. "I have."

"Does Goto-san really believe that that person on Facebook is Daisuké Taniguchi? Who exactly is behind that account? Kyoichi Taniguchi?"

"That is another issue for me to discuss with Sonézaki-san himself. In person."

"Wait . . . please don't go yet. My client is concerned about whether Goto-san is doing well."

"She seems to be. As far as I can tell."

"I have a message for her."

"From whom?"

"My client."

"What is it?"

". . . He says he'd like to apologize."

Kido stared at the black window for a while, lost for words. He almost forgot for a moment that the man could see him.

"Okeydokey. I will convey the message."

"Also, my client says that, whatever happens, he doesn't want you to tell Kyoichi Taniguchi that he can be reached this way."

"You have my word," said Kido. "In any case, I would like to meet with Sonézaki-san to discuss everything in greater detail. Would you mind passing that on for me? I'll meet him wherever is most convenient."

"OK . . ."

"I look forward to hearing back, then."

"Yeah . . . talk to you soon . . ."

When the call ended, Kido sat where he was, looking straight up with his mouth hanging open. He wasn't entirely certain what the apology was supposed to be about, but he guessed it was for vanishing without a word. Either way, it was now clear that Nakakita's concern about Misuzu being a stalker had been needless. Although the man had hardly spoken, Kido had picked up on the remorse he bore toward Misuzu and sensed that it had gained a fresh luster in recent years.

Kido pitied the man his apparently pinched lifestyle and was ashamed to remember the time he had posed as Daisuké Taniguchi in that bar in Miyazaki, going as far as to appropriate his romantic relationship with Misuzu. At the same time, a feeling that could only be jealousy smoldered inside him.

The next day, Kido called Misuzu and told her about the Skype call.

"That is so definitely Daisuké! I can just picture him . . . I mean, first of all, I don't know anyone named Sonézaki."

When Kido relayed the apology, she merely gave a weak laugh.

"Are you going to meet him?" she asked.

"Well, that's the plan. I'm fairly confident he'll agree to see me. Which is great because it's high time for me to conclude this game of make-believe detective."

"Maybe I should go with you."

"Oh . . . You want to come? Shall I ask him?"

"If he says he doesn't want me there, tell him that if he's going to apologize he should darn well do it in person. I guarantee you he'll say yes."

When Kido sent a message to "Yoichi Furusawa" with Misuzu's request, he replied that his client did not want to meet her. So Kido told him what Misuzu had said and after a slight delay another message came: *Mr. Sonézaki has consented to having Goto-san attend.*

The date was set for the first Saturday of March; the location, Nagoya.

CHAPTER NINETEEN

Kido and Misuzu coordinated their plans so that they could sit together on the Nozomi bullet train for Nagoya. Since she boarded at the Tokyo Station terminal and he farther down the line at Shin Yokohama, she was already there when Kido stepped onto the reserved-ticket car, greeting him with a wave and a smile.

"Did you cut your hair?" he asked.

"Yesterday."

"Oh. Specifically for today?"

"No. Just a coincidence."

The hair spilling from her knit cap had been dyed a new, dark shade of brown and now barely reached her shoulders. Dressed in the same style as before, she wore tight denim jeans with a military-style jacket. This was Kido's third time meeting Misuzu, but it was his first time sitting beside her. He caught the sweet bitterness of her citrusy perfume. Kido had come in a suit with no tie.

Although their bullet train left after nine o'clock in the morning, it was mostly empty, and the seats in front and back of their two-seater block were empty. As the ride to Nagoya took an hour and a half, they spent the time catching up on the past few months, during which Misuzu told him about quitting the bar.

"Takagi was coming on to me hard and I just couldn't take it anymore," she explained with a pained grin. "At first I thought he was half kidding, but the lines he fed me kept getting more and more real."

"It was obvious that he was interested in you."

"You could tell?"

"Well, yes . . . I can't say I blame him. Anyone stuck behind a cramped counter like that with a beautiful woman like you is bound to develop feelings."

"It's the same old pattern. They always lust for me like that. No one wants anything serious." Misuzu said this as though it were funny, and Kido watched her smile in profile.

"There were other things too," she said. "I just couldn't get into chatting with customers anymore. Ever since I went to those demos, being in that bar felt like a chore. I wasn't working there for the money. I only got into it for a laugh. If it wasn't going to be fun, there was no point. And standing on my feet all night started to wear on me. I'm not as young as I used to be!"

"I wish I could have gone there one last time before you quit. Your vodka gimlet was superb!"

"Come on. I can make you one of those anytime. But I can't drink when I'm working the bar, so next time let's go out drinking together."

A vision of his future transforming, depending on how he handled this one invitation, momentarily kindled inside Kido and then immediately flickered out.

"You were drinking even when I was there," he said evasively.

"That was the only time," she said with a laugh, seemingly oblivious to the dodge. "I never drink behind the counter."

Misuzu went on to complain how she had been forced to abandon the Daisuké account because of Kyoichi. He had been hitting on her with similar persistence, precipitating a huge argument.

"That jerk doesn't care about finding Daisuké. He was just using it as an excuse to stay in touch with me."

"It's amazing that he would behave that way after swearing with such conviction that his brother had been murdered . . . I don't think he's a bad person, but it's hard for me to see where he's coming from on this."

"Oh, this sort of thing is nothing new. There's a history to it . . . I never told you, but I may have had something to do with the falling-out between the brothers. You see, Kyoichi had a crush on me."

"Oh boy . . . How did I guess?"

"Women flock to Kyoichi. He's not my type at all. Too much of a player. Daisuké is clumsy. He's not all that handsome. And he's the kind of guy that's just begging to be made fun of. He asks for it, acting like he enjoys being the butt of everyone's jokes. He'll be all smiles on the surface until suddenly he can't take it anymore and goes ballistic. Who isn't going to be put off by that? Like, what's with this guy, all of a sudden? But there's actually nothing sudden about it."

The Daisuké Taniguchi that Misuzu was describing struck Kido as completely different from both the one that Kyoichi had griped about and the one Rié had heard about through Makoto Hara.

"Do you think those personality quirks were in the background with the liver transplant dilemma?"

"Yeah, I'd say so, maybe? But that's a far cry from your classmate asking to borrow some money, don't you think?"

"Of course."

"Kyoichi liked to belittle his brother, so he could never accept that I would start dating him."

"He seems to have a lot of pride."

"That's part of it . . . ," said Misuzu with a wry smile. Then, looking around as if to check who was listening, "You know how boys around high school age have a crazy powerful sex drive?"

"Ha, ha. Well, sure."

"Kyoichi just couldn't stand that Daisuké was having sex with me. Like there was something inside him thrashing about in a mad frenzy."

Kido burst into laughter and kept laughing for a while. Misuzu was drawn in by his mirth and began to laugh too.

"So this is not some fairy tale about his enduring love," she said. "Kyoichi just wants to screw me. Even though I'm getting older and

I'm sure he wouldn't get much out of it, for him, it's not even about what I'm really like now. He just won't let it go until he's added me to the notches on his belt."

"I suppose he's hoping to free himself from his humiliation in the past."

"You can relate to that sort of thing?"

"Yup . . . I cannot say that it defies my understanding."

"Really?! So you feel the same kind of desire for conquest?"

"Ahem, it would be dishonest of me to say that I don't, though I suppose it's a question of degree. Insofar as there is the possibility of hurting women, I believe we need to reflect on that desire, whether we are aware that we have it or not. The same goes for the wretched jealousy and competitiveness that can arise between men . . . Have you heard of *triangular desire*? Was it René Girard? The idea is that human beings never desire others one-on-one but develop an attraction for someone because there is a rival that wants them too."

"Wow . . . But then why would the rival have come to like that person in the first place?"

"Oh, right. Chicken and egg . . . Could they be deluded, thinking there's a rival when there isn't? Or could they be some kind of genius or misfit?"

"So you're saying that Daisuké only fell in love with me because he sensed Kyoichi's rivalry?"

"Whoops . . . Apologies. Our conversation seems to have taken a wrong turn."

Misuzu studied Kido's face, wearing an expression he found difficult to read, like she couldn't quite put away the remnants of her smile.

"You're a very honest and serious person, Kido-san," she said.

"I don't know about that. I think I just try to show people the good parts of me."

"People have many different faces."

"We talked about that, didn't we?" said Kido with a smile. He said nothing about his twisted feelings toward the Taniguchi brothers vis-à-vis Misuzu and felt like a pathetic weasel for having brought up Girard in an effort to obscure them.

Misuzu looked vaguely out the window, gazing wordlessly at Mount Fuji as it appeared in the distance after a long stretch of industrial bleakness. Then, turning slowly back to Kido, she said, "This kind of thing happens to me all the time. I don't hate my face, but it always seems to get me into trouble. My problem is that I have no clue how to use it to my own advantage."

"I can see how that might be a struggle."

"When I tell people this, I get a lecture about how it's my fault because I leave a crack in my defenses that gives men the wrong impression. Take Takagi. The way he tried to get me to go home with him after work was just vulgar, but he was never like that when I went there as a customer."

"I don't think it's your fault."

Misuzu smiled sourly. Then, after a pause, she seemed to suddenly realize something wonderful and said, "For the past year or so, I've had a crush on someone."

"Oh, is that right?" said Kido, pretending nonchalance when he was in fact somewhat taken aback. While he told himself it was entirely to be expected that she would, of course, be attracted to someone, he was appalled at his atrociously poor ability to pick up on such feelings in women, which had not improved one iota since high school. It had always caught him off guard when girls asked him out, and rumors about who liked who had never failed to surprise him.

He understood perfectly well that there was another Misuzu besides the one he had met at the bar and with whom he was in contact about Daisuké Taniguchi. And he was aware of how many "friends" she was presumably viewing on Facebook. Nevertheless, out of sheer naivety, he had never thought to direct his jealousy beyond those close at hand, such as Takagi and the Taniguchi brothers. Now, thanks to this rival she had mentioned, though they had never even met, Kido could almost feel his chimeric vision of the other life he evoked through Misuzu being goaded on by triangular desire.

"He came to the bar once," Misuzu continued. "I'm usually surrounded by unsophisticated men who call me 'chick' and 'babe.' But he was different from any of the men I'd ever known. He was the intellectual type. Toward me, he played the gentleman. His language was polite, even online, and he was always honest and serious and intelligent."

Kido nodded along while he listened, thinking that if she just wanted someone who wouldn't call her "chick," he fit the bill.

"Whenever I went to the bar, I found myself waiting for him, wondering if he would ever return. Meanwhile, I was checking his Facebook and giving him lots of 'likes.' He looked super busy. So when he didn't come back, I invited him out."

"What a lucky man. What does he do for a living?" Kido saw Misuzu's hesitation. "That's fine," he said. "You don't have to say. I was only curious."

"It's not his job that's the issue . . . ," she said. "He has a wife and child. You may be surprised to hear this, but I've always had a no-married-man policy."

"I don't see why that should surprise me."

"I'm being serious here! I'm in my forties and I'm still single and here I am, ready to stoop to that in the end . . . He's not just busy. He seems to have a rich, fulfilling life and he's never shown any interest in me . . . To tell you the truth, I've been a mess for the past six months. Such a mess that I've been wondering what's come over me—and at this age too!"

". . . So?"

"Well . . . recently something happened, and I decided to use it as an opportunity to get over him. That's one of the reasons I quit working at the bar. Waiting for him was just too painful. I used to say three steps forward and four steps back, but lately I've been on a stepping backward streak."

"Have you told him how you feel?"

Misuzu fluttered her long lashes restlessly like a water bird startled into flight by a noise. Kido failed to grasp the meaning of her rapid blinking, but when her lips drew momentarily into a faint, closed-mouth smile, he smiled back in the same way and inquired no further.

I guess there's another man just like me, he thought.

✕

For a while after that, both of them were silent.

"If you have any work to do, don't let me stop you," said Misuzu.

"You go ahead and sleep if you like," said Kido, reciprocating her thoughtfulness. "I'll wake you up when we arrive."

"Can I ask you one thing?" she asked.

"By all means."

"Why did that Makoto Hara guy masquerade as Daisuké? I can understand that he would want to get rid of his family register. But what was stopping him from making up a life story to his own liking? Wouldn't everything have been easier for him if he hadn't gone around acting like the story about the transplant and all was his? At least it seems that way to me."

"I don't doubt that some people hide their past with a yarn of their own devising . . . but my suspicion is that he empathized with Daisuké-san, much in the way we all do when reading novels or watching movies. It takes a certain kind of talent to come up with a story that you not only like but can project your emotions into. It's not something that just anyone is capable of—moreover, I think it's important to confront yourself through another. There is a certain kind of loneliness that can only be soothed by finding yourself within the tale of another's trauma."

Kido noted that he was interpolating his own fascination with Makoto Hara into what he was saying.

"Hmmm. I think I kind of get what you're saying . . . but, like, there's the Daisuké I knew back in the day, the 'Daisuké Taniguchi' that started a nice family in Miyazaki and died on the logging site, and then there's the life of the real, current Daisuké we're about to meet . . . It's weird."

"I'm sure we all have an infinite number of possible futures. Only, it's difficult for each of us to realize what those are ourselves. I'm certainly no exception. If I were to pass the baton to someone at this point, they might be able to lead my life better than I ever would have."

"It's like when the president of a corporation is replaced. Or, like, the coach of a soccer team."

"That's the way legal entities have been conceived since the days of the Roman Empire. Even when the people changed, the nation remained the same. Roman law, which is the foundation for present civil law, presupposed the eternal continuation of the empire. But as it turned out, Rome fell, while its laws have lived on . . ."

Kido realized he'd gone off on a tangent but, glancing at Misuzu, found her listening with rapt attention.

"Ahem, anyhow, the situation is different with regard to individuals. There is the human lifespan and death to factor in. Moreover, Hara-san is not Daisuké-san."

"But he's not whoever Hara-san was before either, is he?"

"True . . . Perhaps his life merged with Daisuké-san's or abides alongside it—but if that is so, then when we fall for someone, what part of them is it that we love, I wonder? When we meet a person who will become our beloved, we are attracted to who they are in the present and grow to love them as a whole, including their past. But if a lover finds out that their beloved's past is in fact the past of a stranger, what happens to the love the two shared?"

Misuzu looked at Kido as though the answer were obvious.

"Once the truth came out, they'd have to renew their love," she said. "I mean, it's not as if you love someone once and that's it. You renew your love again and again over the long haul, through everything that happens along the way."

Misuzu's conviction touched Kido, and he looked at her face, aglow with a centered, sensitive calm, feeling overwhelming affection for her. He was reminded of the ongoing influence her perspective had exerted over him this past year, with its untrammeled, somewhat bitter resignation to reality resulting from a certain obstinacy untainted by common opinion.

"Well put," he said. "Love for another might remain the same love even as it keeps on changing. Or perhaps we can go further and say that love persists precisely because it changes."

A voice over the intercom announced that they would be arriving shortly at Nagoya. Kido was sad to think that this trip could be the last time he saw Misuzu. He continued to reflect on her story about her recent heartbreak, watching her in profile as she gazed out the window, pretending that he too was taking in the scenery.

He was doing his best to appear obtuse and hold back from making any moves on her, even while he mocked himself in his head for his lucky misunderstanding of her confession. What he wanted was to make amends with his wife. And he told himself that what Misuzu had said about deciding to "get over him" ought to be taken at face value.

As they were both planning to return from Nagoya that day, neither had brought large pieces of luggage, so there was no need to gather them up before deboarding. Even so, they waited a long time to stand up, remaining seated until just before the train stopped.

In a flash, the urge to stay on the train and go off somewhere with Misuzu budded and then burgeoned in Kido's chest, his pulse rising as though anticipating that he would suggest it. But he considered what Misuzu had said earlier with regard to Kyoichi: *I'm getting older, and I'm sure he wouldn't get much out of it.* He sympathized with her conundrum even as he rebelled against the intent of the statement. *I'm getting older too*, thought Kido. Perhaps neither of them would have got much out of it.

"Shall we?" said Kido. He was the one who stood first, so as to break away from his lingering attraction to her. Misuzu turned to him and nodded with her usual cheerful but languid expression. When Kido extended his hand, she broke into a broad smile as she took it.

"Off we go," she said, standing up. And pleased by his courtesy, she thanked him in a way that left no doubt about her true feelings.

CHAPTER TWENTY

The meeting with "Yoshihiko Sonézaki" was at one o'clock, so Kido and Misuzu had a simple lunch at a restaurant inside the station building. They then said goodbye for the moment, as the arrangement was for Kido to interview the man one-on-one before Misuzu joined them.

The location the man had given them was a branch of Komeda's Coffee. It should have been only a ten-minute walk from Nagoya Station, but as Kido was unfamiliar with the area and got quickly thrown off course by the numerous other branches nearby, he ended up being about five minutes late.

Assuming "Yoshihiko Sonézaki" was indeed Daisuké Taniguchi, Kido knew his face from photos. Then again, as all the photos had been at least ten years old, he wasn't sure if he would recognize him immediately. When he told one of the baristas that he was there to meet someone, she seemed to have an idea who that might be and led him to the smoking area. There, at a four-seater table divided from the one beside it by a movable wooden partition, sat a man in a gray knit cap and an embroidered bomber jacket that somehow didn't suit him. He was looking Kido's way. Kido let out a silent sigh, and his heart throbbed rapidly just as when he had first heard the man's voice on Skype. While he had definitely aged, there was no mistaking Daisuké Taniguchi.

He's still alive.

Kido's cheeks grew warm as though flushing when he thought how he had hung on to his trust in Makoto Hara to the last. The combined stink of coffee and cigarette smoke thickened the air. When Kido reached his seat, he greeted the man and proffered his business card. Without a word, the man bowed, wearing an expression of intense nervousness, and examined both sides of the card.

"Daisuké Taniguchi?"

The man who was supposed to be "Yoshihiko Sonézaki" hesitated, looking harrowed for a moment, before saying, "Yeah."

In response to Kido's smile, Daisuké twisted his cheeks involuntarily. He was supposed to be forty-two, three years older than Kido, but his skin was puffy and lusterless, his eyes exhausted.

Once Kido had ordered a coffee, Daisuké said, "Um, can you call me Sonézaki? And do you mind if I smoke?"

"Go right ahead. Sonézaki-san it is. Apologies."

Daisuké took a puff of his cigarette and, looking more relaxed, said, "You kind of have to experience it yourself to understand what I mean, but once a year goes by after you've swapped registers, you actually become a different person. When you called me Daisuké Taniguchi, I was seriously like, what, you mean me? Because along with our pasts, we switch everything. Before the swap, I hated the Taniguchis. Now it's like I never even knew them. When I saw Kyoichi Taniguchi on Facebook, he just looked like the goofy owner of some bumpkin inn."

"You never think about the old days?"

"If you cut off your relationships and move to a different place, the memories just fade naturally—I mean, if you hate your past, trying to forget will get you nowhere. You can't erase it. You've got to overwrite it. Cover it over with someone else's till it's beyond recognition."

When Kido's coffee arrived, he took a sip, nodding to what Daisuké was saying and realized that he had been mistaken about something. Taking on a new identity didn't seem to mean living the story of another's trauma, as Kido had imagined. At the same time, the impression this man gave him was radically distinct from that of the Daisuké that Misuzu had described on the train. When he looked at his face, Kido had no doubt that the man was her ex, Kyoichi Taniguchi's missing brother, but it was hard to think of them as the same person, just as Daisuké himself had claimed.

"Sonézaki-san," said Kido. "Where are you originally from?"

"A town in Yamaguchi Prefecture. I'm the son of a yakuza."

". . . I see. Did you . . . How can I put this? Were you aware who you were exchanging registers with?"

"You mean Makoto Hara?" To Kido's surprise, Daisuké said this as though he didn't see why Kido was making a big deal out of it.

"Exactly. Was it Omiura that brokered the exchange?"

"Um, that might have been his name. Dude had a face like a blowfish and this super shady vibe to him."

"Oh, then, yes. That sounds like him."

"He talked all kinds of crazy stuff, like, 'I know a guy that lived to be two hundred.'"

Kido burst out laughing and almost tilted his coffee onto the tabletop. "He told me three hundred."

Daisuké smirked, finally beginning to warm up. "What's he doing now?"

"Serving time."

"Really? For what?"

"He was convicted for a scam."

Daisuké closed one eye and exhaled smoke as though he was really enjoying it.

"Did you know about Hara-san's early days?" Kido asked.

"Yup. Father was that killer, right?"

"He was. So Hara-san changed his family register twice? First he became Yoshihiko Sonézaki and then—"

"He swapped with me."

"Why did he trade twice?"

"Why? It was pretty normal in that scene. Actually, someone like me who only did one swap is more in the minority."

"Is that right?"

"Hara-san's past was intense, so Sonézaki was pretty much his only choice for a swap partner. I don't think it bothered Hara-san that Sonézaki was the child of a gangster. The problem was when they met in person. Because Hara-san just didn't like the guy."

Kido saw the pieces of the story coming together at last, realizing that it must have been this man, the original Sonézaki, who foisted Hara's register on defenseless Tashiro.

"The family register for 'Daisuké Taniguchi' was a hot item," said Daisuké, fiddling with a hundred-yen lighter in his right hand. "No criminal record, a real clean past. Actually, it was so popular that one guy kept trading for better and better registers trying to land mine, like the *Straw Millionaire* in that legend. At the time, I didn't care about anything but cutting off my family. I would have swapped with just about anyone. But I drew the line at a criminal record and I didn't want some thug who might cook up a scheme to get the Taniguchi estate. Then I met Hara-san and we talked a bunch and I thought my old identity might help him turn over a new leaf."

"Did Hara-san empathize with Daisuké Taniguchi's past?"

"I'd say so. He listened carefully to my story, said he wanted to do his best to make the most of what remained of my life. If I was going to give away my life, I wanted it to be to someone like that. We only met twice, but I liked him. There was this pureness in his eyes, and he seemed like a really nice guy, even after everything he went through. I could almost taste how badly he wanted to jump ship before his time in this world came to an end."

"So, when you met him, Hara-san would have been going by 'Yoshihiko Sonézaki,' is that right? Was he the one who told you about his original life?"

"Yeah, sure. How he used to be a boxer. Made two suicide attempts."

"Two?"

"That's what he said."

It seemed that Hara had come around to admitting his "fall" from his apartment was a suicide attempt. But Kido had never suspected there had been a second one. "How do you think he made a living after he quit boxing?"

"Um, worked in restaurants, all kinds of places. Then information about him started to spread online, and it got harder and harder for him. Did temp work for a while after that."

As Kido watched Daisuké answer so coolly about Hara, he recalled all the times he had worried that the man might have killed Daisuké since he'd taken on Rié's case more than a year ago.

"And what are you doing now?" he asked.

"Um . . . this and that. Does it matter?"

"Excuse me for prying."

"No worries."

"I just thought that you might encounter obstacles as the child of a gangster."

"It's not like I go around telling people about it. How do you think real yakuza kids go straight-edge? They keep it under wraps."

"Right."

"Just once I told someone who I was, a coworker at one of our bar nights, because he was a real prick. My family is one of the big crime syndicates, so I gave him the name. That douche's whole attitude toward me has been different ever since. In a way, it's almost like a source of confidence for me now, I mean, when I think how I was born to this really badass family but that I'm hiding it so I can try to live honestly."

"I could see that."

"That's why I say I'm not the same me as I used to be—the truth is, I never met the real Sonézaki-san, so I can't picture him directly. I base him on Hara-san. I start by imagining what Hara-san might have been like if he was the son of a yakuza and build up my past from there. There's even a period when I used to be a boxer."

Kido flashed a complicated smile. "Apparently, Hara-san had some real talent for boxing. He won the East Japan Rookie King Tournament."

"Seriously? Wow. He never mentioned that . . . though now, I guess he's . . ."

"He's passed away."

"What a shame . . . Though I do feel kind of relived to know that Daisuké is gone. I wanted Hara-san to keep on living Daisuké for me, but it also kind of creeped me out whenever I remembered that the second son of that family was still out there, alive somewhere."

"On that topic, you should know that the facts have come to light and Daisuké Taniguchi's notification of death has been annulled. Officially, he's a missing person listed as living."

"What? Really?" Daisuké made a sour face and looked as though he were reconsidering the meaning of Hara's death. "What did Hara-san get himself into after he took over being Daisuké?"

Kido briefly related Hara's life from the time he met Rié in Town S until he died. Daisuké solemnly chain-smoked with crossed arms as he listened. When Kido mentioned that Hara had had a kid, Daisuké opened his eyes wide and faced the ceiling, lost in thought.

"So was his wife hot?"

"Pardon? Ahem, well, I suppose you could say that she's cute. With nice, round eyes."

"Isn't that something. Damn. Lucky guy . . . If I'd ended up in Town S, I wonder if I'd have married her too."

"Well, hmmm . . . it's hard to say."

"I feel bad for him that he died young. But actually I'm kind of jealous that he managed to start a happy family . . . Damn. I guess I blew it."

"Are you married?"

"Not going to happen. I'm broke."

"You wouldn't consider going back to the Taniguchis? There is the estate, and I hear your mother wants to see you. For the legal problems, I could—"

"No way!" snapped Daisuké, flinging the lighter he'd been hold-ing onto the table. "If you're going to talk about that, then I'm outta here."

Kido apologized and merely gave a general explanation of inheri-tance rights, but Daisuké had no focus for it.

"Even if I become homeless, I will never meet with the people in that family. Whatever the census records might say, can't we let 'Daisuké Taniguchi' rest in his grave? Misuzu is the only exception. I can't tell you how long I've wished that I could see her again. When I imagine myself on my deathbed and think who I'd want to be there, it's her. Just her. That scene keeps popping into my head. Pretty dumb, I know. You met her, didn't you?"

"I did."

"Is she still hot? Not over the hill?"

"She'll be here in fifteen minutes. She's as beautiful as ever."

"Is she married?"

"You'd better ask her that yourself."

"So she's single, then. Damn! . . . Misuzu is by *far* the hottest girl-friend I have ever had. Most of my memories of 'Daisuké' are just barely hanging on, but not the ones of dating her. Those still come back to me all the time—like when we were in the bedroom and stuff . . ."

Daisuké gave Kido a depressingly lecherous smile.

Now Kido wondered if the two brothers, Daisuké and Kyoichi, however different they appeared on the surface, might in fact be two of a kind, though Daisuké didn't seem to have been like this when he was dating Misuzu . . . So perhaps the change was due to the "confidence" he now derived from being the child of a yakuza. Or perhaps some part of him was unconsciously mimicking his elder brother. Whatever the reason, Kido sensed a kind of psychological deterioration in the man, resulting no doubt from his unfortunate circumstances and irreducible to his innate character.

He regrets what he's chosen, Kido thought. Daisuké had the look of an amateur investor who has just learned that a share he had put aside for more bullish times and finally sold off at a loss has just gone up in value. While his unwavering aversion to ever seeing the Taniguchis again came off as genuine, he seemed to wish that he had thought more carefully about the swap and chosen a life on par with the one he'd started out with. Until now, Kido had felt slightly jealous when he imagined Misuzu and Daisuké's reunion, but realized that he had let his feelings cloud his good sense. The intervening decade had opened a gap between them that he should have anticipated, especially considering that Daisuké had been living the life of another.

As Daisuké's salacious words and Misuzu's story about Kyoichi's unflagging desire entangled in his mind, Kido felt profoundly disturbed. At the same time, he sympathized with Daisuké for the situation that had made him run away from the Taniguchis and was filled with sorrow at the thought of Hara's single-minded adoption of that past as his own.

Kido's cell phone chimed: Misuzu was on her way. Now he wondered if the imminent reunion might bring about some shift in Daisuké. Whether Misuzu would be painfully disillusioned or inspired to extend a helping hand, Kido couldn't guess. Perhaps she would "renew" her love for him—whatever might happen, Kido didn't think he could bear to watch it unfold. He had been planning to stay but now reconsidered, deciding it was none of his concern.

"Goto-san says she'll be here shortly, so I'm going to take my leave now," said Kido with a bow.

"Oh. You're going?"

"Yes. I kind of have plans after this."

"Alright. Damn. Now I'm nervous . . . I was feeling jumpy at first with you too. I was worried I might regret coming. But I'm really glad we could meet. It gave me a chance to ask everything that was on my mind."

Daisuké extended his hand, and Kido reached out to shake it, recalling the touch of Misuzu's hand a short time earlier. Daisuké's was rough and clammy. Kido wondered who that texture belonged to. Seven years ago, when Hara showed up as Sonézaki and left as Daisuké, did he shake hands and part with this man in just the same way? Imagining that interaction play by play through Hara's eyes, Kido paid the bill and walked quickly out of the café.

CHAPTER TWENTY-ONE

After meeting with Daisuké and interviewing him about his register swap with Hara, Kido finished the report for Rié. While there was more he would have liked to know about Hara, he felt it important, for the time being at any rate, to put his investigation to rest after a year and three months pursuing it.

As Kaori had requested, Kido made an appointment with a psychologist at a clinic near his workplace. But because Kido took a professional interest in the way the psychologist asked questions, it ended up turning into a lively conversation in which Kido inquired about the finer details of the technique. And although the psychologist said he would be glad to have him back, Kido never returned.

Kaori was relieved to hear that he had followed through but endlessly put off going herself. For his part, Kido didn't force the issue. Ever since their talk, he'd observed a change in her and saw her scolding Sota to tears much less often. She wasn't necessarily making such changes spontaneously, but he sensed her effort and her desire to rehabilitate the situation at home. And he wanted to reciprocate by cooperating with her as much as he could, especially in light of his newfound understanding of the psychological burden she bore due to the earthquake and the ensuing spread of xenophobia. He felt guilty for having been insensitive to what she was going through and, at the same time, grateful.

Kido has remained unwavering in this perspective on their relationship even to this day. This is why events like the following, which occurred three days before he went back to see Rié, have already never happened for him, becoming just another memory of a typical week-end, hardly worth recalling. Some people may find this state of mind incomprehensible, while others will no doubt feel that they can almost relate.

💢

One morning, Kido and his family went to the Tokyo Skytree, which Sota had been wanting to visit for some time. They arrived at eleven o'clock after riding trains on the Toyoko and then Hanzomon lines.

Two years had passed since the Skytree opened to the public, and they expected the mobs of eager tourists to have mostly dissipated. But this turned out to be naive, especially since it was a spring weekend, and they were told they'd have to wait two hours just to receive a number to then line up for a ticket.

Outside the windows stretched a clear, radiantly blue sky.

Kido gazed at it, relishing his day off.

Suddenly a line from a story he had read long ago flitted through his mind.

"Ah, such a moment of such a day," the character had exclaimed. This expressed how he felt right then perfectly, but the name of the writer refused to come to him.

"What should we do?" Kaori asked Sota with a smile. Although she had been out drinking with her coworkers the previous night and had returned home well after Kido was asleep, she showed no signs of a hangover and had been in a good mood all morning. "Want to line up?"

Biting his thumbnail, Sota looked his mother in the eye and squirmed as he weighed the options.

"Let's go to the aquarium," he said eventually.

Kido checked to make sure that that was what he actually wanted to do. Sota had learned to be attentive to what the adults around him were feeling and to adapt himself to them. Kido wasn't sure if this was typical for his age or if he was just unusually considerate.

"Yeah. Let's go," said Sota, tugging Kido's arm.

So instead of going up to the observation deck, they decided that they would content themselves by merely looking up at the Skytree from the base. Kido then told Kaori his honest impression of the building, the tallest in Japan.

"From a distance, it just looked like some overgrown lattice tower, with no redeeming qualities of any kind. And now that I'm finally up close, it impresses me even less than I was expecting."

"So true," Kaori agreed, smiling again.

The aquarium was in the same building. On the way there, Sota begged them to let him buy a toy in a capsule from a hand-cranked vending machine, so Kido gave him some change and Sota ended up with a miniature samurai helmet and armor. When they arrived, they found the aquarium lobby crowded as well but with a much shorter line. The closest comparison Kido could think of for this aquarium was the Hakkeijima Sea Paradise theme park, which the three of them had visited together. None of them had ever been here before.

Under dim lighting done in contemporary style for couples on dates, Sota hopped his way through the crowd. But despite this apparent excitement, he didn't even glance at the jellyfish, minnows, or anything else that he passed, and when Kido tried picking him up to show him the sea otters in a tank higher off the floor than the others, Sota immediately said, "I'm done."

Presently they came to a tank for viewing sharks and manta rays. It made a grand display, akin to the massive screens in new cinema multiplexes, and the wall of spectators signalled that this was the main attraction. Here too, Sota showed little interest, saying, "It's scary," before hurrying right by. At this, Kido shared a look with Kaori and grinned in dismay.

Next they came to the penguin zone, where a blue tank with artificial boulders could be viewed from above as though looking down
on a big pool. This design seemed to finally thrill Sota, and they went
down a floor to watch the penguins swimming underwater at eye level.
Looking only at the shadows cast on the floor by the whole group in
motion, they resembled birds in flight. From below, the surface of the
water churned relentlessly, crushing the light pouring from the ceiling.

For the most part, the penguins all travelled in the same direction, but Kido was captivated by the way a few birds would inevitably
break away, head deeper, and shoot off diagonally in the opposite
direction until the entire group eventually switched. When he came
to, he realized that Sota and Kaori were gone. He then wandered
about the penguin zone searching for them to no avail. Giving Kaori
a call, he learned that they were in the souvenir shop near the exit
and went to meet them, slightly annoyed.

"Daddy! You lost your mommy!" Sota cried the moment he saw
him, jumping in uproarious laughter as though it were the funniest
thing in the world. When Kido gave him a scowl, it only made Sota
laugh harder. Kaori explained that she'd been hoping to buy Sota some
kind of souvenir. As they found nothing he wanted after thoroughly
perusing the wares on offer, they decided to try a different store after
lunch.

✕

All the restaurants on the restaurant floors had dauntingly long lines,
except for one on floor seven that specialized in beers from around the
world. Once they had confirmed that the menu was child friendly, they
decided to go inside.

Kido was surprised to find that, despite the lack of seating everywhere else, the server led them to a table close to the windows. And as
he gazed out at the blue sky sheltering vast stretches of Tokyo buildings,

with the Imperial Palace in the distance, he felt that the vista here was more than sufficient without having to go all the way to the top of the Skytree.

When the three of them sat down, they all sighed with relief. After walking around for an hour and a half, not to mention the long train ride, they were pleasantly tired out. The restaurant bustled with families and couples talking in voices made loud by the alcohol. Kido noted that they wouldn't need to worry about disturbing other patrons if Sota couldn't sit still.

For Sota, they ordered an orange juice and the kid's lunch that came with a hamburger patty and rice, and for the adults, spareribs and a salad. Kido asked for a Chimay white and Kaori a rare German pilsner the name of which they could not pronounce. The drinks came immediately and the three of them said cheers. Kido drank a third of his glass in one gulp and let out a long, relaxed breath as though he were soaking in fresh bathwater before anyone else had taken their turn.

"It tastes even better when you haven't had it in a while," said Kido when the Chimay's complex fruity bitterness had spread across his palate. He then quaffed another third and held in a burp.

Imitating his father, Sota took a gulp of juice and said, "Whew. It tastes fantastic when you haven't had it in a while," before laughing wildly. Kido and Kaori laughed along with him.

"Want to try some?" said Kaori, proffering her glass to Kido. "This one's pretty good too."

Kido took a sip.

"It is good," he said, nodding as he examined the aftertaste. "Goes down smooth."

The salad arrived, followed, after an inordinate wait, by the spareribs. The all-important kid's lunch was nowhere to be seen. They tried to feed Sota some of the ribs, but after one bite he complained that it was too salty and returned the piece of meat, fork and all, to the plate.

"Hey, Mom, let me play games on your phone."

Reluctantly, Kaori pulled up the puzzle game that Sota liked and handed him her phone. By this time, Kido had finished most of his second Chimay as an accompaniment to the richly flavored meat and was feeling increasingly chipper now that he was tipsy.

"Sorry. Can I have that back for a second?" Kaori asked Sota as she stood up from her seat.

Sota didn't seem to hear her, mesmerized by the screen.

Kaori wavered for a moment about whether to insist, but decided to let him keep the phone and left for the restroom.

"Your lunch is taking forever," Kido said, and suddenly thought of that one night two winters ago, after he had gone to Shibuya to meet with Kyoichi for the first time. He recalled the intense feeling of happiness he had experienced as he put Sota to bed in his room and told himself that he was happy in the present moment as well.

I wonder if there's a life out there that someone is about to part with that I might be able to lead better . . . If I were to hand off my life to someone right now, would he be able to lead the remainder of my life better than me? Just as Hara seems to have realized a more beautiful future than Daisuké probably ever would have . . .

Being "normal" had been Hara's great aspiration and Kido mulled over the meaning of that notion, contemplating all the pain and relief it must have caused people. Then he studied Sota as he stared downward and operated the touch screen adroitly with his small fingers. He noted how similar his features and personality were to Kido's when he was a child. From the perspective of natural selection, was it more advantageous for the child to resemble the parent? Was it because of such resemblance that the parent raised the child with great care, as though they were the parent themselves? Quickly Kido thought up innumerable counterexamples, such as parents who lovingly raise their adopted children, and immediately dropped his hypothesis. Though it was true that Sota's resemblance to Kido overjoyed him, it was not beyond the realm of possibility that the resemblance could one day bring Sota anguish.

I must live properly, Kido thought and, imagining himself making the decision to give up his son, felt as though his heart might split apart in his chest. *The remorse would surely be torturous if I did that. Just as it was for Daisuké—even Daisuké's life might not have attained such enviable happiness if anyone other than Hara had picked it up.*

Kido downed the dregs of his beer and chewed his lip, feeling even more attached to his present life. He pictured how excited he would have been if he had been born Makoto Hara and taken his life over from a man named Akira Kido. Then he might have been leading his present life anew as though he had taken it over from someone else, a stranger to himself at each instant . . .

"Hey, Dad, is my food here yet?"

"No. This is taking much too long. I'll let them know again."

Kido stopped a waitress who was frantically carrying off empty glasses and asked once more that they hurry up. Out of the blue, he realized that he never properly answered Sota's question that night about why Narcissus became a narcissus flower. Sota himself had likewise forgotten about it, but now that Kido had remembered, he made a note on his phone to look it up later.

Sitting at the neighboring table was a married couple with a girl of about two and a baby boy of about five months. The baby had burst into tears, and the mother was hurriedly mixing formula for him.

"Excuse the disturbance," the father said, bowing apologetically to Kido, who was staring at them absentmindedly.

"No, no, not at all."

"It's hard to get him to stop crying once he gets going."

"That's entirely *normal*."

Kido smiled and turned his gaze back to Sota, who remained absorbed in his game. For a five-year-old boy, he seemed to have grown a lot. Rié's second child had never lived that long. She had endured the sorrow of his death. Kido doubted that he would have been able to bear it. Kaori had still not returned.

"Huh?" said Sota suddenly. "Dad, there's a weird screen."

The phone Sota held out to Kido showed an ad for a different game.

"Aha," said Kido. "You must have pressed something by mistake."

Then, just as Kido was tapping the screen to return to the game, a banner appeared at the top of the display. It was a Line notification for an incoming message. And although Kido had no intention of looking, it entered his field of vision: sprinkled around the words "Last Night" were emoji hearts in the style of children's stickers. Involuntarily, Kido gently swiped it away with his thumb as though brushing dust off something fragile. The name of the sender, Kaori's boss, remained in his head after the message had disappeared. Even so, there was no reason for him to suppose that the event had moved beyond his brain's region for short-term memory. And, thankfully, it must have therefore vanished without a trace, like anything else that does not need to be remembered.

When the display went black, Kido placed the phone screen-down on the table as though nothing had happened.

"Dad! I want to play more."

"That's all for now, son. Look, your lunch just arrived. Better eat up."

"Oh . . . Can I play more when I'm done eating?"

"Ask your mother."

Kido finished his lukewarm Chimay and ordered another from the waitress. Eventually Kaori returned.

"The line for the women's room was just awful—oh, it came. That's the kid's lunch?"

"Yup, they just brought it over. Just when I was getting sick of waiting."

"Is that your third drink? Are you OK? Can you make it home?"

"I'll make it back just fine. It's only beer."

Kido smiled and reached out to cut up Sota's hamburger patty into smaller pieces.

The baby at the neighboring table had finally gotten his formula and was sucking it from the bottle in a trance.

Outside the windows stretched a clear, radiantly blue sky.

Kido gazed at it, relishing his day off.

Suddenly a line from a story he had read long ago flitted through his mind.

"Ah, such a moment of such a day," the character had exclaimed. This expressed how he felt right then perfectly.

Motojiro Kaji's "In a Castle Town," he thought, smacking his knee softly so as not to make a sound as he finally remembered where it had come from and withdrew his glass slowly from his lips.

CHAPTER TWENTY-TWO

During the almost two-hour flight from Haneda Airport, Kido gazed outside, engrossed in his own world of thought.

It was April, the spring weather uplifting, and his chest stirred in anticipation of the even greater warmth that surely awaited him in Miyazaki. As his window faced north, the light was bright without being dazzling. He could see expanses of blue sky at eye level, faint clouds veiling the giant map-like form of the Japanese archipelago like delicate lace.

In a stroke of good luck, the seats beside him were empty, allowing him to relax in solitude. When the plane stabilized and the seatbelt sign winked out, Kido reclined his seat slightly and began to turn the pages of his carry-on reading material, Ovid's *Metamorphoses*. It was the bunko edition put out by Iwanami. He had bought it at a bookstore after searching the web in an effort to complete his newly remembered homework from two Christmases ago.

As there seemed to be several competing theories about the myth of Narcissus, Kido wanted a primary resource and had settled on *Metamorphoses* because online comments made it out to be the simplest and most thorough way to learn Greco-Roman myths. But once he cracked the cover, he was immediately puzzled by the immensely intricate symbolic world that unfolded, and lost all hope of explaining it to Sota. Still, the book was captivating in its own right, and he continued to read it for pleasure.

According to Ovid, Narcissus was conceived when the river god Cephissus entangled "azure Liriope the water nymph" in his "winding streams" and "offered violence to her when enclosed by his waters." Kido was amazed to learn the secret of Narcissus's birth, and felt, in light of it, that there was more to the significance of his obsession with staring motionless at water than simple self-love. Rather, for Narcissus, water was at once his parents and the altercation between them, an act of violence that should never have occurred but without which he never would have existed. That is, Narcissus had to look at his origin if he was to see himself, as incapable of erasing the past as he was of reconnecting or returning to it.

The myth of Narcissus was, of course, a story of unrequited love. We find Narcissus "burning with the love of himself," and Echo, a nymph from the utterly foreign domain of the mountains, falling in love with him as well. Echo has been cursed by the goddess Juno so that she can only speak by "redoubling the end of speech" and repeating the words of those she hears.

The result of this dynamic is that Narcissus, only seeing his own reflection, is incapable of loving anyone but himself, while Echo, only echoing the voice of others, is incapable of making her love aware of her existence. Thus, Narcissus is trapped in a world of one from which Echo is permanently barred. It isn't until the moment of Narcissus's death that this lonesome pair fleetingly bridges their isolation, re-echoing each other's voices with the lament, "Alas!" and a final farewell.

When poor Narcissus heard the "youth, beloved in vain" reflected in the water repeat his cry of lamentation, did he experience joy at long last? And what about Echo?! Could that cry and salutation be unique for her, insofar as they were Narcissus's words, while simultaneously being the very words that she truly wanted to say in those moments?

The myth stirred up various ruminations for Kido. The last of these—as he read the passage where Narcissus screams, "Oh! Would that I could depart from my own body!" upon realizing that the reflection is of himself—was that it related to Hara. For both Narcissus and Hara had wanted to depart from their bodies. If this had been possible for Narcissus, he would have been able to love himself, whereas Hara wanted to become someone else, to love another, and to be loved by that other. And yet ultimately, perhaps, by becoming a stranger, Hara too had sought a way to love himself from the very beginning—to love not just the proper noun "Makoto Hara" but the person that should have been.

Sunlight pouring in through the southward windows crossed the aisle and struck Kido's face, dazzling him. Presently, he was shielded by a flight attendant rolling the service cart. Kido ordered a coffee. Then, removing the plastic lid to take a whiff of the aroma and a small sip, he gazed out the window once again at the blue sky and the fine motions of the wing as he returned to his pondering.

True to the title, *Metamorphoses*, the book contained all manner of transformation tales, but nowhere did Kido find an answer to Sota's simple question about why Narcissus transforms. Kido recalled the tragic god Phaethon, who, losing control of his father Helios's brilliant sun chariot, veered toward the earth and might have burned it to cinders if Jupiter had not pierced him through with a thunderbolt. His sisters, the Heliades, the daughters of the sun, wailed endlessly in grief over his death before turning into trees and leaving beautiful amber tears. Then there was the hero Actaeon, who, rousing the fury of the forest goddess Diana merely by happening to see her bathing, was changed into a stag and mauled to death by his own dogs not recognizing their master. And chaste Daphne, who, pursued by Apollo after he is struck by Cupid's arrow, bemoans her own beauty and transforms into a laurel tree.

Allowing these myths to meander through his mind, arising as they came to him and passing away, Kido thought of not just Hara but the whole multitude who had exchanged their family registers through Omiura. Perhaps they too, like such mythical figures—whether in the throes of sorrow, driven by desperation, or pressured by others—had been forced to transform into a different being, some finding love and happiness, others tumbling further from grace.

❌

As the plane made its approach to Miyazaki and began to descend, clouds multiplied as though the clear skies since their takeoff in Tokyo had never been. Raindrops struck the window, streaking past on their myriad thin trajectories. By the time they landed, it was overcast and drizzly but warm. Just as on his previous visit, Kido rented a car at the airport, checked in to his hotel in Miyazaki City, and had lunch.

It wasn't strictly necessary for him to come all this way. While he did want to discuss his report with Rié in person rather than simply email it to her, even that wasn't the whole reason. He had also felt an irrepressible desire to visit again. In this way, he hoped to find closure.

Although his appointment with Rié wasn't until the following day, he had arranged to arrive early so as to meet someone else that afternoon: Ito, president of the eponymous Ito Lumber. Kido had asked Rié for an introduction because he was curious to see where Hara used to work. Ito was initially guarded when Kido contacted him. He seemed suspicious of his motives. So Kido, rather than contrive an elaborate excuse that might backfire and come off as fishy, had told him simply that he was interested in forestry. This seemed to put Ito at ease, and he had agreed to show him around some of the mountains where his company did its logging.

✕

As the worksite was unreachable without four-wheel drive, Ito had arranged to pick Kido up at the branch of Miyazaki City Hall in the town of Kiyotake. When Kido parked his rented car and stepped out into the parking lot, Ito immediately called out to him in a resonant voice that seemed to come from the pit of his belly.

"Kido-sensei?"

A stocky man with a buzzcut, he wore pale sunglasses and held an umbrella against the rain. Kido greeted him, presented his business card, and handed him a box of sweets he'd brought from Tokyo.

"Well, look at that," said Ito, appearing deeply appreciative. "How kind of you."

Ito explained that the mountain was about forty minutes away. While the site they would visit wasn't the one where Hara had died, it was very similar and relatively close to it.

Once they were on the road, Kido reiterated his purpose in brief, namely that he had grown intrigued with forestry while working on behalf of Rié to sort out the estate of Daisuké Taniguchi. (Kido had grown used to calling him Hara in his head but knew the man was still known as Daisuké around here.) As Kido had various sorts of clients, whenever he met someone in a rare line of work, he liked to familiarize himself with it as best he could. While it wasn't clear from Ito's expression whether he bought this explanation, he nodded affably as Kido spoke, saying, "Wow. You don't say."

While Ito's face was dark and forbidding, he was highly personable, both talkative and candid. Playing FM radio on a low volume, he started off by talking generally about forestry to feel out Kido's interest level. As he soon explained, the main business of Ito Lumber was logging national forests, for which they purchased the rights, and they were booked up for the next two years. Although the industry relied on government subsidies and it was difficult to compete with imported materials, all wood was saleable now that biomass generators had been constructed, and the market was, if not booming, in decent shape.

"You may find this of interest as a lawyer. A few cut-rate crews have jumped in on the game recently. Some of them log illegally and get up to all sorts of wily tricks."

"Oh my."

"These days, no one wants mountain land even if they inherit it, so claim holders have been multiplying like rabbits, and now there are these spots here and there where no one can say for sure who owns what anymore. These rotten crews will buy a small plot right beside the mountain. Then they chop and haul all the trees where the owner is in question."

Ito spoke as though this was supposed to be amusing, and Kido couldn't help smiling even as he said, "How awful."

"It's a problem for the whole industry. Something's got to be done. Now and then we look at family registers to check the owner of old mountain land, but it's just a big mess, with claims branching off this way and that."

"I could see that." Kido suspected that by "family register" Ito meant to say "register book" but wasn't in the mood to quibble. He wondered whether Hara had had such conversations with Ito.

The surrounding houses gradually thinned out until soon they turned onto an unpaved mountain road surrounded by groves.

"It's going to get a bit bumpy . . . Did you see those old wooden houses in the area we just passed? Most of those have been forestry households since olden times."

"Is that right."

Though entering the mountain probably had little to do with it, the rain grew suddenly more intense, the wipers hurried. Despite the tree cover that surrounded them, there was a gap in the canopy above from which light shone down. The overgrown branches of low thickets occasionally tickled the windshield, and every time the car swayed, wings of mud flapped out as though startled from beneath the tires. There was something adventurous in the vibration coming up through Kido's seat. Through the drenched windows, only the base of the straight-towering cryptomeria emerged from the mist. Beyond the tips of those trees, as they drove along the steep road, all that should have awaited, if not for the haze, was the sky. As they went up and down the rises of the terrain, a vista would open up occasionally, and in the distance far below, Kido would spot what appeared to be a section of road they had passed a short time ago, surprised how high they had already climbed.

"Do you work in the rain?" Kido asked.

"If it's like this, sure. But there can be accidents when it pours. So we hold off or else we cut it short."

Kido recalled Rié telling him that there had been a torrential downpour when Hara visited her shop for the second time, and now supposed that his work must have been cancelled.

"Oh hell. That's not the way you treat a site. Just look at that mess. How they left the stumps. We would never do something like that. It's an ill bird that fouls its own nest. You've got to leave them tidy—almost there now."

"Once it turns dark, I imagine the roads around here are pretty scary. Very narrow, especially when there are oncoming cars like that one a moment ago."

"Roads can get a heck of a lot worse than this with the steeper sites. I won't buy the really tricky ones. I'm too worried about accidents, not to mention the efficiency is bad and the take-home is slim."

"Makes sense."

After that, they were silent for a while until Ito spoke suddenly in a quiet voice.

"I keep beating myself up for what happened to Taniguchi-kun. I still pray in front of the altar every morning. I never saw a single big accident since I took over the company from my old man. It tears me up inside to think about it . . . That was the one time I took on a site with poor conditions. The client was someone I just couldn't refuse."

"Is that how it happened . . . ? Occupational accidents are common in forestry."

"Yeah, incredibly common. One in a hundred. Not just the logging but machines slipping off cliffs. Also snakes and wasps and that."

"Oh, I hadn't thought of all that."

"When my grandpa was in charge, we had some laborers of Korean stock come work here too."

Kido's jaw fell open in surprise at this unexpected shift in topic, but Ito didn't seem to notice and said nothing more about it.

"What were the circumstances of Taniguchi-san's death?"

"I wasn't on site at the time . . . It's tough, reading which way a tree is going to fall, no matter how seasoned you get. Especially when they're bent. Then they can really trip you up. I tell those boys every morning till their ears fall off to be careful above all else."

Ito sounded distraught, and Kido gave him a slight nod, waiting for him to regain his composure. Though Kido didn't look over, he could tell somehow that the man was holding back tears. It was another vivid demonstration of how deeply Hara's friends mourned his death—whether they had known him in his guise as Daisuké or, like the president of the boxing club, by his real name—and Kido sensed the lingering wound in their hearts. Not a single soul spoke badly of him.

Presently a parked car came into view, then a blue tarp, stacks of wood.

"Here we are," said Ito. He did a prodigious parking job, leaving just enough room for another car to barely squeeze by, and stepped out of the car, unfurling his umbrella. "It's dangerous if you go too far ahead, so better not stray too far from here."

As Ito said this, he led Kido to the site entrance. Past an open space cleared of trees that was wide enough to accommodate a truck was a machine with a long orange neck that resembled a crane. It was clamping on to logs one by one, lifting them, and scraping off their branches. Kido could make out about three figures on site and, sweeping his gaze farther on, saw a flat stretch of stumps, beyond which his view ended at a steep slope.

"Approximately how old are the trees?" he asked.

"I'd say we cut them at about fifty. After that, they become building materials and last another fifty as a house. So I think of each tree in terms of about a hundred years. Fifty years on the mountain and fifty years with people. That's what I tell our workers too."

"Makes sense. I hadn't thought about it like that . . ."

"This way. Watch your step. Over there—we're not doing any logging today on account of the weather. Just jobs like this. Like other industries, everything in forestry is mechanized these days. The heat and the cold take their toll, but the work has gotten much easier on the body. I'm not saying it's a walk in the park, though."

"Did Taniguchi-san operate machines too?"

"He sure did. It takes about three years before you're fully trained in this industry. The government provides a training subsidy called the Green Employment program. Taniguchi-kun learned the whole job in about eighteen months. He was very diligent, decisive too. On the scrawny side but with surprising stamina."

"Did he do some kind of exercise?"

"No. I don't think he had any interest in sports. He said that he practiced kendo when he was a child. As a matter of fact, since I have a *dan* in kendo myself, we used to joke around about us having a showdown."

At Ito's wistful reminiscence, Kido nodded with a slight smile, hiding his surprise at how meticulously Hara had assumed Daisuké's past without the slightest tweak. For, from what Kido gathered, Daisuké had received instruction in kendo as a young child.

"He used to draw pictures a lot. During lunch break and that. Not that he had a gift for it or anything." Ito smiled.

"His widow showed them to me," said Kido.

"Huh, you don't say. They were very honest pictures. Very Taniguchi. The personality you were born with really shows in things like that."

"Yes . . ."

"Oh. Excuse me a moment." Ito accepted a call on his phone and began to walk off. "Yes, hello? Oh, thanks. The other day! Yes . . ."

Alone, Kido gazed at a thicket of rain-soaked cryptomeria for a time. All was quiet. In the silence between the huge globs of rain striking his umbrella and the ground, the sound of his breathing grew crisp. The mist-whitened verdure was imbued with pale light seeping down through the clouds, the mountains overlapping indistinctly into the distance, no sign anywhere that the gloom might break.

Imagining what might have been going through Hara's head each day as he gripped the chainsaw, Kido slipped into a reverie. He thought of the fifty years it took for a cryptomeria to reach maturity. Was Hara aware of the fifty years that Ito had said would follow? The trees that Hara cut had been planted by someone generations earlier, and the trees that Hara planted would be cut by someone generations to come. In the midst of this unfolding time, did he contemplate the duration from his birth until that moment? No, what probably occupied his mind was the desire to finish work early, to see Rié and the kids. When he put the two children to bed after a hard day's work, stretching his depleted body on the futon beside them, he must have felt that he was truly happy, all his many past ordeals only adding immediacy and power to the experience . . .

Kido floated into a kind of rapture in which all traces of who he was were lost. When he closed his eyes, time eased to a stop, and he hung his head in the rain, waiting in perpetual speechlessness. He didn't know whether minutes were passing or hours.

Upon opening his eyes, Kido saw one of the loggers walking on site in the rain and momentarily mistook him for Makoto Hara. He tried to decide what he would have called out to Hara if it had actually been him.

Hara had begun his life anew after his second suicide attempt in order to be alive. Kido wished he could have told him that he understood.

"I was looking all over for you. I was worried . . . ," said Kido. In his mind's eye, Hara stopped in his tracks, turned toward him, and smiled softly. It was as though he had at last come face-to-face with the man he'd been chasing from behind.

Strange that it had never occurred to him before, but Kido realized how much he wished they could have met.

CHAPTER TWENTY-THREE

Three days after her meeting with Kido, Rié told Yuto that she had something important to discuss with him after he finished his bath. He had been withdrawing to his room to read even more of late, and she wanted to make sure to catch him before he vanished upstairs.

She and Hana then went to take their bath first, whereupon little Hana delivered some news, about which she seemed both delighted and embarrassed: one of her front teeth was loose.

"How exciting. Let me see. Oh wow. It really is loose. I bet you'll be one of the first kids in your class to lose a tooth!"

"Yup. In the dove class, Hinano is the only one—guess what. Today I wanted to call to Hinano, but I said *Hinono* by mistake and Hashimoto-sensei laughed at me. I'm such a dumbo-wumbo."

Recently Hana had taken to this refrain about her intelligence, repeating it almost every day. As always, Rié replied, "You're not dumb, Hana," and patted her on the head. But she was beginning to suspect that this response might be exactly what her daughter was after.

It amazed her to recall that only six months ago Hana still often said, "This I think." Rié no longer heard this verbal quirk at all anymore. Growing up was transforming her daughter at such a dizzying pace that memories of her from just a year ago had turned unaccountably fuzzy. Rié felt certain that there was something distinctive about Hana that made her Hana, and yet somehow it was difficult to tease this apart from what made children children more generally.

In spite of this uncertainty, Rié found reassurance in Hana's sense of humor. Given that she had lost her father at such a young age, Hana's high spirits drew special attention at day care. The teachers universally told Rié that Hana was full of smiles, and most pleasing of all for Rié, the parents sometimes called her the most cheerful kid in class.

⋈

Yuto finished his bath at around ten o'clock. Hana and Grandma were by then in bed. This left Rié alone in the living room when Yuto tried to walk by her in his pajamas as though she wasn't even there.

"Hey! Didn't I tell you I have something I want to talk to you about? I've been waiting for you."

"What?" said Yuto with annoyance.

He had been expressing his feelings more openly these days, and Rié thought this might be a positive sign. For what worried her most was the possibility of him holding it all in until one day he became so disturbed that there was nothing she could do about it. To prevent this from happening, she was prepared to take the full brunt of his teenage rebellion, including the share due to both her divorced and late husband.

Yuto seemed to pick up on something significant in her expression and took a seat. "What?" he asked again.

"Three days ago, a lawyer who's been investigating Father for over a year came to meet with me . . . I finally learned everything. I know why he changed his name."

Yuto's gaze turned to the document laid facedown near her hand. Until a short time earlier, Rié had been gripping the edges with her fingertips as she rounded and straightened it repeatedly.

"Who was he?"

"I'm still not sure how much I should tell you. So I wanted to ask how you feel about it. Do you want to know everything now, or are you OK waiting?"

Yuto was silent for a while.

"Was Dad doing something wrong?" he asked. "Something the police might take him away for?"

Rié shook her head. "Just one tiny thing—changing his name . . ."

"Why would he do that?"

"Everything is here," said Rié, pointing to the document. "The lawyer wrote it all out for me."

"Then I'm reading it."

"It's really . . . how can I say this . . . I'm worried you'll be shocked. I haven't fully accepted it myself."

"Ryo died and then Father died . . . What could be more shocking than that?"

Yuto reached out, took the document Kido had compiled, and flipped through to check the number of pages, looking surprised by how long it was.

"I'm going to read it upstairs," he said. "I'll be back."

As her son retreated to his room, Rié tried to fathom his feelings from his footsteps going up the wooden stairs. Watching his body mature as rapidly as it had over these past months, she felt as though she was supposed to have more gray hair. First his voice had changed. Then he had sprouted a smattering of facial hair. Now he had found his dead father's electric razor and was doing his best to shave in imitation of him, without any instruction. (This, Rié recalled, was not the first time the razor had come in handy. It had also provided the hair for the DNA test.)

She had been wavering about whether to share the results of Kido's investigation, but had decided that she couldn't leave him hanging after revealing that their family name had been fraudulent. She'd had no choice but to fill him in, partially at least. And perhaps not just partially, for something told her that there would have been no point in hiding any of it from Yuto, whatever might be appropriate for other fourteen-year-old boys.

She had been doing her best to stop treating him like a child. Otherwise, she was concerned that he might become overly attached to his mother, reared in an environment with no father figure. Since entering adolescence, Yuto seemed to have woken up to this danger, and she could see him struggling to find the right distance with her. Establishing a new relationship with him promised to be stressful, for it entailed accepting that he was an adult, the man of the house, given that no one else was there to fill that role. The prospect was disconcerting, and part of her was tempted to go on babying him forever.

But she also realized that part of him was beyond her ken. It both surprised and delighted her to learn that her son was so profoundly different from her, and she resolved to respect him as his own person. She had stopped speaking to him condescendingly and tried instead to explain her feelings when something upset her. Though, as the elder most intimate with him in the world, she continued to give her honest advice and instruction.

Rié's shift in perspective was due in no small part to Yuto's passion for literature. She had tried reading the Ryunosuke Akutagawa story, "Asakusa Park," that he'd told her about in Burial Mound Park and had since puzzled over its meaning. It seemed to be a sort of script for a short film. Like an anxious dream put into words, it included a variety of surreal imagery, such as the sign that inexplicably becomes a "sandwich man" or the cylindrical postbox that turns transparent to reveal the letters inside. For Rié, who was not much of a reader, these aspects of the story were mystifying.

Of more interest and concern for her was the general plot. It was about a "boy in his twelfth or thirteenth calendar year" who visits the Asakusa area of Tokyo, becomes separated from his father, and searches everywhere for him in distress. The climax comes when the boy sits down on "the base portion of a large stone lantern" and "starts to cry, covering his face." He had mistaken a man with "mouth and nose covered behind a mask" and "a smile somewhat suggestive of malice" for his father almost immediately after losing him, but now, unbeknownst to the boy, this man actually becomes his father.

Rié was unable to work out the overall point of the story. Nevertheless, when the boy began to cry, she found herself crying too. It wasn't so much pity for the character. Rather, her tears began to fall when she imagined Yuto empathizing as he read it. No doubt this was a sign of his ongoing struggle with loneliness and pain, even if he didn't talk about it. But what astounded her was that he had been reading this story *before* she told him that his father wasn't actually Daisuké Taniguchi. Had this been a mere coincidence? Or could he have intuited something without her realizing? What had been going on inside her son when he read it?

Rié's breath caught in her throat at such non sequiturs as, "Hurry, hurry. Nobody knows when death will come." Yuto had only mentioned the uncanny exchange between the boy and the tiger lily; he had never told her that the story was about being separated from one's father. But he must have wanted her to know he was reading it. And even though she didn't really understand the work itself, her son's roundabout effort to share his emotional connection to it had helped her to understand him better. At the very least, she was able to sound the depths of his interiority. How peculiar that she saw her son every day but had only succeeded in drawing closer to him through a book.

Rié had always put readers on a pedestal and unfortunately, neither she nor the men she married had been that type. This could only mean that Yuto's penchant for reading arose from something distinctive in him that he didn't share with any of his parents. While the cause of this difference must have been in his milieu, it nonetheless seemed beautiful to Rié, like a flower budding spontaneously from the wreckage of some disaster.

As if in compensation for hardly speaking to his family, Yuto had been steadily writing in his notebook. As curious as Rié was, she was afraid that taking a peek might irreparably damage his trust in her and had resolved never to touch it. But there turned out to be no need, for she soon came across a portion of what he had created.

The previous fall, a haiku that Yuto had submitted as part of his summer break homework had been awarded top prize in the middle school category of an all-Japan competition held by a newspaper. As Yuto had kept even this to himself, Rié had only learned about it sometime after the ceremony when she spotted a big commemorative plaque lying in the corner of his room. Beside it was the award-winning poem:

> In his cast-off shell
> How rich the singing echoes
> Cicada voices

Rié did not feel qualified to evaluate the poem herself but could hardly believe that Yuto had composed it. The judges' comments, which he had later shown to her with great reluctance, criticized it for "affected ostentation," while also, to Rié's amazement, praising his "precocious talent." In his acceptance speech, published by the newspaper, Yuto had provided this explanation:

"In Burial Mound Park, I saw the abandoned shell of a cicada stuck to a cherry tree. In the upper branches, many cicadas were singing. I listened carefully, trying to find the voice of the cicada that had flown from that shell. I imagined how it must have sounded to the shell to hear the voice of the body that had been inside it under the earth for seven years.

"Then I was staring at the crack along the back of the shell and it reminded me of the soundboard of a violin. When the whole shell started to look to me like a resonating musical instrument, I came up with this poem."

Yuto made no mention of the death of his brother or father. And yet, Rié knew that the cherry tree mentioned must be the one her husband had chosen for himself. And although she wasn't sure whether Yuto had actually visited Burial Mound Park without them and had such an experience or whether it was a fabrication, she pictured her son alone at the foot of the tree, staring at the shell while listening to the cicadas, and couldn't stop crying. It wasn't her place to say whether he had "precocious talent," but it hardly mattered to her, for she could now see how literature brought him solace. On his own, Yuto had discovered a method for coping with the ordeals of life that she would never have been able to recommend or even think of herself.

All this past year, Rié's late husband had gone without a name, and when she learned through Kido's report that it was "Makoto Hara," she felt as though she were meeting him all over again. But overcoming her estrangement was not a simple matter of endowing the man in her memories with this proper noun; she still needed to decide what to call him.

Now that she knew he was two years younger than her, not two years older as she had always believed, Rié finally had a satisfactory explanation for why she had felt compelled to attach the diminutive suffix "kun" to his name. But while she shrunk from "Daisuké-kun," as though it were someone else's possession she had been using by mistake, she could not immediately switch to "Makoto-kun" either. For without being able to receive his reply when she called to him, she had no way of knowing if that appellation was right. It wasn't until Kido left and she found herself capable of looking at the pictures of her husband on her computer for the first time in ages that she felt certain of his wishes. Something told her that he had yearned for the day she called him by his real name, praying that she would love the whole of him—not as Daisuké but as Makoto.

Rié had never heard of Kenkichi Kobayashi. She figured she'd probably seen something about his crimes on the news at the time, but had no memory of it. The details of what he had done were so hideous and gruesome that she wavered long and hard about whether to conceal that part of the report from Yuto. She had thought of murder as something completely removed from the world that she inhabited, and was distressed to discover that it had been linked to her family all along. She recalled Kyoichi's suggestion that her late husband had committed a heinous crime. Did the man feel vindicated to learn that he'd been the child of a killer? She could almost hear him saying, "I told you so." But as it turned out, her husband himself had never committed any such sins, as she had wanted to believe all along.

Rié was deeply moved by what she read of Makoto's sad life in Kido's report and began to suspect that it was this her husband had sought to convey through the unfortunate story of Daisuké. Why did he choose that particular method? She couldn't say. Maybe his intention was simply to let her know about the deep wounds in his heart. After all, even if you misrepresented the cause, an injury was an injury, and pain was pain. Though such distortions would, of course, only confound efforts to find the right treatment.

When Rié read the testimony of the people who knew Makoto during his boxing days, when he agonized over his genetic inheritance, she couldn't help worrying about Hana. While she wasn't bothered in the least by the idea that the blood of a murderer ran in her daughter's veins, it was still possible that Hana might despair if she were to one day learn the truth. Yuto was different in that respect, as he had no biological link with Makoto. If he had, Rié might have been even more circumspect about showing him the report.

After all this, she had to ask herself whether she would have loved Makoto if she had known the truth from the start. Did love even need the past? She wanted to say no. And yet, if she was honest with herself, she suspected that she would not have been capable of embracing a partner with such a tortured history at a time when grieving her own losses and raising Yuto had absorbed all her energy—ultimately, there was no way to know. But the fact was that, thanks to Makoto's lies, they had fallen in love and she had been blessed with Hana.

Kido's report was such a tome that Rié finally began to wonder why he'd gone to such lengths for her. And why had he come all the way out to Town S when an email or a phone call would have more than sufficed? Only when he made one particular statement after running through the main substance of his report, a statement that stirred her emotions more than anything else he said, did she gain a glimmering of insight into his motives.

"I think that the three years and nine months that Hara-san spent with you was the first time that he ever knew happiness. True joy, I suspect. As short as your time together was, it was the culmination of his entire life."

Rié found these words deeply reassuring and realized that conveying them was Kido's reason for making the trek to see her in person. But as she decided not to pry, she never understood why exactly this was so important to him.

𝕏

Yuto remained shut up in his room for about an hour. Rié was just thinking that she should go check on him when she heard his footsteps coming down from the second floor.

"I read it," he said, passing her the sheaf of papers brusquely.

"You're finished?"

"Yeah." Yuto remained standing there impassively for a moment and then started for his room without a word.

"Yuto."

Yuto turned around.

"Are you OK?"

"Sure . . . Dad never killed anyone, right?"

"Never."

"I feel so sorry for him."

"It's kind of you to say that, Yuto."

"Now I understand why he was . . . so nice to me."

"Why?"

"I think Dad . . . he did for me what he wanted his father to do for him . . ."

Seeing the look of tender innocence on his face, Rié's eyes began to sting, and she tightened her mouth.

"True . . . But that wasn't the only reason. He also did it because he cared about you."

"Mom . . . I'm sorry."

"Why? What for?"

Yuto hung his head and burst out crying. As his shoulders shook with sobs, he wiped away his tears with his arm and struggled to get himself under control. Rié cried along with him. When she tried to offer him a handkerchief, he rubbed his wet face with his palms and looked at her with red, puffy eyes.

"So, our last name . . . in the end, what will happen? Are we going to be the Haras?"

Rié smiled and said, "I don't think so . . . How about the Takemotos? Then we'll be the same as Grandma and Grandpa again."

After a spasm of coughing, Yuto gave a slight nod. "What are you going to do about Dad's grave?"

"Good question . . . How about we put him in the same grave as Ryo and Grandpa?"

"Sounds good. Then none of them will be lonely."

"Yuto . . ."

"What?"

"I'm the one who should be apologizing for not keeping you in the loop."

Yuto shook his head and took a deep breath. "Are you going to tell Hana?" he asked gravely.

"What do you think?"

"I doubt she'd understand if we told her now."

"I agree."

"We have to watch out for her."

Rié felt the urge to cry again but held it back, looked her strong-minded son in the eye, and nodded. *My, how he's grown*, she thought.

"Promise you'll tell me if you ever need to talk."

Yuto gave a slight nod and said, "You too, Mom . . . OK, good night."

"Sweet dreams. See you tomorrow."

As she watched her son leave the living room, she tried to imagine how he might spend the rest of the night and felt a lump in her throat. But all she could do right then was let him go.

Once she was alone, Rié put her elbows on the table and hung her head between them, keeping her eyes closed for a while. The only sound was the ticking of the clock on the wall. When she lifted her face again, she gazed at the memorial photos of her father and Ryo adorning the cupboard and then at the picture of her family of four.

He was gone now. And the two children he had left behind were growing up.

She decided that those three years and nine months had been happy for her as well, so happy that her memories of that time and everything that flowed from it might just content her for the rest of her life.

ACKNOWLEDGMENTS

In addition to the various sources I consulted and quoted, this book would not have been possible without the cooperation of many people with my interviews and investigations. I would like to take this opportunity to give them my sincere thanks.

ABOUT THE AUTHOR

Keiichiro Hirano is an award-winning and bestselling novelist whose debut novel, *The Eclipse*, won the prestigious Akutagawa Prize in 1998, when he was a twenty-three-year-old university student. A cultural envoy to Paris appointed by Japan's Ministry of Cultural Affairs, he has given lectures throughout Europe. Widely read in France, China, Korea, Taiwan, Italy, and Egypt, Hirano is also the author of *At the End of the Matinee*, a runaway bestseller in Japan, among many other books. His short fiction has appeared in *The Columbia Anthology of Modern Japanese Literature*. *A Man*, winner of Japan's Yomiuri Prize for Literature, is the first of Hirano's novels to be translated into English. For more information, visit en.k-hirano.com and follow Hirano on Twitter at @hiranok_en.

ABOUT THE TRANSLATOR

Photo © 2019 Alexander O. Smith

Eli K. P. William is the author of the Jubilee Cycle, three novels set in a dystopian future Tokyo: *Cash Crash Jubilee*, *The Naked World*, and *A Diamond Dream*. Originally from Toronto, Canada, he has lived in Japan for over a decade and has spent most of that time working as a Japanese translator. *A Man* is his first full novel translation to be published. For more information, visit www.elikpwilliam.com.